Short Stories

From

Down The Pub

One Team

This is a work of fiction. Unless otherwise indicated, all the names, characters, businesses, places, events and incidents in this book are either the product of the author's imagination or used in a fictitious manner. Any resemblance to actual persons, living or dead, or actual events is purely coincidental.

Copyright © Oneteam 2021

To the teams that work in,

and the customers that love;

The Great British Pub!

CONTENTS

CONTENTS

CONTENTS

CONTENTS

FOREWORD

I can still remember the smell of the cellar; the rich, hoppy, sweet smell of recently tapped kegs and the chemical odour of stone floors, washed religiously by my father, as we passed him out of the back door, on the way to school.

I remember our dogs. The flat. The cat. The customers. Lots of them. From the Colonel in the Saloon Bar to the Rat Man in the Public Bar. The Pool teams, Rugby teams and Darts teams. Tug of War on Boxing Day in the local park for charity. Personalised dart flights and pool cues left behind the bar for the next match. Meat Raffles. Dodgy Phil, who could get you that film.

My Nan, sitting on a stool at the bar over Christmas, topped up on Snowballs by the protective locals. Party Fours and Party Sevens. Babycham and Stingo. Salt and Shake Crisps and Pickled Onions. Ploughman's Lunches and Chicken in Baskets. Ham Egg and Chips, and Seafood Platters.

The brass that I cleaned for pocket money, and the sound of the fruit machine I put it all into. The kids outside, playing in the dark of the garden when we were already in bed. The old lady who cleaned every morning, who my parents invited upstairs for Sunday lunch, with the Potman and our family; every week.

I can remember sneaking downstairs, peering through the crack in the door into the bar. The buzz, the smoke, the smiles and the very loud chatter. I saw relationships made and end. Wetting the Baby's Head, Birthday Parties, Stag Nights, Hen Nights and Wakes.

So much laughter and a few tears too. Stories of real life. Stories of those who came to the Pub, worked at the Pub, lived at the Pub. The Pub; the hub of our social lives, our work lives, and for me and my family, our entire lives.

I then left that world (for reasons best known to me) and chose a new career, 'Putting beans on a shelf,' for the next fifteen years, before returning.

I soon realised, that you really don't know what you've got until it's gone!

Now we all, to some degree, feel the same about our local Pubs. How beautiful is that third place? The place between work and home, where we can go and escape, SIMPLY to be happier than our day to day lives permit. We can meet up with friends, raise the roof or just be on our own in solitary peace, perhaps reading the paper. It's an amazing and very special thing.

Here are some Short Stories about why.

Colin Hawkins

Charles and Annie

The Dog & Duck sat about two hundred yards from a major road junction in Dorset, a thatched pub with a history going back to the seventeenth century. It had a brilliant team from all walks of life, including plenty of students who always came back to work for the busy times, and a great and loyal clientele. On winter nights there was a cheerful woodburning stove to greet customers on their way to the bar. Though many came for a pint (and yet more for a meal) most were there for the company and the 'craic.'

This was a busy pub, but with no buses and expensive local taxi services, it was better known for dining than drinking and not many stayed on till closing time. By the end of a shift your feet would scream for a break, smokers would be desperate for a puff and the chefs keen to snatch a break. Come 10pm the customers were either gone or finishing off the final dregs of their pints. Although licensing hours ran to 11pm, we could happily have closed at half past ten any day of the week, and we probably would've done, were it not for Charles and Annie…

Come hail, rain, snow, sun or shine, at ten-twenty, forty minutes before closing, in would come Charles and Annie. Every night of the week, no exception. Greeting all team members by name on his way to his seat at table three, there was no need for Charles to order his beer, it was already being pulled as he crossed the floor, and Annie was licking the face of whichever staff member had stooped to welcome her. A black and white border collie, she too made her way to table three. Not unlike Charles, no command or request was necessary prior to the delivery of a water bowl for Annie which she gladly lapped at after her walk to the pub.

Charles had no need for taxis, cars, or buses. The two-mile walk was just a stretch of the legs and the real ale a welcome friend on his arrival. A great barometer of quality, he'd let me know without hesitation if the brew was right and, for the most part, it was.

Depending on the night of the week they would be joined by various people who would pop in for their weekly parliament with Charles. The conversation was always cordial, and the depth of debate around most subjects conducted with respect. Some who came also had dogs with them and, like their owners, these all had their own space around table three. As in Charles's case, drinks were being poured long before they reached the bar and more doggie bowls found for the newly arrived four-legged friends.

Every night; same time, same place. Three pints. Always three, never four. The remains of the last pint always lasted right up to three minutes before closing time when Charles would rise, and Annie would sit up, eyes shining, because she knew those dregs were heading to her bowl. As Charles set off for the gents, the last of the best bitter was poured into Annie's bowl which she supped with glee. At eleven-thirty it was "Goodnight" all round and Charles and Annie wandered off into the night; until tomorrow.

Every day for all the time I was there (and for about forty years prior to that) Charles frequented the pub. Now, in his retiring years, he liked nothing more than to end the day at his favourite watering hole. Through Charles, the team and I got to learn the history of the pub (and all the gossip, of course). Our easy-to-please guest and his company needed little from us, and we were able to go about the closedown duties without worry or concern. We knew pretty much by the clock when the next pint would be needed and who would be joining at what time by the day of the week. So, once we saw the dregs of Charles's last pint go into Annie's bowl, all that was left for us to do was lock up and go home…after washing the bowl of course!

I remember the Thursday in September, when the staff all stopped, as if it were yesterday. It had been a busy day. The summer's heat lingered, as did the guests so there was a lot more to clear than anticipated. It was around ten-twenty-five p.m. when, almost as one, the team stopped their cleaning, counting and bottling-up and said, "Where are Charles and Annie?"

We checked our watches again. The bar clock, always five minutes fast, said ten-thirty. But it was twenty-five past ten on a Thursday night and Charles was not in the pub! Sally, one of my bar team who had been there six years, said she had never known it.

"I'm sure we'll find out why tomorrow when he comes in," I suggested.

Charles was fit and well when he left the night before and Annie had looked as shiny and bright as she always did. Perhaps he'd had visitors? I was looking forward to finding out why myself the next day, but we did not need to wait that long. John and Mandy always joined Charles on Tuesdays and Thursdays and, when they entered the bar, it was clear to see that Mandy was in distress. John wasn't looking to chipper himself and even Chaser, their dog, looked subdued. I guessed that we were about to hear some sad news. Sadly, I was not wrong.

As with his ritual of visiting the pub each night, Charles and Annie arrived at the Post Office at nine sharp every morning to collect a daily paper. That Thursday, however, he had not arrived. At nine-thirty, Annie arrived at the Post Office, clearly agitated and alone. Immediate thoughts were that he may have had a fall on the way. The shop's owners reversed the journey to Charles' home only to find the worst possible outcome.

Charles had suffered a fatal heart attack in the night, as he had laid down to sleep. It was sad to hear, and we all stopped what we were doing and commiserated. What a nice man he was, what wonderful company. The staff told how kind he always was and how supportive and understanding. Some were visibly shaken; for many of the younger members on the team, I thought how this may have been their first encounter with a close friend passing. It was incredibly sad.

Several of us attended Charles' funeral. It was a big crowd. Most of the town were there along with family members we had met momentarily over the years. As with all such occasions, it may have been sad but the wake that followed at the pub saw smiles brought back by the memories of Charles and his many friends.

It was the following night at exactly twenty past ten that we got a big surprise; in came Annie. Right across the bar floor, to her place at table three. Head up and proud, as if demanding her bowl. No bark. Once she was spotted, the team were over in a flash to stroke and pet her, which she readily accepted, licking their faces in return. The bowl was brought, and she lapped up the water as she had before on so many occasions.

"But who is she with?" asked Bronwyn, one of the bar team. No-one knew. We checked outside to see if there were any of Charles' regulars there. There were none. We looked at each other and laughed.

"Well, she ought to know the way!" we said in unison.

And there she sat. The last orders bell rang, and she didn't move. The time bell came and went and still she didn't move. This will be interesting, I thought. She could be here all night.

It was at eleven-twenty-five when the strangest thing happened, Annie got up and started to nose her bowl at the time that Charles would've headed off to the loo. I came over with an inch or so of bitter and poured it into her bowl and she lapped it up with glee as she had so often before. Then she wandered over to the door and waited.

I asked Sam, one of my team with a bike, to wait outside and follow Annie. When I opened the door, she went off without so much as a backward glance, into the night. Sam called twenty minutes later to say that Annie had walked back to a house and been let in.

It happened again the next night…and for the next two weeks. It was amazing. Same time, same routine. It gave us such a lift after the sadness of losing Charles so suddenly.

It was a Thursday night when John and Mandy came by again. We had not seen them for some time. They said it had been all too much and only now had they felt it right to visit the pub again. We understood, of course, and brought drinks to their usual seats at table three. The only missing piece was Charles.

14

"Should we tell them?" asked Bronwyn and Sam.

"Why not," I said, "it will cheer them up, as it did us."

Sam and Bronwyn went over to table three and told them to sit back and wait. It was quarter past ten.

"Wait for what?" they asked.

"Just wait…," said Sam.

Ten-twenty came and in bounded Annie, as if she owned the place. She ran over to John and Mandy as if they were long-lost family. The joy on their faces brought joy to us all. Smiles and beers all round for everyone was the order of the day!

Then they sat and watched with us and many of Charles' friends as Annie had her water and waited until the right time before nudging the bowl for her beer and making her way out.

We soon discovered how Annie was able to carry on with her routing, one of Charles' relatives was taking care of Annie and let her out each evening when she pined at the door.

I often wonder if she was longing for Charles, or that drop of beer at the end of the night…

John Paul

Snow Day

One of my fondest memories, was an eventful snow day back in January 2010, when I was working at a fifteen-bed hotel in Horndean Hants.

The weather had been steadily deteriorating in the aftermath of the festive season, and by the time the new year was getting its legs, the elements were becoming disruptive up and down the country; the A3 was snowbound and then eventually closed, which unfortunately left many motorists stranded, far from home. Heavy snow continued to fall, and an amber weather warning was issued by the road's authority.

Although all our fifteen rooms had already been booked for the night, we expected it to be a quiet day, due to the severe weather putting off all the regulars. However, as the day went on, we were getting rather busy.

The placement of the road closure had left a steady stream of customers visiting the pub, who had decided to abandon their cars alongside the motorway and look for the warmest and safest place to stay. We just so happened to be a couple of minutes from the turn off and we were soon alive with the frosty hum of chattering teeth and fresh rosy cheeks.

To compound the misery of the day, at around 6pm we experienced a power cut which lasted for most of the night. This left us with no tills, beer pumps and half of our kitchen equipment. It would have been easy at that moment to accept defeat and call it a day, sending the mismatched social rabble before us out into the night to find solace elsewhere.

Not to be deterred however, we decided to continue letting people into the warmth, so they could defrost around the roaring open fires and stay somewhere safe. We lit candles and continued to lift spirits by talking to one another to pass the time. Despite being our job as hoteliers and staff, it was a levelling experience; after all the staff were very much in the same situation as the snow continued to pile up against the frozen brick exterior of our cosy sanctuary.

The tired kitchen staff quickly rallied together to come up with a choice of hearty meals to provide a satisfying and warm belly to all the people in the pub. We handwrote all the individual tabs of meals and drinks by candlelight, running with an open till draw while the power was out.

It was a real test of our basic mathematics without the reliable help of the register, and many of us came out with a heightened appreciation of our pub predecessors, who had to carry out the job without the aid of technology. This meant that those that had cash could pay and those with cards could be charged as soon as we were able to do so.

The reason this day stuck with me so vividly was not just because of the heavy blizzard, but because of the kindness of others. Knowing that most people in this pub wouldn't have a place to stay for the night, many of the hotel guests who had already booked twin rooms, offered to share their rooms or even beds for the evening.

Staff were unquestioning and even happy to stay on well after their shifts finished to keep people happy and provide their phones to those that needed to contact home and say they were safe, if not perhaps a tad drunk!

As evening drew in, we moved all the tables into the dining room and raided the laundry room for any spare pillows and duvets, so that people would be able to sleep in the bar areas. The stories and jokes that were told as people settled down for the night, were quite something and the laughs could be heard echoing the whole way through the pub. People from all walks of life were happily chatting away until everyone, exhausted from the eventful day, finally fell asleep.

The next morning, we were up nice and early to cook up a full English buffet breakfast, so that no one left without a full, warm stomach. Some of the people who had stayed the night lingered around into the afternoon, until it was safe to drive again, but by the end of the day it was just the regulars who had come down desperate for a pint after being stuck indoors for a day!

Hatton Garden Planning

'Hurry up love, we're gasping over here!', says a raised but jovial voice. Then muttered under their breath, 'Doesn't she know how much we spend in here?'

If you've ever worked in a pub, you will have probably come across customers like this. Usually, a group of men of a certain age who would come in at the same time, on the same day every week. They always head for the same table which would be close to the bar. Their rounds of drinks rarely change, and they expect to be served at once, regardless of how busy you might be.

There was one such trio who frequented a popular pub in Islington. These three pensioners used to visit every Friday evening where they sat at 'their' table, deep in conversation, consuming their quota of pints. Then for no obvious reason they weren't seen for some time, until their mugshots were splashed across our TV screens and newspapers. They had committed the biggest heist in UK history.

'The Hatton Garden Robbery'.

Unbeknown to both customers and staff in the pub, during their regular Friday get-togethers, they were hatching a plan on how they were going to break into the Hatton Garden Deposit Company. They planned to drill a hole through a concrete wall, and empty its boxes of gold, diamonds and cash. Their visits to the pub continued for a brief period after the heist and prior to their arrests, during which time they were caught on CCTV discussing the raid and what they were going to do with their loot.

Now, rather than worry about how much time it will take to be served; they are worrying about how much time they are serving!

Victoria Pac-Pomarnacki

The Mystery Extension

In 1995, I was working as a property surveyor for a small managed house pub company, and we were just completing a major investment at a site in the south of Bristol. Part of the project was to create a larger trading area within the pub, and we decided to do this by encroaching into an adjacent outbuilding and storage area.

It's probably worth mentioning in those days, we were a little more cavalier when deciding to seek permissions for everything we did as the priority was to get in and out and move onto the next project as quickly as possible. It's also worth saying that the company was owned by an entrepreneur, who grew up in Bristol, and was known for visiting his sites during projects, getting involved with hanging pictures and being in the way.

But let's get back to the project for now.

The work was going well, the completion date was rapidly approaching, the new room was big enough for around 40-50 covers which made building the extension very worthwhile. However, there was no time to seek licensing approval for the extra area. Any licensing officers reading this story, please look away now!

The day of the grand opening arrived, and it was all hands-on deck with me, the team and our owner on site making sure the property was looking as good as it could be.

Then the site took a call at around three in the afternoon from the local licensing officer, to inform them that they were making visits in the area, and that they would be visiting the site to meet the General Manager and have a look at the work that had been done. Knowing it was re-opening on that day before 5pm, they told us they would arrive around that time.

Well, to say that information put the cat amongst the pigeons is an understatement! It was like a panic at the disco. I was only twenty-five years old and didn't know that grown adults could go into quite such a frenzy or revert to their toddler days. I was instructed to go to the local builder's merchant and pick-up sheets of plasterboard, skirting and dado rail. I managed to get back to the pub at 4pm with the materials and a plan was made and laid out to me in earnest.

I was requested, with the remaining members of staff, to construct a non-load bearing stud wall between the pub and the new, unlicensed area. To an untrained eye, it would appear that the new area did not exist.

We set to it, and within half an hour we had knocked up a full height wall complete with glued skirtings and dado, and we were painting merrily, slapping paint onto plasterboard that should have been plastered first. The owner of the company then decided that he would screw some pictures and light fittings to the wall to also to make it more convincing.

The licensing officer did make a visit just after 5pm with their line manager in tow. They were offered a drink and met with the new manager; at the same time customers were arriving at the site for their first jar. The grand tour was started, and everything was going well until two things happened.

We had forgotten to lock the door from the rear trade garden to the new internal area, and customers had made their way into that area on the other side of our wall and were happily chatting away whilst we were on the other side. Even more embarrassing, was that one of the lights which had been put up, decided to fall to the floor due to the way it had been hastily fixed.

The licensing officer, not oblivious to the noise on the other side of the wall, was told that the staff were having a training session in the adjacent outbuilding, and that this was normal practice. A staff member was quickly dispatched to quieten the customer noise down with a promise of free drink and food, if they obliged. One problem overcome!

The issue with the light fitting was covered off with a story I made up. I explained that 'we had no wires connecting the light to the wall as we were trying a new type of lighting that didn't need wiring, that had just come from Japan.'

Unbelievably, they turned to me and agreed that they had heard of this invention and would be interested to see how we got on using it. The visit was over by 5.45pm, and by 6.30 the newly built wall, pictures and lights were gone, and the customers who had kept their end of the bargain were eating and drinking on the house. All courtesy of the owner, who was stood with the broadest of smiles.

As an aside, I know that the new area was given retrospective permission, later down the line with our licensing friends. I never did contact them to update about our wireless lighting experiment!

Ben Jones

Honey the Pub Labrador

Honey was the most fabulous loving dog; albeit not a guard dog. All our customers completely adored her.

She would take herself off every morning to do the rounds of the local shops, where she was given meat scraps at the butchers, and ten chocolate buttons at the sweet shop.

They used to say at the sweet shop, that they sometimes tried to give her less, maybe seven or eight, but she knew, and would not leave until she had had her tenth!

She became quite fond of the odd Snowball, (Advocaat and lemonade) which was a fashionable drink of the 1970's. I don't recall how it all started, but after Honey had some surgery, and was just up and about, unbeknown to us a customer gave her a whole bottle, poured into a clean ashtray, and she lapped it all up. She was seen later that evening zig zagging down the passageway to her bed.

Anyone who has owned a Labrador knows only too well, that they love their food, and Honey was no exception. She was often given a few crisps and pork scratching's as the customers couldn't resist her soulful and appealing eyes. She was overweight, and as hard as we tried to discourage the well-meaning customers, we never won the cause. Having said that she still lived to a good old age of fifteen and she was happy, and greatly loved.

When she died, our local community was so upset that we even had big tough northern men crying into their pints of beer. Every pub needs a dog like Honey. She was as much a part of the community as anyone else and will always be missed.

Naked Dinner

The Castle Inn is the second oldest pub on the Isle of Wight and is, in fact, the sixth oldest pub in the county of Hampshire. It dates all the way back to the fifteenth century and has only ever been a public house, not like some of these church-converted, soulless night clubs we now have. It was purpose built for weary travellers to wet their whistle, fill their bellies, and allow the hard-working steeds a place to rest. The Castle Inn has had an eventful past and if the walls could talk, they would have a fair few stories to tell!

The pub is built on the thirteenth century boundary wall of Carisbrooke Castle, which was used as a residence, then a prison, for King Charles I, and during the 1600's there was a tunnel that ran between the two. In his happier times the King himself secretly used this tunnel to frequent the pub for a jug of ale but could not use it to escape his civil war captors, and ultimately, his beheading. I have looked for said tunnel but cannot find it, which is probably just as well as I wouldn't want to pop up in the middle of a royal game of croquet on the Carisbrooke lawn and risk having my own head lopped off!

As you can imagine with a pub this old, it is quite haunted… And these are just a few of our spooky inhabitants.

We have the legend of the stable boy; a poor young lad that was to be executed by hanging, but his neck did not break so they cut him down rather than letting him choke to death. *Great!* Thought the stable boy, just before they gently bled him to death…*This is* so *much better! Not!*

He was sentenced to death for a debt he could not repay, and now leaves us shillings (5p coins) anywhere and everywhere you can think of, which is obviously the closest to the money that he had in his day. Unfortunately, he is clearly unaware of inflation, and we would much prefer fifty-pound notes!

There are original beams from the stable in what is now the cellar, hence the name Stable Bar, and it is claimed that on July fourth you can see him hanging from the third beam along, and this is definitely somewhere I do not go on that date.

On the less morbid side, we are blessed with the ghost of a cat that wanders around the old pub, which is supposed to bring you good luck if you see it. And amongst others, there is also a robed priest that strolls around on the stone floor, which of all the ghostly stories I've heard, this is the one I think would scare me the most.

A tragic fire in 1684 damaged much of the pub, which then had to be rebuilt with bricks imported from France, although some claim Dutch bricks were used, and The Castle Inn was up and running again. At one time, the public house had a brothel running in the first-floor rooms, and what a fitting piece of history that is for the risqué venture it would undertake in April 2019.

The Naturist Association hold various 'naked dining events' throughout the year, in different locations, and approached us with a proposition. I must admit to being a little apprehensive, but I was reassured that the evening would be handled in an extremely tasteful manner. The evening was very well planned by the society, with us aiding where we could, and although we tried to keep it under wraps and low key; we are a very small island.

It wasn't long before the local county press got wind of the event, and it erupted over social media like a volcano! The news couldn't have travelled quicker if a town crier had bellowed it from the gate towers of the castle itself.

I remember the night very well, and don't think it is one I will ever forget. It was a private and tasteful event on a Saturday evening in late April, for which tickets were sold in advance. We had separate toilets put in for their use and obscured all the windows to preserve the guests' modesty. The curiosity of the locals got the better of them, and as you can imagine we had a very busy night in the main pub, with plenty turning up for a pint, and to see if they could get an eyeful of the action.

"Give you a fiver / tenner to get in and see the nudes?" was whispered to me several times in various forms, which I would laugh off, and decline. We still had a few customers asking about the on-going 'swingers' night, to which we had to correct them; naturism is not 'swinging!'

Myself and my business partner, Liam, did most of the serving and clearing of the tables, as we had a lot of young staff who were pretty nervous at the thought of revealing themselves – we would never put them in a situation where they felt uncomfortable – but we did have one very outgoing team member who asked to be a naked server. Wow, you think you know your team!

The tables were laid with very thick napkins, the hired seat covers were thoroughly laundered before their return, and each guest had their own modesty towel.

We had twenty-five guests on the night and served a three-course meal. Now I have to say that I envisaged a predominantly cold food menu, and I was very surprised at some of the options chosen! I mean, soup, whilst naked... SOUP! Hence the very thick napkins.

The menu had a wide selection including a burger option, garlic prawns, a chicken dish, and fish pie. There were plenty of potential disasters on offer, and anyone who has ever had fish pie knows it has the ability to be hotter than the sun, but the evening went without a hitch…. or stitch!

I regard myself as a rather outgoing person and shyness is not a forte of mine, but it was a very bizarre moment for me when I first walked into a room full of jovial folk who were literally only wearing a smile. I really didn't know where to look at first, so decided that maintaining eye contact was the best course of action. It felt odd being the only dressed person in the room, the complete opposite of the childhood nightmare of being stood in front of the class naked.

Each guest had a fantastic night of dining, dancing, playing games and just generally frolicking around. So much so, that the ambience of the room was enough to put me at ease and forget they were in a state of nature. It wasn't too long before I was joining in conversations and making cheeky comments along the way. My business partner is not as outgoing as myself, and I caught a few glimpses of his blushing cheeks (the ones on his face) and that made me chuckle. I think he would have had a few days neck ache from the amount of time he spent looking at the ceiling.

I was genuinely surprised at what a fantastic night this was… drinking, dancing, playing board games, just a good, wholesome, fun evening; without any sleaze. There were people from all walks of life, ageing from their twenties to seventies, and discretion was of course the key. As a publican, it was a surreal experience and a big eye opener for me. It is not very often, or ever, that you invite a group of people into the premises to get naked and relax. I mean, I like to make myself feel at home in any pub, but I've never stripped off and just gone around chatting to people.

As the evening was coming to a close, they asked for a picture with us all together, two fully clothed landlords and twenty-five totally naked people. What a very peculiar situation, indeed something that felt a whole lot easier at the end of the night than it did at the start!

And when the story made it to the local paper, they cut it out, signed and framed it, and presented it to the pub. In fact, this press article made it as far as Manchester, where a friend of mine read it, and rang me for the juicy details. I had to tell him what a wonderful night it was, a society of happy, fun-loving folk that we would welcome back to The Castle Inn with open arms.

Lord Simon Cant

Robin and the Regulars

Our pub is a quaint, old, family affair, deep in the heart of the Midlands. Wooden beams, a warm fireplace, and a view from every window of huge trees and green leaves. Through the long beer garden, at the rear of the building, sit the old stables, long since overgrown with vines and foliage.

But each year, within that lush mass of greenery, the robins build their nests. Over several weeks, they fly in and out preparing a home for their chicks. To the untrained eye, this meticulous labour of love goes unnoticed, just a metre above the farthest table in our beer garden. The careful construction of a beautifully woven nest of twigs, leaves and grass slowly emerging above the blissfully unaware pub guests. Two worlds so remarkably close, yet entirely unaware of the other's existence.

Until one day, the two worlds collide. A fluffy young chick makes its first dive from the nest, crash landing amongst the pint glasses, crisp packets, and startled guests on the table.

This first chick creates great excitement, and the staff rush to organise the guests into a rescue team. Forming a lengthy line, the guests help to guide the chick across the long beer garden until they find the nest that the little chick calls home.

This has now become a lovely local tradition for the last seven years, and we hope it is one which will continue for many years to come.

Neil Carruthers

Ghostly Carry On

Imagine hopping into a time machine and being dropped off in Newcastle in May 1646. The English Civil War is coming to a climax, and England is reigned over by an often arrogant, self-righteous, and unscrupulous King in the form of Charles I. Scotland had besieged the town two years prior and, rather than face the wrath of Parliament, the King decided to throw himself at the mercy of the Scots.

While safely in the hands of the Scots, the King lived in opulence at Anderson Place and was free to come and go as he pleased, whilst disrupting church sermons, playing golf on the Shield Field to the east of the town, and regularly popping into his local, the Old George, for a swift pint or two.

Fast forward to February 1647, where the King's comfortable, relaxing down time was rudely ended, when the Scots handed Charles back over to Parliament. The landlord of the Old George was not particularly happy losing such a valued customer, and having a famous empty seat in his pub, which still resides in the pub to this very day.

The final stop on our time travelling escapade brings us to Whitehall, January 30th, 1649, where we find our Monarch kneeling over a chopping block, with an executioner's blade separating his head from his body, and birthing the short-lived English Republic.

Although the King has long left the Old George, there are tales of supernatural goings on throughout the pub. From haunting whispers to apparitions. Workers at the treasonous King's old watering hole have never been alone, and these three tales will leave you asking yourself questions, and looking over your shoulder……

The Whisper

Two trusted and senior staff members were locking up the pub one night. Most tasks had been done, all that was left to do was the usual walk around, checking that all the windows and doors were locked, and that the pub was safe and secure.

They briefly stood outside the function room to check that it was locked when, at the same time, they both heard an incoherent whisper in their ears. As though someone was feigning a conversation. They both stared at each other, neither of them had spoken.

Overcome with shock and fear, they momentarily froze to the spot, speechless, and questioned this experience and whether it was really happening. Neither of them had encountered anything so spine chilling. They were terrified and quickly set the alarms and left the pub. Neither staff member would do the walk around alone after that.

The Visitor

It was 1:30am and Ashley, the Deputy Manager, was alone on his computer. He had been finishing up some last-minute administration, essential when you work in a pub. Ashley lived in the pub's accommodation opposite the venue. Ashley's baby daughter was sound asleep in her Moses basket in the living room down the hall.

Ashley, initially, heard the floorboards creak outside the room that he was in. This would arouse some suspicion but, given the age of the building, it could be easily rationalised. Then came the quite excited voice of a female saying "Hiya!!" echoing into the room in a tone of excitement at not having seen someone in a long time.

Immediately after this, his baby daughter stirred and made quite a loud groan. Ashley was terrified and dashed to check that all was well. It could have all been in Ashley's mind, however, something told him that it wasn't.

It was later suggested that the "Hiya" sound was his daughter, but he is adamant that it was not. He says that the word, the way it was said and the volume of it was just too clear, and it was right outside the room where he was sitting.

Ashley has lived there for four years and not seen or heard anything. He was a nonbeliever but now, he is unsure. He simply cannot explain it.

The Woman in The Attic

Fast forward a few years, and the figure of an old-fashioned looking woman was spotted by a staff member, who was visiting the accommodation opposite the pub. The figure was standing at one of the attic windows and the staff member presumed that it was a colleague up in the attic. When working later that day, she asked her colleague if she had been up in the attic earlier. The answer was no! Who was the lady? Where did she come from? Where did she go? There was no way a customer could have gotten up there. There were keypad locks on the doors.

Many mysterious encounters happen at the pub that was once frequented by royalty. Are they a result of confusion? Overactive imagination? Or are they ghostly encounters with the long since gone patrons who are trying, in Charles I's final words, to go 'where no disturbance can be?'

Sweeney Todd

In 1995, I had the great pleasure of running a gorgeous pub called The Digby, in Birmingham. It was situated in an area called Erdington and had previously been a social club for workers at the local Spitfire factory. Many of its patrons' families had been drinking there for many generations. It was what you might call a 'locals pub,' where it was not unusual to see the same familiar faces every day.

The memories I have of my time there are endless, but there is one memory that tops them all.

One of the regulars Nick, also known as 'Slim,' had been suffering severe toothache for about a week, and we had been listening to him complain about it endlessly. He had tried to ease the suffering with his daily intake of whisky, but to no avail. By the end of the week, Nick could take no more, and rather than take a trip to the local dentist, he decided his drinking buddies could help him out. 'I'm going to get me bloody pliers!!' shouted Nick.

Within a minute, Nick was pinned down on one of the benches in the beer garden by two of his mates. Another stood menacingly over him, with the pliers in his hand. We couldn't believe what was happening, or that they would go through with it. It was horrifying and brutal. A swift yank was made, and the ordeal was over. Nick stood up, came back to the bar, and took a final swig of his whisky. His toothache was no more.

Handing the glass over, he asked in a broad Birmingham accent, 'Can you chuck that in the bin for me bab?' and headed home. There in the bottom of the glass was his tooth. I nearly passed out with laughter.

Colette Sarjant

Pub Dog

My dad wanted a 'big' dog for the pub. A 'proper pub dog,' this time. We had been broken into a few times; the fruit machines had been 'done' and it had been pretty worrying for my parents.

The pub was separate to our well-secured flat, but it was unsettling, mostly to my mother. My brother and I didn't seem too bothered about the break-ins as I remember, but we liked the idea of a fierce dog to scare people and tell our friends about. You know, typical boys.

Sally, our poodle, had recently been put to sleep and we still had an old white cat, who was deaf and appeared increasingly disinterested with us.

Sally had been our first dog in the family. Dad had completely surprised us one day after school by presenting us with her. She was, at first sight of indeterminable breed and looked like some sort of small Ewok type creature; a ball of apricot and white matted fur with a small tail, and big brown eyes peering through the unkempt hair. In the first few days we were unsure about her habits. Being a couple of years old, she already had her own ways, which included insisting on sleeping under my parents' bed, which I think they quite liked.

There was an embarrassing episode on the second day of having her.
Sally started walking around in circles, slowly, and a large bulge had appeared at her rear. We had just brought her back from an early walk and were outside the pub in the main street. We called my dad outside to help.

There was something wrong. She was having a baby! There was no time to lose, it had to be delivered there and then in the street. It didn't matter that there were onlookers. Hot towels and a bowl of water would be needed and were quickly fetched. After about twenty minutes of anticipation and preparation, she delivered a poo the size of a premature puppy and then ran off inside, done with the deed. We went to school quickly and no more was said of it.

So, the years passed. We had good times with Sally, who eventually died; and after being recommended a breeder, it was time for a new era – A German Shepherd puppy.

Sabre was an immediate joy. His ears and paws looked like they had been transplanted from a much bigger dog, and they promised the size of the dog he would soon become. He grew exponentially. Bowls didn't seem big enough to hold adequate food for him. He was soon eating out of a large plastic washing up bowl, filled to the brim with a stinking tripe-and-cereal mix, which he bolted down every time like it was his first meal in months.

The cat was not keen, and her place by the fireside was soon under threat. The spiteful clawing that she had given Sabre several times when he was tiny, was turning out to be a bad move. The dog now hunted her like a maniac every time it got back home, for pure sport. She gradually moved into my sister's bedroom with access to the outside world via a small window onto the balcony. The food went in there too. The cat was exiled, and the flat was now Sabre's.

Sabre was getting rather large, and people were noticing.

"The dog's taking Bryan for a walk again!" customers would joke, as dad was dragged out of the pub into the street by the huge black wolf, wheezing at the collar, whining with desire to run free.

It was clear that the dog needed training and a tough hand, and so a retired police dog handler was recommended, and we boarded the dog with him when we went on holidays to reset his behaviour. When we returned to pick Sabre up, he was like a different animal. However, the new disciplines never lasted very long, and his old habits soon returned.

We couldn't leave the flat without throwing a bone down the hall and running out of the door. This would be followed by a whining, barking, black missile that would hit the glass panelled door with alarming force and scare the wits out of anyone who saw our exit.

The pub staff wouldn't go up into the flat to get a box of peas or chips when we were short downstairs. It was only *family* that could enter. The job was done on the intruder protection front, but we were also somewhat imprisoned into the bargain.

Things settled, and the bond grew between family and dog. Man, and dog. My dad became the alpha. He dished out the food, did the walks and spent most of the time with Sabre. They were an unruly team.

The dog would be let out when the last orders bell was rung.

"We've had your money, now drink up and piss off!" My dad would shout in jest to the public bar regulars. The dog would be released behind the bar and dart around frantically, looking for a way out into the main customer area, lfor that cat or anyone else occupying his territory. My dad would throw ice at the dog, who would catch it mid-air and crunch it up like frozen biscuits.

Drinks would be quickly quaffed, and farewells exchanged before the dog would be allowed to barge through the bar flap and race to the window, barking, covering the window with spit and steaming up anywhere on the glass where it pressed its hot muzzle.

One night someone wouldn't leave that easily. A stranger had settled in a corner in the lounge bar. The regulars had remarked on his presence. He was rumoured to be trouble.

He had just 'got out' and a few nervous locals had bought him drinks as a gesture of submissive goodwill, so he hadn't been up to the bar much himself.

"Time now please, drink up," my mum had called over. The dog was doing the rounds from the other bar and circling; waiting to come out.
"I'll go when I'm finished," he called back, dismissively.
My mother, not one to ignore a verbal challenge, cocked a brow.
"You'll go now, thanks," she retorted.
The stranger got up and came to the bar.
"I'll go when I've finished, you old cow," he snarled and swiped his arms in an attempt to drunkenly pat her around the face, patronisingly.

The dog raced forward and leapt up, scrambling his front paws onto the highest glass shelf, roaring. He viciously growled and flashed white teeth at the would-be attacker.

"You have ten seconds before I let him out – we're closed," My dad called firmly from the other bar, not fully aware of the scenario, but sensing there was something wrong. The man was gone in less than five.

34

Time passed, and Sabre remained unruly but fulfilling the brief; a deterrent to anyone who thought to burgle. Looking the part. Playing the role.

In the summer, he would race up and down the balcony on the flat and everyone in the garden could see him, standing up against the parapet wall, running at speed dangerously close to the edge of his high stage, but somehow never threatening to go over. He became famous with our friends who loved the fact that we had a guard dog for the pub.

One day, we came back from school and dad seemed unsettled. The dog was still relatively young but had started bumping his head gently on the walls now and again, and his head seemed to hang to one side.
"Sabre's not well," he said. "I'll take him to the vet."

A few more days passed, and the symptoms seem to worsen.

A week later, and Sabre returned from the vet. One side of his face was shaved, exposing his white skin, which was stark and shocking against the rest of his thick black fur. It was very upsetting for us to see. His head was surrounded in a large plastic cone to stop him licking his own wounds. There had been an exploratory operation. He looked tired and he was losing weight, sleeping increasingly. Dad took him back to the vet later the next week, and then brought him home again with no news. We didn't ask any more questions.

Then it was Friday, and we came home from school. Sabre was not there. Dad was having a lie down in the bedroom. He rolled over and looked at us, sorrow crumpling his brow. "You become too attached to them. We're not having another dog, boys."

Our Pub dog was gone.

Colin Hawkins

Love is in the Air

I will always remember one fine early spring afternoon, when I was working on my own in my local pub. I was accompanied by a gaggle of local firefighters, who tended to stop off for a drink when on their way home. The only other company they had in the pub, was an older gentleman enjoying one of his many afternoon tipples, and a young couple who had just entered. Rosy-cheeked from the cold outside, they could barely bring themselves to look for a table, as it would mean taking a break from staring longingly at one another.

The young man approached the bar and ordered some food and drinks. He did not seem to notice the rowdy firefighters, as he handed over his money, a glazed and giddy look slapped across his face. He seemed to float back to the table, which certainly caught the attention of the firefighters.

When the food arrived, the couple ate in silent conversation, a whole language reduced to facial expressions, winks, and smirks. And they laughed hysterically. What could be so funny without words? Love was clearly in the air. A passionate fire of affectionate smoke, I am sure the men at the bar were more than willing to cover with foam and water.

After about an hour of such shenanigans, the couple sauntered out of the pub, thanking me as they exited into the car park. About ten minutes later, one of the firefighters followed suit, although seconds after exiting the pub, he rushed back in, with what can only be described as pure glee cascading from an ear-to-ear grin. Barely able to find the words, he simply gestured hurriedly to his colleagues and myself, to which we jumped up and hurried out of the door after him and into the car park.

At first everything seemed normal, but then came the faint squeaking of metal, like the cry of a small animal, but far too rhythmic. I squinted as I tried to place the noise, although I found all my answers when I saw the young couple's car rocking away in the far corner of the lot. Far from an ordinary suspension check, the windows were fogged with young love as the metal frame bounced steadily away.

36

In unspoken synchronicity, the firefighters and I began to loudly clap and cheer, applauding the pair from the back door of the pub as the squeaking came to an abrupt stop. With a loud whoop from yours truly, the couple shuffled into the front of the car and scrambled to start the engine.

As the car pulled past us towards the exit, an even larger grin clocked us as the young man gave us a brisk wave, much to the delight of the firefighters. His partner on the other hand, had the sudden urge to bury herself deep in her handbag, fancying herself as the new Mary Poppins.

With a final cheer, we returned to the pub. One of the lads turned to me and informed me he would be bringing his wife in the next day, and that they would be eating whatever that young couple had ordered.

Whitewashed

In the early 80's, I was making use of The Jolly Pirate, an excellent real ale pub, located deep in the Hanover area of Brighton. This remarkable spot was one of the first in the area to serve decent beer, which attracted a diverse range of customers.

On the evening of one unforgettable day, I decided to pop into the pub on my way home from work. I parked around the corner and noticed that a telephone line had broken and was lying across the road. Being the responsible citizen that I am, I pulled it back and wound it around the bottom of the telegraph pole adjacent to my car. Upon entering the pub, I bumped into my friend Loco, who seemed to be just on his way out. We shared a few jokes and the usual mickey-taking, then off he went.

After a couple of beers, I made my way home for dinner. When I got to the car, I was astounded to see that it was completely tied up with telephone wire; carefully fed through the door handles, wrapped around the bumpers, then round and round the car. It was also tied to the telegraph pole, Loco the -------!

A short time later my old school friend George, who was the part-time barman at the pub, was getting married at the Registry Office to the part-time barmaid Janine. I was to be best man and would arrange a 'bit of a do' at my house in the afternoon.

Right now, I should probably mention, George's admiration for his car. He was always tinkering with it and kept it in pristine condition. With this in mind, prior to the wedding, and unbeknown to anyone else, myself and the other lads bought some whitewash and painted his treasured car completely white. The car was to be used the next day, when they were off to some distant exotic resort... Eastbourne, I think.

I'll just point out that whitewash doesn't do any serious damage to the car and can be eventually washed off, although for many weeks later every time the windows are wound down, a nasty white streak is left.

Continuing with the story, we were all meeting in the pub before going off to the Registry Office, so instead of taking the remaining whitewash home, we left it in the bucket with the brushes behind a wall close to the pub, with the intention of picking it up the following day.

The ceremony all went well, and everyone piled back to our cosy place for food and beverages. When the drinks had all disappeared, we decided to make our way back to the pub, where a few more friends would be joining us for the evening. Before going in the venue, I noticed that Loco's car was parked around the corner close to where my car had suffered its bondage session. It turned out that he had to work the next day, so he wasn't staying for the evening.

I suddenly had a brainwave, well, the sort of brainwave you get following a day of merriment. I shared my mischievous idea with a couple of fellow conspirators, and off we went through the pub's side door. We retrieved the bucket of whitewash, and in an extremely artistic way, changed the colour of Loco's red car, turning it completely white. The bucket was replaced behind the wall, and we returned to the pub without anyone noticing we had gone; most importantly the victim of our joke.

A short while later, Loco made his way home, and as soon as he left, the whole pub burst into hysterical laughter. We expected him to come back screaming and shouting, considering he was not what you would describe as a quiet man, but I think he knew our condition and thought better of it.

I have no idea why, but just before closing time, a few of us decided it was a clever idea to go into town to a steakhouse; who surprisingly let us in, and, as far as I remember, we had our meal and a few more beers. Eventually the staff showed us the door, and we had ordered a taxi to take us home.

Our ride arrived, and the driver, Dean, turned out to be someone we knew well – yet another regular from the pub. We told him the story of Loco's car, laughing aloud; but Dean was already aware – the word had got around. We suggested that he should drive past Loco's house to see it for himself.

When we found the car, there was a white ring around it where he had scraped most of the whitewash off, in fact, he had made an excellent job of it. As we drove away, we looked at each other laughing; it was clear we all had the same idea – we asked Dean to drive us back to the pub. He said it was well past closing time, so it was pointless, but decided to take us back anyway for the hell of it. We jumped out, collected the bucket, and asked him to drive back to Loco's place. He was not keen but eventually agreed, probably bribed by the offer of a large tip.

He parked up, and we soon started to repaint the car. We were not being the quietest bunch of artists as we soon aroused an annoyed neighbour, who came out and asked angrily what the hell we were doing. One of us innocently explained that we were just painting the car; the now pissed off neighbour asked some other question, to which "Dulux Brilliant White" was the reply. He freaked out and threatened us with a call to the police.

Naturally, it didn't take us long to complete the work, and we soon disappeared laughing our heads off.

A short time after about 2 am, there was a knock at Loco's door. At first, he didn't react, but the persistent bang eventually got him down the stairs.

"What the hell is someone doing, banging on my door at this time of the morning!", the unhappy bunny shouted.

"It's the Police, we need to speak with you, can you open the door?"

"I'm not opening up, just tell me what you want, I need to go back to bed as I'm getting up early for work in the morning", came the reply.

"Please open the door," patiently ordered one of the officers.

"No way just tell me the problem!"

"If you insist sir, but we need to inform you that a bunch of louts have painted your car."

"Yes, I know all about it, please leave me alone."

"Sir, do you know who the perpetrators are?" they persisted.

"Yes, now please go away. I need to get some sleep."

"OK sir, if you insist, but if you want to press charges, please come to the station."

"Look, please just go away, I know all about it," shouted back an unsuspecting Loco. "I know who did it and anyway, I've washed it all off!"

It was only the next morning that Loco realised we had been back. His face was a picture when we next met in the pub. "If I'd have known you did it twice, I might have given your names to the police" he said in jest.

We knew he would dream up something in the future and the fun would continue, so from then on, instead of leaving my car near the pub overnight, I walked to the pub as often as possible!

Cheeky Cheeky

I am going to break the "what goes on tour stays on tour" code. Sorry, I have over promised already, but hopefully this provides the hook to encourage you to continue reading!

I am proud to say, that I was a founding member of my local pub football team at the tender age of sixteen. A lot of my fellow players, including Belgian John, Big Al, Richard, Simes, Lloyd, Mark, and Pete D (who was good enough to go professional if only he had wanted to) like me were still at school. The rest of our team lived and worked in and around Ealing in a variety of trades and professions. The Grange was a quintessential community pub and reflected its local community.

We played friendly games during our first year, before joining the Chiswick District Sunday League. I am not too ashamed to admit, that I would occasionally nip into the pub, particularly after training and our competitive matches on Ealing Common. We always had the best intentions just to stay for one, why do we always say that? It never happens does it, but usually these are the best times. This was back in the day when a half a pint of dry cider would have set you back the regal sum of twenty-six pence, but I will not reveal my age! It was here that I discovered my love for pool, but that is another story involving local gangsters in the now defunct Three Pigeons pub!

As our team developed and friendships blossomed, Mike, our new centre forward arranged our inaugural tour over Easter Weekend to Kettlewell in the Yorkshire Dales. This was close from where he originated. While this might not seem your obvious destination for a Sunday league team from West London, it turned into a stroke of genius and Kettlewell became an annual pilgrimage for years to come.

What made this tour standout from your archetypal "boys will be boys" jaunt, is that we all invited our wives, partners and, in later years, children as well. Our itinerary was structured and inclusive and everybody was expected to participate. We would make the journey from West London on Thursday, so that everyone was booked in and ready for the first of our two long hikes up and through the Dales on Friday morning. I have never looked forward to a sumptuous homemade pie as much as when we would land at The Fox and Hounds in Starbotton at the halfway point.

Mike arranged games against two local teams on Saturday and Sunday, to ensure that everyone in our large party got a game, before a second hike on Easter Monday. The Buck Inn was another standout venue for our halfway point and provided the motivation to keep walking.

Our Kettlewell Tour became a rite of passage that bound us all together. Even though players, including myself, would leave West London over the years, we invariably were always welcomed back, and once in each other's company it felt like we had never been away.

While we spread out across Kettlewell and stayed in different hotels and guest houses, we would always meet up at The Kings Head in the evening after having either conquered the Dales or vanquished one of the local football teams. We would occupy the whole of the main bar, with a circle of tables formed in front of the glowing fire.

It is here, that we would play our initiation game for tour first timers, never ceasing to be hilarious, however many times we played it! It is at this stage, I am wondering if I am about to describe one of those "you had to be there" moments. Oh well, I have started so I will finish!

Andy, as always, would hold centre stage, and announce that he was going to start the "Cheeky Cheeky" game. In front of him was a used ash tray – do you remember when smoking was allowed in pubs? The tour newcomer would then sit next to Andy, who would proceed to rub his cheeks while saying "cheeky cheeky." The tour newcomer would do the same with the person sitting next to him, and this would be repeated by everyone in our circle until it was Andy's turn again. The exercise would then be repeated with a different part of the face, for example "nosey nosey," for as long as it took for the tour

43

newcomer to realise, that Andy had been rubbing ash into his face during every round of the game!

Amazingly, this game could take hours, as it would be interspersed with drunken stories and much hilarity, and it was usually only when the newcomer went to the toilet, that they would realise that they had been duped.

One famous year, we discovered that George D our fearless, and recently recruited right back, alarmingly did not wash his hands after visiting the toilet. Unfortunately for him, this meant missing the opportunity to see his ash covered face in the mirror above the sink. He twice returned to the table enabling "cheeky cheeky" to continue, although I do remember that he looked a little puzzled as the laughter levels increased significantly when he re-joined us!

George was a real character, the first into any brawl on the football pitch, and there were quite a few in Sunday football back in the day. He was famous for his "Chris, you doughnut" exclamation when Chris missed a sitter! He spent his first tour telling us that is Grandmother was a bit of a "Fire Sparrow" although to this day, I am not sure what this means, although it did give birth to his new nickname. George had the last laugh however, when he left us after a couple of years to play for boot money in a semi-professional league.

Being in Lockdown, has given me the opportunity to reflect on my life and career in the hospitality industry. While it has been my livelihood for well over thirty years, visiting the pub has been the cornerstone of my social life since the formation of our pub football team. I have made lifelong friends; I have shared in their successes and heartaches and am now watching a new generation of family and friends find their feet and initiate their own fun and games.

It is not surprising, that the majority of my funniest ever moments seem to have been in and around a pub. I have recently found myself reflecting on these moments (including my student pub days) which are best to save for another day or edition. Anyone drinking in The Lansdowne in Torquay between 1982 and 1985 will know what I mean, particularly when the annual three-legged pub crawl took place. They are a major source of amusement and comfort as I head towards my dotage.

Colin Cassels Brown

Tarantula Revenge

As a rookie Area Manager, working for a national pub company, I was responsible for an idyllic twelve-bedroom pub, come hotel-restaurant. It was situated close to Barrow in Furness and overlooking Morecambe Bay. It was a lovely location and a charming business full of character. Little did I know the horrors that were to land in my lap, on one particular weekend at this unassuming business.

One Easter weekend, I received an urgent phone call from the site General Manager, with what was to become my ultimate business challenge. A long story was relayed, whereby the live in Head Chef (who had just split from his girlfriend) had decided overnight to break into the downstairs bar and consume copious volumes of vodka. After which, he had stolen the keys to the manager's car and driven off into the town to drown, beyond oblivion, his sorrows. After crashing said car, and being arrested by the police, our chef was returned to the hotel by the boys in blue.

"Wow," I said. "What a mess!"

"That's not the problem," the manager explained to me, "It gets a lot worse."

Without too much thinking, I quickly advised the manager that he was to sack the Head Chef on the spot, (not the correct procedure these days!) and instructed him that the chef should also vacate his live-in accommodation immediately. (Another breach of procedures).

I was spared the colourful exchange of expletives that I am sure punctuated the required employee discussions, and I began to consider the number of HR issues that would no doubt require a resolution. It was after that, that my manager called me again and said;

"That's all dealt with boss, but look, that's where the real problem has started."

What *other* problem? I thought to myself. Wasn't *this* the problem? Wasn't it now dealt with?

I could not believe that this issue could get any worse – but it really did. The manager continued;

"Well, we were not previously aware, but the chef kept tarantula spiders in a glass tank in his bedroom in the hotel. When he was instructed to leave the premises, he decided to empty his tank into his bedroom. We believe that he had up to four tarantula spiders which are now loose in the building, and the hotel is completely full of guests."

My manager then committed the ultimate abdication by asking;

"What do you want me to do - boss?"

Despite my youth, I have always had a dry sense of humour and my initial reply was "Don't worry, I will look it up in my area manager manual – under S for spiders and T for tarantulas, but I'm guessing that page might be missing." Call it sarcasm or gallows humour – but I thought it was an appropriate response at the time, whilst I was really thinking "What the hell?!!."

"Leave it with me" I said. "Don't do anything yet whilst I make some calls – AND DON'T TELL ANYONE."

And so, the journey began…

As I worked for a national pub company, we had specialist contractors responsible for pest and vermin control. I won't state their name here, but they were renown for killing things. It was an Easter weekend and therefore finding an account manager to deal with the problem was difficult. I eventually tracked one down and quickly gave them a stripped-down version, namely- "We have a 12-bedroom hotel with four escaped tarantulas, can you get one of your team over A.S.A.P. – like now?"

I suppose I shouldn't have been surprised with the reply from a dour vermin terminator contract manager, which was, "I am very sorry, but tarantulas are not covered by your contract."

Despite the temptation to let out a range of aggressive expletives, I had the good sense to not let this rat killer off the hook,

"Is there anyone you can recommend for handling tarantulas?" I asked.

Now that is a sentence I had never expected to use and have never used since, but it was probably the most sensible thing I said all day. My exterminator of vermin had a very blunt answer, "I suppose you could ring a local zoo."

So, just recap, it's Easter weekend, we have a twelve-bedroom pub restaurant that's full of residents, we have four (more or less) tarantulas running wild and our contracted national bug killer is washing their hands of the problem. And it's now probably four hours since the eight-legged monsters were catapulted into freedom.

Was it hope or desperation, who knows – but I rang Blackpool Zoo and asked to speak to someone in the entomology department. Somehow my education had taught me that entomology covered everything creep crawly. As you would expect, zoos are pretty busy during an Easter weekend and after a long, long, long hold (would there still be any customers alive in my business by this time?) I was put through to a staff member in the creepy crawly department. I cut my story even shorter;

"Help, four tarantulas loose in a hotel – what should we do?"

I still don't know the name of the person I spoke to, by now good manners had escaped me. However, this very pleasant person absolutely howled with laughter. I kept calm, "Please, please, please, what would you recommend?" (Note the slight hint of desperation).

I can paraphrase at this point for brevity, but my zoo creepy crawly expert advised me that tarantulas really need a better P.R. Manager, because their bite was very rarely dangerous unless you were over 85 years of age, or under 8 and was more like a bee sting.

At this point I did wonder the statistical odds of how many residents were in that age bracket, but I quickly gave up on the calculation. I was also advised that there are varied species of tarantulas that can easily be discerned from their knee colour, and apparently the ones with the brown knees are the vicious buggers. The obvious request was "Please, please, please, what would you recommend?"

I was then given the crystal-clear information I needed. "Tarantulas are from the Amazon and need a minimum temperature of 20 degrees or they die very quickly, certainly within 48 hours". Hallelujah, I had a solution, and I thanked my zoo expert. I then made a business decision which still bears heavy on my conscience.

I rang the manager and advised him that looking under furniture for the colour of the spider's knees was not required. Somehow, I don't think he was up to the task. And so, I instructed him that the plan of action was to immediately switch off the heating for forty-eight hours (Barrow in Furness is not blessed with average temperatures above twenty degrees over Easter, and not even in the peak of summer). Our customers were to be advised that there had been a boiler breakdown and that it is almost impossible to get a heating contractor to come out over Easter.

In recompense we gave each room a bouquet of flowers, a box of chocolates and free bottle of "chilled" wine with their chilly evening meal (no expense spared!), and after forty-eight hours we all breathed a sigh of relief and switched the boiler back on.

And so, the story ends of the worst Easter of my working life. However; to this day, my imagination still runs riot as to whether any of the eight-legged critters managed to crawl to the pub boiler, nestling into the warmth for dear life.

The pub was also located within twenty miles of a nuclear power station. Is it possible that those spiders survived, adapted, and multiplied in those conditions and genetically mutated from nuclear radiation?

Soon after this event I moved on from managing the site and so did the manager. I have checked on a well-known search engine and the business is still running under new owners. But who knows if a giant, nuclear charged arachnid break out is due at some time in the future? But if it is, I deny any legal liability (your honour!). And thereby rests the case for the defence.

David Lee

Elvis flees from Whitney's Mum!

In 1994, I was working as an Events Co-Ordinator for Greenall Whitley, organising events such as 'Karaoke Copycats' – a twist on 'Sing like the Stars.' The popularity of the event, along with the two-hundred-and-fifty-pound winning prize, meant we hosted the final in the largest venue possible in Liverpool, and tickets were quickly sold out. There was an electric atmosphere on the night.

After the eight heats and two semi-finals, we had our six acts deservedly chosen for the final, including Liverpool's own answer to Elvis Presley and Whitney Houston. The acts had all brought huge support with them, with family and friends thundering their support for their chosen contestant.

All in fact, but the Elvis impersonator, who despite quickly emerging as the clear favourite, had evidently forgotten his supporting cast! The growing support for the other contestants, from a clearly biased audience, suggested that favouritism was trumping talent!

As the alcohol continued to flow, support from family and friends became even louder, and as the judges made it clear to us that Elvis was the obvious winner, we began to get concerned about how the decision would be received.

As the designated company representative, I was the person to announce the decision, so as I nervously stepped on stage, I took a deep breath and announced Elvis as our winner.

To describe the crowd's reaction as complete silence would be an understatement, despite the best attempt of the judges and myself to clap loudly enough for the masses. And even though not having much experience in the pub trade, it was clear that the atmosphere was becoming unpleasant and uncomfortable, so I quickly brought up the two runners up, which to my relief accompanied huge cheers. Unfortunately, the worst was yet to come!

As we left the stage, the mother of our Whitney Houston impersonator, who had one of the largest followings on the night, decided to confront Elvis, inexplicably claiming, "My daughter has been robbed!"

Sensing that things were about to take a turn for the worse, we knew we had to get out.

Thankfully, with the aid of the Manager, the now unpopular group headed by Elvis, and including the judges and myself, were quickly ushered through the back-exit doors, with the belief that our presence would only fuel the tense situation.

It took a while for things inside the venue to settle down, and at one point the police had to be called to assist the venue and help disperse the crowd, although thankfully no injuries or arrests were made. Despite being relieved at making such a hasty escape at the time, the headline in the local paper the next day did make us all smile – 'Elvis flees from Whitney's mum!'

Unsurprisingly, that was the last time we held any karaoke competitions in that particular pub!

International Toilet Confusion

It was a pleasantly warm summer in England's South Coast, in 1983. Every Saturday lunch time was hectic. A bout of pleasant weather had boosted the business, and our spacious beer garden was full to the brim. The bar was packed with locals and a mix of tourists and students from the local university. Queues of families gathered with their hungry kids and elderly relatives, patiently waiting in an orderly queue for tables.

I'd been the manager at the pub for two years. I loved the job. It was hard, but every day was different, and I enjoyed the buzz. The people, the banter… it was almost fun just to work. I couldn't imagine the monotony of a desk job or working in a factory. Bar management suited me.

This one particularly thriving afternoon, we were a little stretched for staff. Summertime wasn't only busy for trade; it also meant dealing with staff holidays, student staff going back to their hometowns, and on this eventful day, some staff sickness was thrown in for good measure. We were just about coping. The kitchen team were stressed, and the waiting staff flew busily about from bar to kitchen and back again, like manic bees to and from a hive. Everyone was focused, and there was little time for the usual jokes and chat until the rush was over.

During the 1pm frenzy, I noticed a lanky male student who looked suspiciously stressed and pained at the busy bar. He was impatiently waiting his turn behind the crowd, but I sensed he was keen to ask something rather than order drinks or food.

"You okay mate?" I called over to him.

"Toilet please", the guy responded in a heavy French accent. His voice was almost shaking with that "I REALLY need to find a toilet" vibe that can sometimes take over you unexpectedly. We often had foreign customers in the pub during summer, mainly due to an exchange programme at the local university, but also due to tourism. Slap bang between Brighton and Portsmouth, we were a natural base for holiday makers.

I pointed over to the toilet sign above the entrance to the pub, which was not particularly well signposted. It was easy to miss, and customers often walked straight past it on their way in. The building was old and not well designed like modern premises, and the small gents toilet with a single trap and a large, long urinal looked like it had been added as an afterthought, sometime in the 18th century.

The guy urgently hurried towards the toilet, and I continued serving. Time flew by and we were winning the war. Empty plates were flying back into the kitchen and bar staff began to look happier. Cheerful glances at watches confirmed it was 2pm, and we all knew we'd beaten the worst part of the rush. We didn't have all day trading back then, so service was always short and sharp.

As I was washing up, in the corner of my eye I caught a glimpse of the Toilet Man, leaving with his group of friends. They appeared happy, but he seemed a little less relaxed… almost agitated. As he turned to leave, I noticed that his pale, blue shirt was soaking wet across the back of his shoulders.

I waved them goodbye.

"Strange," I thought to myself. "Perhaps a weird, sweating pattern or a mishap with a spilt drink?"

I continued washing up and then checked on staff to see if everyone was ok. I also did a quick stock check, replaced some spirits and topped up the fridges, ready for the evening session. Lastly, a quick round of the tills to take out excess notes, and my mid-day routine was almost over with only a toilet check to do.

As usual, the ladies' toilets were fine. The men's toilet in the saloon bar, apart from some missing toilet roll, was also in a serviceable order for the next session. Finally, I paid my visit to the toilet in the public bar, opposite the main entrance.

As I opened the door, I was caught with an unpleasant surprise. Sitting proudly in the middle of the long, ceramic urinal was the reason for our foreign visitor's haste.

I tried to work out how this had happened. A joke? No, I thought - even the rugby boys wouldn't do that, and besides, they hadn't been in today. I didn't recall anyone being paralytic who might have been the culprit. It wasn't unusual to occasionally find human faeces on the cubicle floor or a soiled pair of boxers, when someone had become legless and been unable to navigate the toilet or perform the simple task of undoing their own belt and lowering their trousers.

After pondering the strange situation, my mind swung to our French student with the wet shirt, and my detective skills started to solve the riddle. There was only one cubicle in that toilet, and he had looked desperate to go. By the look of the deposit in the bottom of the urinal, he must have been close to bursting. It seems that having finally found the toilet, that the single cubicle was no doubt already occupied during the busy session, and in his desperation, I imagined, the stressed-out student must have gently lowered himself into the old urinal, with his back against the urine covered wet ceramic, and relieved himself.

To add insult to injury, it appeared that he must have been caught in the process by a quick shower from the water jets at the top of the urinal that go off every few minutes to wash away the stale wee. Hence a wet shirt and an unhappy young Frenchman.

As I contemplated how I was going to remove the offending item, I attached a "toilet closed" sign to the door and retreated from the unfortunate scene. Such fun being a bar manager, I chuckled to myself, as I went off to find a hose and some strong bleach. Fun at work... perhaps not completely fun!

Clive Hawkins

Bath Time

It was the bodacious eighties, and The Jolly Sailor in the Hanover area of Brighton had become my local. It was run by Harry and Joan, who, despite a certain trait to be explained shortly, were both very friendly and welcoming.

Harry was a big character who prided himself on being the face of the pub, whilst Joan would spend her time doing what she loved the most – serving her customers from behind the bar. The clientele were a mixed bunch to say the least, but they all seemed to gel well, and between the Mickey-taking and the banter, there was genuinely never a dull moment.

If you've ever been down to your local on a weekend, it shouldn't be too hard to envisage this scene: It's Saturday evening and approaching eight o'clock. The six o'clock crowd are still going strong and the thirsty later arrivals are just now coming through the door – the pub is buzzing! Two superstars, Gill and Erica, are completely rushed off their feet trying to satisfy the demand for drinks whilst Harry is stationary, holding court on the pub floor.

Harry summons the two girls and declares that he is 'off for his bath now' and slinks upstairs. For context, this was not the first time that the eight o'clock bath had been announced. It was actually a frequent occurrence – you could even say that Harry's attraction to the tub shared similar exuberance to that of the drinkers to the pub – and the poor remaining team were always left to deal with it.

One thing that everyone agreed on was that getting served by Harry was a major achievement. One regular, Potato Pete, even had t-shirts printed with 'I Got Served by Harry' for any customers that were rendered fortunate enough.

The fact that Harry would vanish to his precious bath as soon as the pub got busy, leaving the workaholic landlady Joan and her bar team stranded, was a common cause of gags from the patrons. However, this was water off a duck's back to him; I think there must have been a solution of Teflon mixed into his bath water, as the berating just bounced right off him.

Back then, I was an alarm engineer by trade and one day Harry had asked me to give him an estimate to install a security system in the pub and living space. This was approved, and I started work, but half-way through the job I had an idea that would wreak havoc upon Harry's bath time. I was left alone in the living space as I had the floorboards up, and nobody noticed that I was secretly installing cables and equipment into the bathroom with an ulterior motive.

A few weeks later, the word had spread that something was going to happen at Harry's bath time. Everyone was sworn to secrecy, except for Harry and Joan's son Jimmy, who had helped me perform a test run whilst his parents were out.

Underneath the bath I had fixed an extremely noisy electronic siren with a loudspeaker. Alongside this a microphone was set up in the bar and connected to an amp and another speaker which was placed strategically under Harry's sacred space. The pub was getting crowded and had a great atmosphere, fired up by the anticipation of a legendary stitch-up in the making.

Sure enough, just before eight whilst the bar was even busier than usual, Harry made his disappearing act to the bath. A couple of – you might say – 'more vocal' regulars, set themselves up at the bar with the microphone. We waited for our signal from Jimmy, who in time gave us the nod that Harry had just settled comfortably into the tub. It was time - I pressed the button generating an almighty din.

The two lads then proceeded to bestow upon Harry a stream of verbal stick about being in the bath when the pub was so busy, the fact that his naked body was being videoed, and that he was now in full view of everyone in the bar!

Unfortunately, it was only a one-way speaker system and no actual cameras, so we were unable to see or hear any of Harry's responses, which I am sure would have been unprintable anyway. However, Jimmy had been stationed outside the bathroom door and heard it all, and he did say it was his dad's shortest bath to date!

As you can imagine, the bar was in fits of laughter and the pints were flowing generously when eventually the door to the stairs opened and out came Harry to a cacophony of clapping, cheering and laughter. He must have had an extra dose of Teflon in his bath that night, as he simply took a bow and went on *not* serving people.

How Strong is this Wine?

One of the key roles of working in a pub, or dealing with the general public, is responding to their various enquiries. Questions can come in all shapes and sizes, and often after a few alcoholic beverages they can be a little bizarre, yet we do our best to give an informative answer. I always try to be helpful but sometimes mischief does get in the way, despite my best intentions.

I recall one particular occasion; we had a group of friends drinking in the bar. They had spent the evening enjoying each other's company in a relaxing atmosphere, and by now had consumed quite a few drinks. One of them, a young lady, approached the bar, waving a large glass of sloshing wine enthusiastically in the air.

"Excuse me." she said, "Can you help me? I was just wondering, what is the percentage of alcohol in a glass of wine? I know a bottle is between ten and 15 percent, but don't know what a glass is?"

I tried, I honestly did, but the wicked side of my brain took over and I teasingly responded. "Depends on which part of the bottle you got it from as all the alcohol sinks to the bottom. So always try to have the last glass from the bottle, either that or shake the bottle before you open it."

The lovely polite young lady looked delighted with this 'technical' explanation and returned to her friends to share my words of industry educated wisdom.

If you have been the victim of anyone shaking wine, or heaven forbid, champagne bottles before they open them, then I am sorry, and I can only apologise!

Gary Joines

The Marsden Grotto

It was a bright and pleasant Glasgow morning as I set off early, ready for my commute to meet the engineers who were assessing the maintenance required to get the pub lift repaired. We were beginning to get ready for the fast-approaching Easter holidays and the inevitable peak trade that it would bring.

As I drove towards South Shields Bay, watching the dawn break, I found myself pondering the history of my workplace, The Marsden Grotto. I was debating exactly how much dynamite would have been necessary for Jack Bates to blow a cave large enough to build a home for his family in 1782, before the site became a pub in the next century.

Soon enough I arrived at the pub's cliff car park. As I pulled in and got out of the car, I saw the manager standing by the pub signpost, looking rather stressed and shaking his head in disbelief.

I wished him a good morning, to which he replied,

"Yup, it's definitely morning. Not sure about the good part though. Those kids have been meddling with the signage again."

This wasn't the first time we'd had this problem, so I turned around to see what had been done. As I turned, I couldn't help but have the Fawlty Towers theme tune start playing in my head.

Our sign no longer said,' WELCOME TO THE MARSDEN GROTTO'. It now read' WELCOME TO ARSE ROT'.

I bet Jack Bates didn't have to deal with this kind of nonsense; and where was that dynamite?

Count your Chickens

If anyone has had to prepare for a visit from your new boss to your business, then (if you really care about your reputation) you will understand the stress and worry involved to make every single detail perfect. The panic, the double checking, the sheer agony of waiting for the boss to arrive. You don't get a second chance to make a first impression and all that.

This was exactly how one publican felt when he had a scheduled visit from a Business Development Manager (BDM) to his rural pub several years ago.

The preparations were made and the 'coal painted white' for the big day. The BDM was on his way. The Publican lived in a cottage in a field to the rear of the pub and had its own, long, separate driveway. The BDM (himself preparing, looking for notes on his passenger seat as he was driving) passed the pub quickly and headed on up the empty road towards the cottage.

Except the driveway wasn't empty, which the BDM realised after a soft thud on the bottom of the car.

The publican and his family kept chickens which they had brought with them to the new pub as a family petting zoo. Much to the BDM's horror, and after a quick inspection of the front, newly feathered wheel arch, he realised that he had managed to run one over. Being very embarrassed, and after a quick look around to see if he had been spotted, he hid the deceased chicken in his boot, silently praying he would not be caught.

A short time later, after a successful and positive meeting, the publican cheekily asked the BDM if he had any Heineken goodies in his car, stating "Come on then, let's see what you have in your boot!"

It was often common for BDM's who were visiting pubs to bring promotional items with them, which meant it was difficult for the BDM to deny having any at all in his car. Sheepishly, he came clean to the publican, admitting he had hit a chicken on his way up. It was hidden amongst the bar towels and other goodies he had stored in the boot.

After an initial outburst of restrained anger from the publican, he was able to see the funny side of the situation and they were able to share a laugh about it.

Now, he had one up on his new boss, and perhaps he would not be as stressed out the next time he visited. He might even plant another dead chicken on the road and then he would definitely get some free merchandise!

So, I guess there is a moral to this tale, which is, always come clean if you make a mistake, and perhaps, something about counting your chickens!

Phil Preston

Tom

Just another Sunday night.

It was early August, and the weather had been glorious for the entire weekend, keeping the pub garden full of happy faces. Faces we had only just started seeing again as the national virus lockdown had ended a little over a month prior. The day had been typically unexciting. I start every day with a game plan, always have, probably always will, and Sundays were no exception.

By midday, I'd prepped the reports and envelopes for the end of week financial returns, made my kids their lunch, and grabbed a quick piece of toast.

In the early evening after the lunchtime rush, staff breaks were taken, and I usually cleared the cellar ready for the evening stock count. This Sunday was following the perfect routine.

As the sun started to go down and the kitchen was closing, there were just three of us left on the bar. We busied ourselves cleaning tables, filling up napkins, clearing the last of the glasses from the few remaining occupied tables. By 9pm there were only a few outside seats taken so another staff member was sent home. I was cleaning down the front of the bar and chattering away to my colleague Alisa, when we noticed an unfamiliar face coming from the garden doors, down the few steps towards us.

We watched as he wobbled and nearly collided with the table at the bottom of the stairs. Both of us trying to hold in an innocent giggle, we continued to watch him stagger past us towards the toilets. Andy, our chef had finished his shift and was having a well-deserved drink in the front garden.

"Do us a favour hun, check on a guy in the gents for me?" I asked him. He popped his head round the door of the gents.

"Yeah, he's alright, he's having a piss." Reassured, I carried on cleaning.

A couple of minutes passed by, and I hadn't seen the man walk past me back to the garden. I went to check myself, and as I walked past the open lobby door to the gents, what I saw caused my heart to race.

There was a large crimson mark on the wall, and fresh blood on the floor. I stuck my head round the internal door and was greeted by a smear of blood around head height above the corner urinal. I continued my journey through the front doors to the car park. There, standing extremely unsteadily, essentially clinging to the metal barrier, was the guy I was looking for.

As I approached him, I could make out a large gash on his forehead and blood running down his face. I ran back inside, grabbed a pair of gloves and hospitality-grade paper towel while shouting to Alisa to find his friends in the garden and get them outside. As I returned to him, I started talking to him.

His eyes welled, his face a mess; I began to worry about the injury to his head. I told him my name, who I was, and that I was going to clean his face up. While I attended the wound, I realised he was completely unable to respond to me, and then one of the group that he had been sitting with came out.

"Tom mate, you alright? What have you done?" It was Chaz, one of our regulars. He looked at me.
I explained that he'd wobbled down the steps, gone to the loo then obviously made his way out here.
"How much has he had to drink?" I asked. I hadn't served him once that evening and Alisa was only aware of him having one pint, as she had taken their order out to their table shortly before he'd gone inside. Chaz told me he'd only been there with them less than half an hour.

"Shall I get him home?" asked Chaz. "I'll call a cab."

I looked at Tom. His face was cleaned up, but the cut was quite big. And he could barely stand; he was holding on to the rail for dear life.

"He needs an ambulance. No taxi will take him. He needs to be checked out," I replied.

Chaz got out his phone to call 999.

Tom was looking worse so getting hold of him under the arms, I lowered him from the hunched over position he was in and rested him on the edge of a flower trough. From there I moved him to the ground, then put him in the recovery position. Alisa came out from the bar, seeing him on the floor she looked panicked.

"It's OK," I tried to reassure her. "I'm with him, Chaz has called an ambulance. Just get everyone to drink up and go turn the tills off and do what you can, I'll be with you as soon as I can." She nodded and went back in.

Another couple from the group who had been drinking with Tom came out. They were laughing and joking.

"Bloody hell Tom, you'll do anything for attention! What a lightweight, you'd barely had a pint!" They stood across the barrier from us, watching me watching over their friend on the ground.

I was growing increasingly concerned every time I looked at him, the colour of his skin had turned sallow. I felt his wrist. His pulse was weak and faint. The thin cotton of his shirt was wet, his hand felt clammy. Having seen my dad in the same state many years previously, I knew things had gone rapidly downhill. I pulled my phone from my pocket and dialled 999.

I explained who I was, what was happening, and the voice on the other end spoke very calmly back to me. "There is an ambulance coming, but there's traffic, they will be with you soon. Are you alone with him?"

Chaz was about ten metres away; the others had returned to the garden to finish their drinks as Alisa had told them the bar was closing. I called out instructions to Chaz as they were given to me.

"The pharmacy, Buckleys, just down the road has a defib kit, you need to run and get it, there's a code on the box. Just get it, NOW!"

I could see the reality of what was happening dawn on his face.

Still listening to the responder, I carried out the directives given to me. Turning Tom onto his back, I placed his legs and arms flat and tilted his head back to open his airway. With the phone tucked under my chin, I unbuttoned his shirt. His chest was barely moving. I kneeled next to his ribs. Clasping one hand other the over, I pushed his sternum down, once, twice, three times, four times, five – rest to the count of five. Again., One, two, three, four, five, rest.

The voice kept coming through the phone, which I had now put on speaker on the ground next to me. I could see Alisa coming towards me. She looked terrified. I kept going. One, two, three, four, five. Rest. Again., One, two, three, four, five.

I called to Alisa to hold my phone next to me. There were now more faces in front of me, his friends open-mouthed, watching. I looked at Tom; there was frothed spittle at the corners of his mouth. A foul stench came from his slightly parted lips and the edges were now a deep blue. I knew he was dead, but I was not stopping. I shouted my observations to the mobile in Alisa's outstretched arm, and a less confident voice assured me help was on its way.

"Where the fuck is Chaz, where the fuck is the defibrillator?" I shouted to no one. I knew time was not on our side, and with each round of compressions I feared I might not be able to keep him going much longer. I breathed a loud sigh of relief a minute or so later as Chaz appeared, with a green bag in his hands. His expression turned to horror as he registered Tom's lifeless form. "Get it open, follow the instructions!" I yelled at him.

He and another from the group set about trying to get the kit together. Not missing a beat as I pumped Tom's chest, I watched as they removed the charging box and pads and cables. Unable to help them, they scrambled in their unfamiliarity to try to set it up. A button was pressed that issued verbal instructions.

As they were nearly ready to attach pads to Tom, a loud siren sounded in the distance. Almost instantly, a medic car pulled up. Still fighting to keep going, I gave as much information as I could, while he got out equipment and got ready to help me. "Are you OK to keep going while I check his pulse?"

"Of course. I'm not stopping," I replied.

He opened Tom's eyes and shone a light in. I could see the lack of reaction in them. Feeling his neck, the medic made out a very weak, very slow pulse.

"Keep going, you're doing great," he told me.

Another siren could be heard, getting closer. Very close. The medic was telling me he was going to take over from me to rest my arms. "After this five, we swap." I nodded my agreement, and we counted together. "...three, four, five." I removed my hands as quickly as I could. The medic, hands interlaced at the fingers, took over.

I stood as the ambulance pulled in, and went over to the team that were frantically pulling out bags of equipment, donning gloves and masks, and answered every question they asked - who is he? His age? What happened? How long has he been unconscious, and how long had I been doing chest compressions?

I realised then it had been nearly twenty minutes. Bloody hell!
Another siren sounded behind me, a second ambulance. I relayed the same information to them and then went back over to where the first medic was still pumping up and down on Tom's chest, while the two new crews worked around him. There were tubes everywhere and a small oxygen cylinder. Sticky

pads were stuck on his chest and connected to a portable monitor. Someone else was cutting clothes off to attach more tubes.

"Can you take over again? He's getting tired," a masked faced asked me. "Of course," I said, and on the count of five I resumed my position on my knees beside Tom, keeping the rhythm going. The monitor behind me beeped slowly. There was an occasional heartbeat.

He was still with us, but only just. The work going on around me was borderline frantic. One person opened his airway and put an oxygen line in, another set up a drip. Blood pressure was being taken through an arm cuff, and a SAT's monitor was put on one finger while blood sugars were taken from another with a quick prick. Boards were placed either side of him, ready to lift him to the waiting trolley behind us.

"We're going to move him now. When I say stop, stop." I nodded in response. In one swift movement, he was lifted one side, then the other, and the boards clipped together.
We all lifted him up to the waiting trolley, which was then wheeled to the open ambulance, and as one they set about rigging up more monitors and preparing to take him away.

"Are you OK?" It was Alisa. I just nodded.

"uh huh, mmm." My legs felt like jelly.

We watched as the ambulance doors closed, and one of the team got in the driver's seat. The lights went on, and as they pulled away the siren started. The second crew and the first medic tidied the last of the bags.

"You did great, well done. He's got half a chance because of you. "It was directed at me.
I shrugged in response and could only say, "thank you. Thank you for everything."

"Come on then, let's get this pub shut," I motioned to Alisa. We walked into the pub together, locking the doors behind us.

The next day we were both on shift together. Neither of us had really slept, and it showed.

We were both shell-shocked after we had finished clearing up, I'd still had the tills and the paperwork, plus the stock to do. Once finished, it was nearly 4am, and Alisa had stayed with me; she hadn't wanted to go home and think about it anymore than I did.

Later that day, I got a phone call. The voice was unfamiliar, and I'd had to ask who it was. It was one of Tom's friends. I felt tears running down my face as he gave me the news. Tom was in intensive care, very frail, very poorly and in need of major surgery. But he was still with us. That was enough for me.

It was over two months before I saw Tom again.
He had been in hospital for seven weeks, recovering, and was on the waiting list for heart surgery. He had arrested three times in total and had essentially been *dead* for nearly twenty minutes while lying there on the ground. I hugged him tight while we both cried. He thanked me.

I was just thrilled to see him with my own eyes. Alive.

Jo Fuller

Kids will be Kids

The Pack Horse on Briggate is the oldest pub site in Leeds. It was built around 1550, and in 1982, following the discovery of some fifteenth-century elements of the original buildings, it had a major refurbishment and finally became the pub we all love today: The Pack Horse.

The thoughts are that a drinking house has been on the site since the 1130's and it has an iron Templar Cross on the gable end. The cross tells us that it was part of the manor of Whitkirk, which was owned by the Order of St John of Jerusalem, successors to the Knights Templar. To cut a long story short, it's old!

The pub has a traditional feel - proper pub cellar, bar on the ground floor, toilets on the first floor, kitchen, and a secondary bar upstairs, with this second floor also housing storage and some accommodation.

As to be expected, there's loads of dark wood knocking about, stained glass, mirrors, some very questionable wiring and grade II listed beams that breathe generations of history throughout the building.

I moved in there in spring 1998, a young, single male not needing much space other than for my games console and CD collection, and the top floor became my home for the foreseeable.

I arrived there to a good set of regulars who gave the usual friendly words of advice and wisdom for any budding new landlord: You won't be as good as John; We'll miss Eric and Dawn; I'll give you six months; You need to watch him; and of course, have they told you it's haunted?

I knew Eric and Dawn, and to be fair they were big boots to fill, but the pub did very well, and I didn't give much thought to the rest of the advice. My accommodation housed two small bedrooms, a bathroom, boiler room and kitchen come office; if you're wondering what a kitchen come office looks like, it was a regular kitchen with a table covered in administrative documents shoved in the corner.

I lived upstairs on my own for a couple of weeks before the deputy manager, Jeannie, moved into the other room. I'm probably not the tidiest person but everything has its place. Keys, wallet - always in the same place. The "office" had to be organised, it being a table in the kitchen. So, when things started to go awry it freaked me out a little; I had a few chats with Jeannie about putting things back properly, but she said she always did and so that was that.

Then it started to be a bit more obvious. I'd be filling in the huge ledger book that all landlords had back then; start at the top left on a Sunday morning and finish bottom right on a Saturday night. I'd get up from the chair, walk the two steps to the kitchen to make a coffee and be back sat down. No calculator, I've left it next to the kettle, ok. Then the next time it was the pen, and then I couldn't find the calculator at all until I came back to the desk, and it was where I'd been using it.

I presumed a practical joke or perhaps just madness, but Jeannie confirmed the same thing was happening to her too, nothing ever serious, but a little mischievous. Surely this wasn't the hauntings that the regulars had warned me about; I thought ghosts were scary not simply mildly inconveniencing!

The pub was always busy right from the get-go, so I found early on that a lot of time was spent here. All the while in the main bar you could feel something around you, tapping on your lower back, a little pull on your belt, sometimes even a little tickle on the ribs. It was very weird, but we put up with it, and it did happen to all the staff.

One day though, it was like a scene from Jumanji. It was an ok lunch, not too busy, when suddenly, there was a sort of drum sound. Customers could hear it, as well as staff, and it was as if the kegs in the cellar were being rhythmically banged with mallets. It got louder and louder, even causing glasses to vibrate on the tabletops, until…

Suddenly it stopped, and so did the flow of beer from all the taps. I very slowly, and rather reluctantly I might add, as could be seen by the sweating expression painted across my face, crept into the cellar with Jeannie a few steps behind, only to find that all the keg connector handles, which allow the flow of beer to the pumps behind the bar, had been lifted up!

There was nobody in there, and the only way out was through the bar where we had been stood listening to the commotion. That did raise the hairs on the back of my neck, but stoically we put the handles down and carried on, rather than burning the place down and running for the hills as was my first thought.

We also had spirits hung upside down on optics, mirrored on either side of the bar, and one evening both bottles of schnapps shot forwards from their optics and over the bar, shattering into a thousand pieces on the floor, at least a six-foot jump for both bottles at the same time. We put it down to user error on the optics but, again, very weird.

Then came the main event.

We had a Christmas display to do, it was our first, so we were going big. Papier-Mache mountains, with a train set running through them, Canadian Mounties drinking Labatt Ice. The works! At around 3am I went upstairs to the flat to get some more stationary, when the intercom went mad.

'Have you just been in the upstairs bar?' Jeannie asked.

'No, just up here at the minute, why?' I answered suspiciously.

'Then there's someone up there, I've just heard a load of footsteps and banging', she said in a panic.

'I haven't heard anything, but I'll go down now.'

There was nothing and no-one there…

'There's no-one here' I said, 'I've not passed anyone, we'll check the toilets.'

They were also clear, but I could see Jeannie was shaken up, so we went downstairs, grabbed a large stiff drink, and talked it through. After a short while, myself beginning to believe that Jeannie had simply made the whole thing up, sure enough the sound of footsteps crashed on the ceiling above.

'Oh, like that!' and I ran off upstairs to again find nobody on the top bar!

Another drink was needed. We listened to it, repeatedly. It was like two children banging through the two sets of double doors, footsteps running across the top section, down the steps, across to the wall and then back again, giggling as they went, as if they were playing and having a race. It went on for around an hour then stopped. None of us were working the next day and it was light before we dared go back upstairs.

We would often go out after work, or just go for a chat with managers from other pubs, and if we came back late enough, or early enough in some cases, sure enough we'd hear the same commotion. You couldn't hear it from upstairs, but clear as day from the main bar. We started to just say goodnight if we were going up at a normal time, and if we were downstairs when it was happening, we just waited it out, until one day I shouted up:

'Can you stop that please, it's late and you shouldn't be running around!'

There was a bit more giggling and then the running stopped. Magic!

A few months later it was our area manager's leaving do. We'd had a few drinks in The Pack Horse, had a walk round a good few pubs in Leeds and then back to mine for a couple more. There was only a few of us left – the area manager had already gone, but Tracey, a pub manager from Halifax, was staying in Jeannie's room as she was away on holiday. It was getting towards 3am as she grabbed my arm.

'I've just seen someone moving over there.' She said, with a terrified look, 'And again, look, over there.'

'In the mirrors? I asked, 'Don't worry about it, it's an old place and it's late.'

I managed to settle her down and she seemed ok, then the running started.

Now, in hindsight, I should probably have warned her beforehand, but it was such a common occurrence that I didn't really think about it anymore.

'What the hell is that?' she screamed.

'Ah,' I said, hurriedly explaining the story before she ran for her coat, 'You just need to shout up and tell them to be quiet.'

71

After a few expletives and head shakes I managed to take her by the hand to the bottom of the stairs and she shouted up to them, but nothing happened.

'Excuse me!' I shouted up, 'This is Tracey, and she is a friend of mine, now you should listen when she talks to you.'

'Try again,' I said to Tracey.

'Can you stop running around please!' she shouted upstairs, 'It's late and you shouldn't be running around!'

There was a couple more giggles and then it all stopped.

'There you are. All sorted. Now where were we? Shall we have one more and then go up?' I asked.

But Tracey's coat was already on, her bag was on her shoulder, and she was off to get a taxi back to Halifax. With a sigh, I switched off the lights and went upstairs.

'Well thank you very much for that,' I said, 'next time I'll warn you if someone is staying!'

But we never heard them again. And I can't believe I'm putting this in writing, but maybe I was a little harsh on the two ghost kiddies that were just having fun.

You can shout all you like sometimes but usually you are wasting your time, even if it is hundreds of years! Kids will be kids.

Wake up for Pool

"Boys are you awake!"

A shout came up from the pub downstairs to the flat above. This was our father's preferred method of communication to our childhood home. He was often rushed off his feet, lacking the enthusiasm and energy to climb up the long narrow stairwell to deliver a politer and more personal message.

"I need you for a second," he shouted. Although we could sense a slight softening of his voice.

He sounded flustered, slightly desperate. Unusually polite compared to his normal tone.

My brother and I were twins and had lived in various pubs for as long as we could remember. It was a constant source of amusement for our friends, who often joked that we could spend our lives dining like royalty on crisps and peanuts. The reality was less than ideal. Parents working long hours including evenings and weekends, and rarely any family time together. But we did not mind. We did not know any different and the lack of parental supervision gave us our independence. Also, it was the 80's. Kids didn't moan as much as they do now.

I sat up in bed. Should I continue this shouting conversation from my room? Probably not a good idea, I thought to myself. I grabbed my glasses and swung my legs out from under the bedclothes, putting my feet onto the cold wooden floor. In the half-light I lazily searched for my slippers with my toes. I had not been asleep.

It was the beginning of December and my mind was filled with pages from the latest Argos catalogue of potential Christmas presents. I was obsessed with getting an Evil Knievel stunt bike, images of the many interesting accessories available had plagued my mind, making it difficult to nod off.

I walked to my bedroom door and opened it.

"What's up?" I shouted down the hall.

"Do you boys want a game of pool? We are short of some players," Dad responded.

It took me a second to process but I quickly realised it was Thursday night. Pool Night, no doubt it was our pubs turn to host a home game against one of the other local pubs.

"We've had two people drop out and we will have to concede the night if we can't find anyone." Dad added. "Come on…". His initial polite request was quickly becoming an instruction.

As my brother's head gingerly emerged from his bedroom door, it quickly occurred to me that the idea of two ten-year-old boys dressed in Superman pyjamas competing in a noisy, smoke filled bar full of drunk men was not the best of ideas.

Firstly, would the person we were playing even accept this as worthy competition? They might see it as an easy night, but equally, they could see it as kind of insulting. Secondly, how would they take it if we beat them? What seemed like a fun idea could quickly turn sour as they faced becoming the butt off all jokes. Who would want to be known as the only man in the village to be thrashed by a speccy ten-year-old boy in furry slippers.

"It will be fine." Dad said, sensing my unease.

I turned to my brother, whose face told me that he required no explanation of the situation and was also running through the scenarios in his head.

Our dad disappeared from the bottom of the stairs. Seemingly, despite any actual agreement, the deal had been done. He was no doubt already filling in the locals on the plan as we both could begin to hear some increased chatter and laugher drifting up from the public bar.

As we often did as twins, we just gave each other a look. No words were needed. We both knew this was weird. We grabbed our cues and silently made

74

our way down the stairs, resigned to our uncertain fate and potential humiliation.

The public bar was busy and as I had imagined it was noisy and smoky. An intimidating place for a couple of ten-year olds. Supportive smiles and nods came from the familiar faces of the locals as we made our way quietly past the back of the bar and then out into the main area, cues in hand, dressed in our matching blue pyjamas and slippers.

We quickly noticed that the opposition were seated in the far corner. The vibe coming from their camp was distinctly edgy. What was clearly a source of amusement for the locals was not resting as easy with them, but they were staying tight lipped about it. Perhaps sensing an easy opportunity whilst also mulling over the potential disaster of defeat.

The pool table was laid out ready to go. The triangle was placed ceremoniously on its end on the table as if to signal something important was about to happen. I never really understood why people did that.

Sensing a need to break the tension, a local stepped forward.

"Heads or tails?" he asked me politely.

"Heads," I responded.

It was tails. Without any introductions or shaking of hands, one of the visiting team stepped forward, removed the triangle and instantly broke with an earth-shattering crash. It was the kind of break that said "Boy, I'm the man here, and you are about to be crushed."

I had tried to do one of those breaks before, loud, powerful, and so hard that it sends every ball to every part of the table guaranteeing several balls to be potted. and giving the opening player a big advantage in terms of sinking their colours. Much as I tried, I could never do it. You needed to be a proper man with big thick hairy arms to achieve the necessary power. Not skinny ten-year olds limbs. This break was no exception, two red balls were potted, and the other balls scattered around the table under the immense power and energy of his manly break.

Refusing to acknowledge my existence and sporting a wry grin, he positioned himself purposely for the next shot and proceeded to sink another red. Another quickly followed, but in his haste and impatience to impress and seal a quick victory, the white became out of position. It left him no easy shot. He had practically snookered himself and his run of success was temporarily over.

I could hear him swearing under his breath in a deep and menacing Glaswegian accent, as he returned to his seat, still refusing to meet my gaze, and clearly frustrated by the charade he was now deeply involved in. This game had suddenly become quite important to him. There were going to be no niceties.

I stepped forward. Ignoring the frosty situation and lined up my shot.

Now at this point in the story, it is worth pointing out that although my brother and I were not amazing at pool, we were well above average. In those days, pubs were closed from 2pm to 7pm on a Sunday, and whilst we were not afforded all the luxuries of a typically normal upbringing, we did benefit from being able to regularly enjoy several hours of pool on a Sunday afternoon.

So, with a deep breath and ignoring the glare of the visiting audience, I managed to sink three yellows, including one impressively long shot before eventually missing. A balance was restored to the game. The half smiles and whispered jokes from the visitors had stopped. They were now sensing that a proper game was emerging.

This time another visitor stood up and made his way over to the table, surveying the situation with serious eyes. I had not realised, because no one had mentioned, but this was clearly a doubles game. This meant that there were two people on each side who would take turns to play. Had this raised the stakes? Maybe if they lost they could blame the other person? This made the game less personal and as the new player missed his first shot I realised that this had now become a winnable situation for me and my brother. I began to relax.

The pace of the game slowed, as nerves and careless shots from the opponents, mixed with some good safety play and patience from my brother and I, carried the game on for what seemed like an eternity.

Finally, I found myself positioned on an easy black ball, with an air of silence hanging over the once rowdy public bar.

Steadying myself with a deep breath, I cleanly pocketed the black to a huge roar of applause and shouting from the pub regulars, (our prize for saving the day) then scurried off back upstairs in our pyjamas to leave the banter to the real men.

We do not know what the visiting team made of us beating them or whether it was discussed again.

Oh, I never did receive my Evil Knievel stunt bike that year. I got a new pool cue.

Clive Hawkins

First Week in the Haunted Pub

Eighteen years of age and a spotty cliché- I decided to get a job behind the bar of the nearest pub to my accommodation, in order to pay my way through my undergraduate degree; beer and regret doesn't come cheap after all. I heard through a friend that the pub down the road was hiring, and their selection policy was little more than a charming smile, bingo! The catch? Outside this five-hundred-year-old pub hung a sign branding it as "The Most Haunted Pub in Britain." Whatever - right?

Like I said, I was eighteen years old and sweating false confidence through the pre-pubescent dusting of a moustache disgracing my upper lip. I ain't afraid of no ghosts!

Fast forward to my first night on the job and a procession of black-veiled customers filtered through the bar and up to our disused first floor dining area; they had hired the room for the night in order to carry out a séance. Unfazed that they were trying to contact the dead, I was more perturbed by the fact I would have to ferry their drinks upstairs all night.

My brazen arrogance even left me more amused than scared when my presence with trays of double vodka oranges seemed to break their clairvoyant spell throughout the night. They left disappointed and seemingly ghost-less and I returned to my student flat without giving their endeavour a second thought.

After a sound night's sleep, I returned for the early shift the next morning, assuming a consummate air of professionalism (this lasted the entirety of my first week on the job, first impressions count after all). I got myself busy learning the trade; prepping the bar for service, making the coffees, and looking busy while the General Manager did his stock-take.

I miss the days where my job was 90% acting and 10% spilling drip trays. As the lunchtime crowd filtered in, I'd almost completely forgotten about the events of the night before; this haunted pub wasn't scary, just dark and old like half the others in the city. It was then that I noticed the hunched frame of a frail old lady approach me. Her face was hidden under the brow of a black straw hat and the hand that gripped the bar was riddled with purple veins and more wrinkled than a Shar-Pei puppy. As she looked up, she revealed a pair of milky eyes that seemed to look straight through me. I opened my mouth to ask how I could help but she cut me off with one question.

"There was a séance here last night wasn't there?" She croaked.

I gulped audibly as she cocked her head slightly, revelling in my discomfort.

"There was," I replied, barely audible through my dry mouth.

"I can tell," she said. "There are some very troubled souls in here." And with that she left.

Certainly, one of the creepier encounters of my life, I stood pondering the conversation with a furrowed brow for several minutes afterwards. How could she know? Was this the rest of the staff playing a joke on the new guy? As my mind rattled through the various possibilities my supervisor called for me.

"We need some more vinegar for table twelve" he said. "Pop up to the dining room and grab one, would you?"

Oh perfect! That's exactly where I'd like to go actually, having just been informed by the Wicked Witch of the West that it's full of angered demons who don't take too kindly to their eternal sleep being interrupted. But I'm the new kid, I can hardly say no. So off I went, creeping up the stairs as quietly as I could. Slowly turning the handle of the great wooden door to the dining room I slipped inside.

It was cold in there. So very dark and given I hadn't learnt where the light switches were at this point, it would have to stay that way. As my eyes adjusted to the dusk, I saw a figure stood in front of me and what a devilishly handsome figure it was too, for I found myself opposite a large ornate mirror.

Still, the initial shock had really got my heart going, this was fight or flight and my delicate hands weren't taking on any ghostly opponents if I could help it. Think, vinegar. I peered into the darkness and snatched at a basket of condiments, rifling through for that precious maroon cap. As I did so, I heard a rustling in the corner which stopped me dead. Not daring to turn to the source of the noise I rifled faster, casting ketchup and mayonnaise bottles aside in search of my vinegary treasure. Found one!

Trophy in hand I made a run for the door, very aware of a presence looming over me from behind. With a final lunge, I flung myself free of the darkness and into the relative light of the stairwell, slamming the door behind me and gulping for breath. Standing up straight I found myself nose to nose with a heavy-set silver man whose arms seemed to lunge at me; I had dived straight in front of the pubs very own decorative suit of armour, an heirloom I now know affectionately as Alan the Knight. However, this first meeting of ours ended with a rather effeminate squeal and the launching of my precious vinegar.

Returning to the bar, I had been truly humbled by the haunted pub. My supervisor sighed at my empty hands and trudged upstairs to complete the task I had clearly failed.

As for me it took an early break and a stiff drink to calm my nerves, and to this day I take a deep breath when passing Alan in the corridor…

Alfie Edge

Salcombe Lifeboat

I was in Salcombe in Devon for the opening night of one of our pubs called the Kings Arms, which had recently undergone a refurbishment. The night was an enormous success.

In the town was the Fortescue Hotel, where my wife and I were staying.

The drinks were flowing, and the locals were enjoying the Kings Arms and complimenting us on the sensitive changes we had made to the pub. The pub was so busy that we were sorry to have to leave, but with a long drive the following day, we retired with a group of colleagues to the Fortescue for supper.

After a wonderful meal and a few glasses of Doom Bar, we booked an early breakfast with Dave, the Landlord, and retired for the night.

On arriving in the bar in the morning at 0800, there was nobody to be seen and a noticeably quiet kitchen. There was, however, a note on our reserved table from Dave, saying that he had been called out at 0400 in the morning with the lifeboat and would be back as soon as possible!

Dave, I discovered, has been a key member of the lifeboat crew for many years and, as I looked out of the window, there was a gale blowing and I was quite concerned for the safety of everyone out on the sea that morning. Thankfully, a kettle was on hand and a toaster available too.

At 0820, Dave came running back into the pub, having completed a successful mission to save a rudderless yacht and its two-man crew. Without missing a step, he headed straight to the kitchen and promptly rustled up breakfast for both of us (with extra salt brushed from his lifeboat uniform!). It was the last thing I expected. This man has been out saving lives and yet, his first thought was to cook us a breakfast on his return. I told him this and with a broad smile he said, "that's all part of being on the lifeboat crew, every one of the team will have gone back to their day jobs just like me".

It was a fitting reminder of the community service that many of our publicans, along with other business owners, give to their local towns and communities.

In chatting with Dave, he did point out, with a twinkle in his eye, that the Salcombe lifeboat crew base themselves at the Fortescue for their 'down time' so the business also benefits a little too!

Andrew Younger

The English Welshman

It was 1999, Wales were playing England at Wembley in what was to be the last ever match of the Five Nations, and my little pub was packed full of England supporters. Well, that was apart from two solitary Welshmen – my husband Dion and… let's just call him Gethin. Self-proclaimed Welshman Gethin was born to Welsh parents but had never actually set foot in Wales. He spoke with an English accent and his brothers and sisters supported England, but Gethin was steadfastly Welsh.

On the day of the game, the atmosphere in the pub was electric, full of happy, singing, rugby supporters. The match was in injury time and England were seconds away from winning the Grand Slam. They were leading the match by six points and both Dion and Gethin had been subjected to endless Welsh jokes throughout the game, which I must give them some credit for taking in good spirit. Suddenly, there was an unexpected turn of events, history shows that Scott Gibbs scored an amazing try and Neil Jenkins kicked the two points which won Wales the match.

It's fair to say, that the mood in the pub had altered drastically. Once everyone had eventually got the two Wales supporters to settle down, there was silence. You would have been able to hear a pin drop for the intense ultimate minutes of that game, where a drop goal from England could have changed everything once again. Sadly (for most present), this was not meant to be – the final whistle blew, and the raucous sounds of 'Bread of Heaven' could be heard being sung badly by my husband Dion.

"Come on Gethin, sing along!" he shouted.
"I don't know the words" was the sheepish reply.
"What, call yourself a Welshman, what songs do you know then?" asked Dion.
"Hmmm none really…" muttered Gethin.

As the English fans drowned their sorrows, they were beginning to tire of Gethin's joy. By now he had situated himself on a chair by the bar. Someone took off their belt and strategically wrapped it around both Gethin and his chair, and gradually several others proceeded to join in the fun. They cunningly moved his chair so that he could no longer get to his pint, followed by a popular suggestion from one customer: "let's put him on the bus!"

Just for context, my pub was at the end of the bus route. The bus would finish the run, wait for 5 minutes, drive around the one-way system and then start off again from the front door of the pub. We were the best bus stop in England. People would often pop in for a pint whilst waiting for the bus, knowing they had just enough time to finish it whilst it drove around the one-way street.

Unluckily for Gethin, someone had noticed that the bus had just pulled off and was due to appear at the stop shortly. A quick whip around for some change was orchestrated and soon enough, Gethin and the chair were being carried out of the pub and onto the bus. He was soon plonked in the space for the prams and the driver was presented with the fare contributions. The request was then made to the driver to take his new passenger as far as the money would get him, and with that, off he went.

A couple of hours later, the pub door opened, and a large cheer could be heard. There stood Gethin, the chair and a handful of belts, still smiling after his round-trip to Brentford. Whether or not he was Welsh was still up for debate, but one thing that he was for certain, was a good sport.

Fast forward to 2001, and it may have been a new millennium, but not much had changed for Gethin. Not only was he Welsh, but he also happened to be a Liverpool fan and this year Liverpool were in with a chance of winning the treble. Gethin had placed a bet earlier in the season that Liverpool would win the treble that year and was anxiously awaiting the outcome of the UEFA Cup final. In a pub full of Chelsea and Tottenham fans, once again outnumbered, Gethin took a lot of stick.

It appeared that Gethin's nerves eventually got the better of him, and he unfortunately could not wait until the final whistle, before nipping to the toilet. Whilst he was in there, it became time for another elaborate joke at his expense.

One prankster got the keys and locked the outer toilet door, whilst another got the whole pub primed to cheer. They gave him just enough time to have done what he needed to do and then the pub erupted with fake cheers of a goal scored. The inner door to the Gents flew open, and then Gethin's desperate face became visible as it pressed against the pane of glass on the outer door, whilst he tried with all his might to prise the door open. Eventually he was liberated, and he howled with rage after the realisation that he had been set up.

And that's the story of my favourite English/Welsh regular, who brought about many laughs in that pub of mine. Despite poor Gethin's treatment over the years, he did have the last laugh that night – Liverpool went ahead and won the treble, resulting in Gethin picking up a nice four-figure sum from the bookies! He could have certainly got a few more round trips on the bus out of that, or maybe even a trip all the way to Wales.

Helen Marshall

A Horse walks into a Bar

"Why the long face?" is a question I have invariably asked many a customer over the last decade, although never quite so literally as when I found myself opposite Alfie the Shetland pony, staring curiously up at me, clearly bewildered by my attempted humour!

The Woodman Pub in Woodmansterne, Surrey, has traditionally had a *No Dogs Allowed Inside* policy, something I continued upon becoming landlord. It was quickly pointed out to me, whilst looking slightly aghast upon Alfie's first visit, that there was no mention of horses, or specifically Shetland ponies!

Alfie, who belongs to one of our regular customers, Sharon, is now a regular commodity at the Woodman and his popularity continues to rise. Thankfully, he has become so familiar with a lot of the patrons and staff, he has stopped following Sharon to the toilet, which, as you can imagine, saves a few yelps of surprise!

After becoming poorly, and requiring 24/7 attention, Sharon – craving a pint – decided to bring the little equine along on one of her quick visits to us. Being house broken enough (thankfully!) to not make a mess inside, Alfie quickly won our hearts and we agreed to let him stay.

Sharon has said that Alfie hates being left alone, but to his credit, it is to our benefit. Alfie has attracted more visitors than our last ale festival! We have even named a meal after him on our food special's board, although this consists of sugar cubes and carrots, so it tends to be solely Alfie who orders it.

There has been some talk about who our next four-legged guest will be, although I may have to put my foot down. Alfie might object to the competition anyway! For now, the upcoming Grand National is keeping us both occupied!

When Customers are nearly Family

There are always a few customers that become more like family in the pub trade. At the Amber Rose one of those customers was Sue Thompson. The family member she most closely resembled? Definitely the mother in law. She loved us but wasn't afraid to give very honest, and at times, very brutal feedback when things weren't to her liking.

She would visit us at least once a week and always brought people with her. We've seen her grandchildren grow and met the whole family over the years. She was always forthcoming with what she liked, so by now we had it perfected- drinks ready before she ordered, food cooked to her preference and speedy service even if it meant she skipped a few customers in the queue.

Christmas was always Sue's time to shine. She would come four or five times over the festive period, try every course on the menu and bring plenty of family and friends.

One year at the Amber Rose we had a particularly busy Christmas and Sue's booking of three happened to be at the same time as our biggest Christmas party of sixty-eight people. In a small pub like the Amber Rose sixty-eight people is a lot. In order to accommodate this booking, there obviously had to be some furniture rearranging, and of course, Sue's usual table had been taken over by the group of sixty-eight.

I was dreading breaking the news to her, and sure enough as soon as she arrived, I could hear her voice across the busy pub, "Jackie, why are there people sitting on my table?"

"I'm really sorry Sue, we had to sit that big group together, so we can't seat you at your usual table. I've set up another table in a quiet corner, you've got Santa hats and crackers there for you and I promise we'll look after you." I replied.

"I hope this group isn't going to affect our meal! I bring people here all the time and I've never seen any of *them* here before."

"I know, don't worry, I will look after your table myself, I'll make sure all your meals are perfect and you won't notice any difference." Sue huffed and puffed a bit but went and sat at her table. All the staff were fully briefed- the big table is important but above all else look after Sue. "If she doesn't have a good time we will never hear the end of it!"

After that we were off and running. Sue had loved the first two courses and we were just about to serve the large group their mains. I cleared Sue's table, "We are ready for out desserts now" she trilled.

"Okay" I replied. "We just need to get the large groups order out and then I promise your desserts will be next."

"Sounds like you are giving them special treatment!" Sue sniggered.

"No not at all, we just don't have room in the kitchen until we have the mains out of the way." At that, off I quickly went.

There were three chefs and four servers in the kitchen, shuttling the mains out, everyone was breaking a sweat and everyone had their hands full trying to serve the big group. We had around half of the group's meals out and things were going pretty well, when I heard her voice again in the kitchen

"Jackie?" Very swiftly followed by Sue appearing in the kitchen. She had walked past the busy bar, past the bar staff, past the office and joined us in the kitchen. We were all in shock.

"Sue you can't be in here!" I gasped

"Oh, I just thought, as you are busy I'll just come in and get the desserts myself."

"Sue you really can't, I promise we will get them out to you as soon as we are done with this." Sue then stood in the doorway to the kitchen, blocking everyone's path.

"Well if that's the case I just need to say a massive well done to all of you, we have really enjoyed our dinner. I just wanted to come through and help."

"Okay great, if you could just go back to your table I'll be out with your desserts as soon as I can" I said, trying to hustle her along.

"Okay before I go, can I just give everyone a hug?"

The staff all looked at each other, stress levels were getting high. The big party were waiting on the rest of their food. I figured the quickest way to get her out was to do this. "Right okay, quickly please!"

She stood in the kitchen doorway and hugged everyone in turn, regardless of them being covered in gravy, midway through plating up turkey or hands full of plates.

Eventually she was happy, and we got her back to the table and the rest of the mains out to the group. They weren't too happy at the delay for half of the group, there were a few grumbles and a few drinks had to be complimented to keep them on side. Once that was done I took the desserts over to Sue's table.

"Here you go ladies, sorry about the delay."

"Oh no problem Jackie, that other group didn't seem very happy! That's a shame there was a bit of a wait for their mains. I guess they probably won't come back next year. Can I book my table for next year now?" she said with a smirk.

So, from that day onwards we have realised that there is no point in fighting it- some customers like Sue will always get their own way!

Jacqueline Weston

Hopping Mad

I have been in the pub trade for many years and have enjoyed great laughter amidst some great times throughout those years. One of the funniest things I have ever seen, however, occurred over twenty years ago and makes me smile whenever I think about it.

It is sort of one of those 'you had to be there to appreciate it' stories, so I hope I can get the picture across for you.

I was the manager of a very busy pub in Old Street, London. It was a massive venue with a large dance floor and raised areas that we used to hire out for corporate events. We always had large company parties every year, and this December it was a local office annual Christmas party.

There are a couple of things to note about Christmas parties. Firstly, you get people attending your pub who normally would not or have never even been into it. It might be because they don't live or work in that particular office or they go home early from work so there are a lot of new faces around.

Secondly, though these people work together they may not socialise together, and there is always an awkwardness amongst the throng as the managing director is now being challenged to "down in one" from the boys in the sorting office. Then there are those who have harboured a crush on one of their work colleagues and are now chancing their arm fuelled with alcohol and Dutch courage.

Now, back in the day, we used to have the Hells Angels working on the door. They weren't exactly the well attired agency door staff we have today, but nobody would dare mess with them because of their fearsome appearance. They could look after themselves, but they were the nicest most pleasant guys I had ever worked with, and never overtly aggressive to anyone, even those wanting to 'have a go'.

As the night wore on, I received a call from one of the door staff to say that one of office party goers had obviously had a little too much liquid courage, and had started to become quite boisterous, showing off, and embarrassing his colleagues.

I let it slide initially but kept half an eye on it. After all it was his Christmas party, but eventually he got to be too much and was making a scene, spilling his drink, and starting to become aggressive towards staff, door staff, and other customers. I spoke with the party organiser, and they agreed that he would have to leave as he was now out of hand. The requests from his colleagues fell on deaf intoxicated ears, so I asked the door team to remove him from the premises.

They came up to him, one either side, to escort him down the grand staircase and out of the building. As always, they were very polite and asked nicely, then a little more encouragingly until eventually they had to aid him with one of them on each of his arms.

He went quietly enough, and I thought the problem had been sorted. Apparently, this was not the case, and something else was clearly happening as there was a stream of excited people flowing down the stairs towards the entrance. Including most of the office party.

Wondering what all the fuss is about I joined the crowd moving towards the front entrance and I was about halfway down the stairs when my eyes landed on a sight I will never forget.

The gentleman we had removed from the office party apparently had a false leg. How do I know this you may ask? Well, because he had whipped it off and thrown it up the stairs as a weapon at the door staff!

He was now hopping energetically and skilfully around on his one leg, fists up and hurling manic, threatening abuse at the door staff. Nobody had any idea how to react to this man who was quite literally hopping mad. It was so funny to see. If I had booked it as an act it would have received rave reviews.

The whole gathering was in fits of laughter including the door staff. He looked like a cross between Charlie Chaplin, Norman Wisdom and Lee Evans. In his current state, he would be unable to fight his way out of a wet paper bag but at that moment he was happy to take on the world.

And from that day to my last day, I will never forget the image of that prosthetic leg, laying randomly on the stairs amidst all the commotion, and the faces of my door team, who were in utter confusion as to what to make of the one-legged attacker, and what to do with it his leg!

When it had all calmed down, the leg was duly returned, a cab was called, and the guest was driven off into the night.

David Whelan

Spartans Assemble

Some people say; "you don't have to be mad to work in hospitality, but it helps." Long unsociable hours. Weekends, bank holidays and annual holiday periods given over to serving the public at what are our busiest times, and yet so many people remain in the industry for a lifetime. Many knowing no other work nor wanting to; such is the enjoyment you can get from this crazy world.

There are people who have worked in hospitality for many years, who have travelled from the bottom to the top when they only took a part time job on for the summer one year, and then never left. It's not only the people you work with that make it such an enjoyable place to work, but also the people you serve. Your regulars, your community, visitors from everywhere with an abundance of stories and tales to tell.

Having left military service after twelve years I found myself in a sales job, and whilst it was quite a large company the work itself was solitary and independent. I missed working with a close-knit team, A lot.

My brother worked in the industry and asked me if I could spare a few weekends to help him out in a new pub he had taken on in London. Now at that time in the late eighties the mortgage interest rate was 16%, yes, that's not a typo, it really was 16% so any offer of work for extra income was more than welcome. So, for the next four weekends, I set off from Hampshire to London on a Friday to work from Friday night through to the end of Sunday lunch at his pub.

Saturday was always an 'AFD' shift. For those of you not in the hospitality industry that is an 'All F…...g Day' shift! Not because of poor planning or lack of staff, just the way it falls to the needs of the business. In this pub that meant 11am to Midnight, naturally with a break for lunch; if you were lucky!

I really enjoyed these weekends. The team in the pub got on well, fully supportive of each other. The regulars and visitors meant there were new tales and variety daily, and the ebb and flow of the peak rush hours in the pub kept a steady flow moving through the business all day long.

Saturday, pre-live satellite sports channels, might see Chelsea, QPR and Fulham all playing at home on the same day. The morning crush followed by the 2.30pm exodus to the grounds would have you rushed off your feet, then give you a breather before they all returned around 5.30pm for the post-match analysis.

Yes, I liked this industry. My brother and his wife were very content and enjoyed it too. They had come into it quite by accident and it looked like I was about to take the same path.

Some thirty-two years later I am still in that same industry. I have worked for large companies, small companies and even set up my own business when I lived abroad. On returning to the UK, I knew that the industry was the place to re-establish myself and the route back was a familiar one.

I have collected glasses, washed pots, flipped burgers, flambéed lobster, cleaned cellars, pulled pints, mixed cocktails, scrubbed toilets, worked the door, worked the cloakroom, been a commis chef, a head chef, a deputy, a dogsbody, a wedding planner, a wake planner, a furniture mover, a party planner, sports planner, counsellor, social worker, shoulder to cry on, general manager, father figure, arbiter of disputes, referee to arguments, diplomat and friend to many.

So, still in the business, I am now an 'Area Manager' having been in that role for over thirteen years. Despite that title, my experience of the past has still had me flipping burgers in some kitchens quite recently when the needs of a new development were greatest.

I was with one of the larger companies in the UK for over fourteen years when the need for change arose. A new challenge was needed. I still wanted to stay within the industry, and a colleague who had moved to another company had extolled the virtues of this new company and had highlighted a vacancy that I might be interested in, knowing that I was looking to move.

Interviews arranged, and tests completed I was taken on.

The contrast between my previous role and this was stark. Previously I had worked in picturesque destination diners, all thatched roofs and roses around the door. Now I was back in the urban nightlife and community boozers where I had first cut my teeth at the start of my career. It provided the fresh challenge that was needed.

As with any new job there is a period of induction, and this was no different. Four weeks of new systems. New 'IT'. New 'jargon' and of course getting to know the wonderful support staff who will be there when you hit the ground.

Oddly enough, the last people you get to meet are the pub managers who form your area, and your fellow area managers. You are not let loose on them fully until induction is completed. When you do get to meet them, naturally you want to make a good impression, and give a good account of yourself so to speak.

Little did I know I would be doing this in the guise of a 1970's rock star or as a Spartan Warrior!

The end of my induction coincided with two events that had been in the divisional diary for months. The first being a divisional get together to report on the previous year's performances and new initiatives for the coming summer, and the second a major fundraising charity event, both in London and only one week apart. My induction over, my attendance was a given, as I was now part of the division, and my new area team would be at both events.

The divisional meeting was in a venue on the Embankment in London which could house the whole division of over 100 pubs. The theme '1970's glam rock'. Now in my previous company matching my tie to my suit was my only worry when attending such events, so this was a whole new challenge. I wondered how seriously they took these events. I quickly found out.

I was met at the door by Sonny and Cher and realised immediately that 'they take it very seriously'. My new boss accepted that I had not had enough time to get an 'outfit', so I had arrived in a summer sports jacket and chino's and stood out like a lighthouse on a beach. Being given a nylon wig, gold medallion and some big sunglasses by 'Lulu', helped slightly and I now resembled a well-dressed member of the 'Hair Bear Bunch!'

It's customary for the operations team to arrive before the pub teams and this was no different. I was looking forward to meeting them all. It would have to wait till later though, as I was introduced to Mick Jagger, Jimmy Hendrix and everyone else from the Beatles to Ozzy Osbourne. Even a little Italian guy who looked like Julio Iglesias! I did my best, but apart from my old colleague who had brought me to this new and crazy world, I knew I would not remember their real names or faces just yet.

The meeting presentation began. Many of the pub managers dressed up in various costumes and were getting into the swing of things. So here we were in this psychedelic pub surrounded by people in psychedelic clothes about to be addressed by a cross between Roy Orbison and Lemy who came on to 'Lucy in the sky with diamonds' blaring through the ample sound system. Indeed, it was the only thing missing from this 70's colour fest.

I am beyond matching ties and thatched roofs now!

The meeting was great fun and informative. When it was all over, I got to meet my team and my divisional colleagues and really began to feel the 'Fun' that plays a large part in the company and the division.

Before leaving, my new boss reminded me about the fundraising charity event the following week which was going to be just down the road.

"And I'll expect you to be in costume for that one" he said.

I spent the weekend scouring the dressing up box and fancy-dress shops. I knew the standard of 'joining in' was high based on the previous week's trip back in time to the 70's.

The following week the ancient people of Sparta Invaded the city of London. In various shapes and sizes from 'Hercules to Hagar the Horrible' and from

'Wonder Woman to Blunder Woman' the whole gathering had put their heart and soul into this event as:

"The Spartan's Assembled"

It was a tremendous sight. At a pub called the Minories, built under the Arches near London Bridge Station, more than a hundred 'Spartan Warriors' assembled to do battle in chariot races around the ancient city of Londinium. But in true pub company style, not before a good round of sausage and bacon rolls with their various toppings!

The 'Chariots' duly arrive with not a horse or 'Ben Hur' in sight. These were the modern steel version that seated ten gladiators who would pedal their hearts out to get around a three-mile circuit of the city streets.

Now this was not the 'London Marathon' that sees the streets closed off to traffic. Amidst the traditional 'Route master' buses and black 'Hackney's' the speeding chariots of Sparta would appear in fierce competition. It was a tough gig. These new modern chariots took some moving. Luckily, there was room for refreshment in front of each rider so plentiful amounts of various liquids were eagerly consumed.

Midway point in the route was a forced stop at another of the company pubs for more refreshment and minor respite.

The first rotation was over, and a leader board took shape. The competition was truly on. Post lunch, and more refreshment, many of the Spartan Warriors were now wobbling somewhat, so glad of a perch on the chariot for the afternoons second rotation of the same route.

Timings on the second run were much faster as those in the team with no seat had realised, they could turbo charge the machines by pushing from the rear. It was not considered cheating as every team was at it.

Back in time for the mass BBQ and results. The team that won the first round had only increased their lead in the second. Driven on by their 'Adonis' of an area manager who appeared to be carved from the granite hills of Sparta themselves!

The real winner on the day however was a well-known cancer charity. This charity initiative had been going on for some time before I even joined the company, and this event was the finale of all the effort. The final push if you will pardon the pun.

Looking like Gerard Butler himself in the movie, magnificent in his Spartan outfit and helmet, the divisional Director called us all to order before the evening entertainment began.

There were prizes for the winning team. There was recognition of those who had raised the most individually, the pub who had raised the most and thanks all round to the organisers of the day's events which to this point had run without a hitch and would continue to do so into the wee hours of the following day.

But the best prize of all belonged to everyone and he kept it to last. The fundraising activity throughout the year, culminating in the days gathering, had raised over one hundred thousand pounds for the charity. (£100,000.00).

I was amazed. I had been at such events and involved in similar initiatives but never realising such a vast amount. It was very impressive. I felt proud of my team and my new colleagues. I like to think I played some part in the raising of that sum, but truly it belonged to those before I arrived. Everyone was a winner that day and I felt genuinely proud to be a part of it.

Then I heard it for the very first time.

The boss shouted, "Spartans Assemble!" I was then deafened by the immediate and tumultuous response from everyone at the event:

AWOO! AWOO! AWOO!

John Paul.

My First Pub Halloween

I will never forget my first Halloween shift in a pub. I had been eagerly anticipating the day, and it turned out to be one of my fondest ever memories. You must dress up of course, especially when there is a bottle of Jäger as an incentive prize!

I spent some time choosing my costume and eventually decided on Hannibal Lecter, but unfortunately, I did not win this time. A Captain Jack Sparrow took the prize – damn you, Captain Jack!

So, I was working the floor collecting glasses, and taking in all the sights and outfits. Every customer and team member had gone to so much effort, some of the costumes were outstanding, but it was the interactions that made the night.

If you do not know who they are then please google them, but picture if you will: Princess Peach and the Incredible Hulk getting overly friendly; Bill and Ben, the Flowerpot Men, having a lightsabre battle, complete with sound effects; Sherlock Holmes banging down shots with yet another Jack Sparrow (loads of Jacks, one Hannibal, just saying); Fred Flintstone in a face-reddening arm wrestle with Superman... the list goes on. I have got to say that the icing on my cake was Poison Ivy slowly swaying over, passing her number, and seductively whispering in my ear; "You can have me for dinner."

The night was going well, and this was better than I had dreamed off, although unfortunately, there was no time for said dinner.

It had been a pleasant enough evening, the garden was full, and the autumn sun was beginning to set. There were still people outside, as the fun and good spirits continued into the night. We were clearing up the garden, when we heard a glass smash and voices being raised, so myself and Aladdin made our way over to where the noise was coming from. An argument had begun, I was unsure of the origin, but the forthcoming affair was a remarkable sight.

We arrived to witness the outstretched blade-laden hand of Freddy Krueger, jabbing the air towards the rotund blue body of Tinky Winky. It appeared, on the face of it, that it was a complete mismatch, but Tinky was giving it his all, as though he was protecting his very own Teletubby Garden.

It then began to escalate; Tinky Winky's best mate Po arrived as back up, along with Stone Cold Steve Austin. This now seemed a slightly more balanced conflict, but Freddy's entourage was epic… Dracula and Batman! Half the Teletubby crew and a wrestler had no chance against this night crawling crew, and just for good measure (or in case of a medical emergency) a scantily dressed nurse had joined the heated debate.

The situation was now starting to get a little tense, and myself a little nervous. The protagonists had spent a long time drinking in the sun, and tempers were becoming more than frayed – I was fearful of an all-out war breaking out.

But it was then, from out of nowhere – like a beacon of light, whose whole life had been leading up to this one very moment – Mahatma Gandhi appeared with beers in hand. He gave Freddy a beer, he gave Tinky Winky a beer, and he very calmly proclaimed these unforgettable words:

"Gentlemen, we don't need to settle things with violence, we need to settle things with… more beer! We are going to down these beers and whoever finishes last, buys the winner a beer. Go!"

Peace ensued and we all learned one of life's great lessons.

For those wondering, Tinky Winky downed his pint quicker than a bowl of tubby custard, whereas Freddy Krueger's attempt was a bit of a nightmare!

Hauntings of the Olde George

You will find the Old George pub quietly nestled in a corner of Newcastle. It is well known as being one of the oldest pubs in the city. Rumours have abounded, for as long as anyone can remember, that the building is in fact haunted!

In the 17th century, King Charles was being held prisoner nearby on a local estate. This was not too arduous as King Charles played on his royal status. No dark and dank windowless dungeons for his royal highness, prisoner or not. Instead, he was escorted on regular trips to a nearby pub of his choice!

He would visit the Old George for a drink so often, that a room in the pub is still known as the King Charles Room. It is complete with his favourite chair carefully preserved as a fond memento. Many of the pub's regulars claim to have seen his ghostly form floating above it like a grey mist, although there is no record of how many drinks had been consumed prior to making this claim!

Over the years, the pub team have reported many strange experiences of their own that sent shivers up their spine. An apparition taking the shape of a phantom man with his sheep dog, has been seen standing at the bar. But he simply fades from site whenever anyone summons the courage to approach him. Footsteps have been heard coming from empty rooms many times over the years. There are even rumours of lost CCTV tapes, which the old proprietor swears had captured footage of a glowing orb floating down the corridors in the middle of the night!

A year ago, George, and Ralph were carrying out the routine end of night closedown. This included the checking of windows and doors to ensure that they were locked.

"George," a voice whispered. Laughing, George turned around,

"Don't be funny Ralph….," he began to say. But the words died on his lips as, having turned around, he saw no-one. Striding hurriedly back to the bar, he saw Ralph coming around the corner from the other end of the pub.

"George," Ralph cried out looking thoroughly relieved. "How did you manage to sneak up behind me and then get all the way over there?"

Hearing this George froze. "What are you talking about?" he asked, a faint hint of panic creeping into his voice.

"You were the one who snuck up behind me……right?"

Suddenly, words did not seem to be what either of them wanted to hear. With an unspoken agreement they set the pub alarms, locked the doors and both ran home. After that, they always refused to close alone and somehow always managed to get out the pub before anyone else could.

Just last month my Deputy Dan, who lives in a flat above the pub, had his own scare. He was working late in the office, whilst his baby daughter slept soundly in her cradle in the living room. Squinting at his computer screen whilst going over the latest figures, he glanced at the clock and realised it was already two in the morning. A creaking floorboard outside the room caused him to raise his head.

He then heard the excited, high pitched tone of a young girl. "Father" she cried. Confused, he leapt from his chair and burst into the corridor to find it empty. The only sound he could hear was the plaintive cry of his baby daughter, who must have awoken when he opened the door in such haste.

When he told me the tale, I tried to reassure him that it must have been his daughter. He claimed, however, that this was not the case. While Dan had always been very sceptical about the existence of ghosts, he is now not so sure. One thing is certain, we are both far more alert when working on our own in pubs – particularly late at night!

Not all Pub Dogs are Good Dogs

In my early 20's, I was lucky enough to have a generous and kind girlfriend called Sophie, who worked in one of the pubs in the town centre. This was a real locals pub where everyone knew everyone! This really worked for me as, after enjoying a night out with my friends, I would stumble into Sophie's pub and charm her into giving me a lift home at the end of her shift!

One particularly blurry night, after a few too many pints, I stumbled through the front door and begun to carry out my usual puppy-dog routine. Compliment her hair, sympathise about her difficult day, and try to stop belching – who says chivalry is dead?

After I had managed to get a promise of a lift home, I leaned unsteadily on the bar, hugging my final drink of the night, whilst trying to bring the bar back into focus. The Landlady Brenda, who would normally have ejected someone in my state, looked me up and down with a smirk and told me, since I was there, I might as well make myself useful. She asked me to let her dog George in from the pub garden.

Now this should not have been too taxing, but in my befuddled state, I struggled to even open the door! Once I staggered outside, I was confronted by a fifty kilo Doberman glaring at me with its teeth bared. I froze to the spot and, thinking I was some sort of post, George decided to relieve himself all over my jeans! I was in no frame of mind to move, while clearly George, once started, was going to finish despite Brenda's belated, and I felt half hearted, cry to stop.

Once George had finished his business, and Brenda had ushered him away, I was left a sodden mess. A subsequent trip to the toilet, I seemed to have sobered up very quickly, failed to repair the damage and I returned to the bar to much amusement from Brenda and Sophie. My only redeeming quality was that, by now, all the regulars had gone, leaving just the giggling Landlady and my girlfriend. Surely my secret was safe.

Despite what had happened, Sophie lived up to my opening description, and drove me home, although insisted that I wore a plastic bin liner. Not surprisingly, she decided not to join me for a night cap, although after my harrowing experience, I would have appreciated at least a reassuring cuddle.

The next day, having forgotten my jacket due to the previous night's kerfuffle, I returned to Sophie's pub hoping to nip in and out unnoticed. Not a hope! As soon as my first foot crossed the threshold, I was treated to a chorus of barking from the not so funny locals!

To this day, it still amazes me how news could travel so fast, with both Brenda and Sophie off duty and without the benefit of social media!

While my relationship with Sophie sadly ended shortly after my urine riddled encounter with George, she still works in the same pub, and I do see her from time to time when out with my friends. We share a knowing smile although I steer well clear from the pub garden and make sure that I am not the last customer left in the pub!

Bean Bag. Everyone said it was a Bad Idea!

All my staff said it was a poor idea, and in hindsight I must agree with them!

For the start of this short yarn, I would like you to cast your mind back to the1990's; yes, indeed there was life before the turn of the century.

I was just a young man living in a pub back then. I didn't earn much, but we had wonderful times and we learnt a lot; quickly. The pub was a huge affair with three bars and a function room. It had everything that an old pub could ever want, except a TV.

Great news for me as World Cup Italia 90 rolled into town. I got the time off to watch the England Belgium game and enjoyed the match with my mates. It was the match with that David Platt goal, (YouTube is available for those under the age of 40ish to view) and the pub we were in went wild, with beer, glass, pool balls and pool cues all ending up in places they were not designed to be in.

I caught the gaze of the pub manager, who was trying to clean up and he stared back at me with the expression of the 'proverbial rabbit caught in the headlights' and, as I offered my condolences to the quivering wreck, I thought that no way would I run my future pubs like this!

Amateurish at best I exclaimed to myself with a serious amount of incredulity. How could he not have been prepared?

Fast forward to 1996 and I was in my first pub as a landlord. Nice pub, just the right side of the M25 Junction 25. South Hertfordshire 'don't you know' when it came to selling your property.

It was the summer of Oasis and EURO 96 'football coming home' and all that. I was going to put on a festival of football for all my customers. England v Spain, June 22nd and that Stuart Pearce winning penalty.

I did put on a festival, but it did not go according to plan. The impromptu buffet I put out was now hanging from the place where the chandeliers should have been, and the chandeliers where in the road where cars should have been, and still were!

I looked in the mirror and looking back at me was that 'proverbial rabbit caught in the headlights.' I had seen before, *but this time it was my face*. Had I learnt nothing?

Let's fast forward once again to the summer of 2018 as we eagerly awaited the World Cup hosted in the eastern regions of Russia. New pub, new company and a million miles away from those days spent running a pub in the 90's.

Times had changed. I had grey hairs for starters, and health and safety had taken over from common sense and experience. I moved with the times. We had lots of staff available and risk assessments by the bucket load. Meetings with local police and councillors had been attended as we progressed towards the opening games. We also had a lot more screens.

I gathered the team around and we laid down our plan. Lots was discussed and they all listened. I told them of my experiences and now, that I, at the tender age of just being the right side of fifty, 'knew best'.

Amongst other things discussed I wanted the finals to be female friendly. Women in the pub with their partners I always thought had a calming effect on the guys, and to underpin this idea I ordered five huge beanbags for the ladies to sit on, whilst drinking their wine and enjoying the experience. Even though we knew the guys would just throw their beer in the air and laugh.

Awful idea the staff claimed! They'd be ruined, soaking wet and a complete waste of the £100+ that I had somehow legitimately sneaked through on expenses, thanks to a forward-thinking Area Manager. Not even the online expenses lady, Selima, had questioned my idea; whoever she was!

The day of the game began, and the atmosphere built. Given the nature of the area that the pub is situated in, there were a few paparazzi hanging around looking for a cheap story for the 'Red Tops' about how Britain was a war zone and had lost control of its senses. The pressure was on, but with a high covert police presence and my bar fully staffed we had a chance. The wine bar opposite knocked out a steady rhythm of Mediterranean tunes to help create the atmosphere.

As I surveyed the pub from outside, I crossed my fingers. The game was England v Panama June 24th, and it was an extremely hot day. It was a cagey start, but the atmosphere was great, and I was confident. Then, my worst nightmare happened. England scored and my best laid plans of providing the girls with somewhere to sit and safely observe the outrageous behaviour of their future husbands, exploded into a winter wonderland of a trillion; I kid you not, small white polystyrene balls, as all the beanbags exploded from their zipped shoring's. They went everywhere.

TVs were obscured, the open window that had aided ventilation was now spewing white foam. The customers exited choking on them as if they were escaping the Towering Inferno; (where's Paul Newman when you need him?) and worst of all, given the amount of beer thrown about, they stuck to every bit of wet surface. I cut a sorry figure as my snowman of a glass collector came up to me and wagged an annoyed finger, to remind me that 'he told me so.' The 'rabbit in headlights' scenario threatened to rear its ugly head again!

We survived the rest of the game, avoided any major problems and we lived to fight another day as England won the match. The clear up included hoovering the ceiling, and me sweeping the problem out and into the high street drainage system... A river of white meandered up and down the roadside kerb stones and as I walked home at something like 1am, a small gust of wind blew some more polystyrene balls into my path, and I sighed a small apologetic laugh.

But this isn't where my story ends if you can read a little further.

Several weeks after the footballing festivities had finished, I was completing a banking in the local Barclays. I stood impatiently behind two elderly gentlemen in front of me. One was moaning about how several weeks ago he awoke to find his front garden covered by a mysterious layer, of what appeared to be a white foam that he had at first thought was snow, but considering it was high summer found that conclusion very improbable.

On inspection he discovered that they were thousands of small polystyrene balls, but how they had got there was a complete mystery.

The gentleman he was talking to, claimed he knew the answer as he had seen this mysterious phenomenon blowing up and down the high street for several weeks, but didn't know of its origin.

I listened intently, and then felt compelled to interrupt and whispered, to tell them that the polystyrene balls had come from exploding beanbags, bought by the manager of a nice wine bar opposite my pub.

Although his intentions had been admirable, the result had obviously been of some embarrassment to him and I apologised profusely on his behalf. The gentlemen groaned a little and gave a resigned chuckle to each other. I completed the banking and exited the branch hoping that the truth would not come out.

The irony of the whole episode is that I had tickets to go and see The Sex Pistols at Finsbury Park on the day of the Stuart Pearce penalty. Given the nature of the day I had to give it a miss and my chance of seeing them had gone. Gutted was not the word, but I needed to deal with the aftermath of the recent games. Euro 96 needed my attentions.
Recently I was listening to an interview on the radio with the said Mr Pearce, and he was asked about his greatest moments. He went on to describe scoring that penalty, and then introducing The Sex Pistols onto stage the very next night. Great, I thought to myself, and then suddenly; I had a promising idea for a story....and a new plan for my next big football competition!

Paul Marshall

You're not serving Beer then?

I have many memories from my long time as a pub manager, but this one never fails to makes me chuckle. Allow me to set the scene.

I was the GM (General Manager) of The Crown Wood in Bracknell, a nice local estate pub. Not long after I started, we were lucky enough to get the go ahead for a refurbishment. Once all the plans had been made, the contractors turned up and began stripping the interior. Almost everything went, carpets, furniture, light fittings; the only thing that stayed was the bar itself.

I was up bright and early every morning to let the contractors in, and I would then return to lock up in the evening. Every day I would check in, just to see how everything was getting on, and if I am honest, just to be nosey!

So, one morning, I was downstairs standing behind the bar, having my daily nose around. At this point, all the light fittings had been taken out and so the contractors had several halogen work lights, dotted about the place on stands. The walls were stripped bare, the bar, having no fonts or dispense taps, was little more than a block of wood. All this, accompanied by the sound of drills, hammering and a wood saw.

On the floor, were two rolls of carpet and various piles of timber waiting to be used. Overall, not exactly your usual pub atmosphere or decor....

The front door was open, as the contractors were in and out to their vans all day. Health and safety signs were pinned everywhere around the entrance, so it could not be missed on entry. As I stood there, looking at what was practically a building site, a middle-aged chap walked in. Dressed smartly, wearing trousers and a shirt. My initial thought was that he was from the building firm or perhaps the council.

As he walked towards me, carefully stepping over the two rolls of carpet and walking around various piles of lumber, he arrived at the bar and just stood looking at me. Still a little unsure as to who this gentleman was, I asked if I could help. His response was not one I had expected.

109

"Can I have a pint of Heineken please?"

I didn't know if this guy was making a joke or not; so, trying not to laugh, I asked him "Are you serious?"

Once again, he replied, "I would like a pint of Heineken please."

Trying to be a consummate professional, but honestly expecting Candid Camera or Jeremy Beadle to pop up, I politely told him that we were shut for a refurbishment and to just look around.

He glanced around at the shell of the pub, and proceeded to grumble, then said "I can't order a pint then?"

Keeping as dead pan as I could, I told him, "Sorry, unfortunately we are not serving at the moment, but if you come back in a couple of weeks, we should be back open."

He turned around and left with the parting comment, "What a crap pub!"

I have seen some oblivious and self-absorbed people in my time, but that guy totally took the biscuit!

Stuart Ward

110

Chutzpah

This is the story of my first and most challenging pub. I was a newly appointed Area Manager, and The Vasey Arms was the thorn in everyone's side. The pub had a long and proud history. A meeting point for working class men and women of the East End community, that, through the 60's and 70's, had morphed into a notable venue for live music.

The 80's and 90's had hosted many anniversaries, birthdays and family celebrations, before it fell out of favour allowing the darker side of the community in. Gone were the families coming together on an evening. Gradually, in came those with menace and an agenda to sell drugs, overindulge on drink and prey on the vulnerable.

The business had recently played host to many frightening incidents and was on its last legs. In truth, it was a proper headache. It was on the Police watch list, and I had recently walked through the issues with officers, resulting in a lengthy list of security upgrades needing to be actioned, to prevent enforcement and the potential closure of the pub.

These were dark days and The Vasey Arms needed huge change. I knew the key to success was to appoint a good publican. The alchemy of pairing the right manager with the right pub is worth its weight in gold, so I was delighted to be able to recruit a young man called Cian.

Cian was in his late 20's and had packed a lot in since leaving County Clare. An ex-solider, he had already travelled the world in various postings. Military service had come to an end when a nasty injury had ruptured his leg.

However, Cian was shrewd, and had learnt several skills in the army, one of which was as a Sous Chef. So, after discharge, he started working in London pubs, progressing from the kitchen to front of house, before being promoted to manager. Along the way, he had met his future wife and was ready to settle down and start a family.

As with the military, one of the perks of being a publican was the free accommodation that was often provided with the role. This was the redeeming factor of the Vasey, for despite its reputation, the 3-bedroom flat with kitchen, dining room and separate flat for two others was a massive plus point. This particularly applied to London with rental costs being so high.

When Cian walked round the pub, he could see past its unloved façade. He focused his attention on the curved wooden bar that arched as the centrepiece of the pub, the legacy of the saloon, the large gardens, both front and back, and the stage in the side room that had once hosted up and coming local bands. Cian was smitten - the opportunity to restore the Vasey to its former glory was too tempting to turn down.

I admired his passion for the pub from the start. As he set about the restoration, he recruited ex-comrades from his old regiment and friends from previous pubs. The place was scrubbed, painted and kitted out with furniture he had cadged. He revitalised the drink range, upgraded the food, and revamped the music on a weekend.

Good weather was met with family days at the Vasey. Celebrations of Halloween, Burns' night and Valentines all took on a new level of fun and engagement. The community started to switch onto Cian's broad smile, his ability to talk ten to a dozen, along with the steely stare that only an ex-squaddie can give to those wanting to cause trouble.

Every opportunity was taken to include the community, so all that chose to come through the front door were greeted with a booming "How are yer?" And the love he showed the pub was returned by the locals. I was proud of him. He was flying.

One afternoon, the magic he had bestowed to his pub was fully realised. It was one of those slow mid-week afternoons. A local was nursing a pint as he read the paper, and Cian had got chatting to a couple at the bar. They were football coaches who had hosted a training session in a nearby sports centre. The more Cian got them talking, the more he realised this wasn't just a local team but something more professional. Unbeknown to him, nearby was the temporary training ground of a big team - the Arsenal youth team. The men were in the Vasey to debate a problem they had to sort for a first team player.

They had been asked to organise a meet and greet event for a newly acquired German player. The player had recently moved to Arsenal from his childhood team, Koln. Still adored by the Koln fans, he had asked the coaches to help him find a location to host a coach load of fans post Arsenal's home game, and then via satellite, beam a Q&A session back to Germany.

Cian always knew when to chance his hand, so seized the opportunity. He convinced the coaches that the Vasey could play host to the forty odd fans, the old stage being perfect for the player Q&A and, with his culinary skills, he could rustle up fish and chips for all.

A deal was agreed. Free venue but with the guarantee of drinks and food. The German fans would go to the Arsenal game, get the coach from the stadium to the pub, where the Q&A session would start, and then everyone would retire to their hotels afterwards. There was no need for contracts, a firm handshake between men was enough to seal the deal and planning began.

Cian, with the faith of a child, could initially see no issue with the plan. Superstar player hosts "An evening with…." for a coach load of Germans in an East End pub with a history of trouble on a Saturday night. It took his wife to throw a few possible spanners in the works, so the plan was revised and signed off by me.

Locals kept to the front of the pub, (except trusted regulars), no Arsenal or Koln colours to decorate the venue, table service so no one wandered around and strictly no advertising of the event to stop crowds appearing. It was a risk, but it got the adrenalin pumping.

Obviously, word of mouth spread round the locals. Happily, no one could quite believe it. How does the Vasey, a community pub in the backwater of the East End, get to play host to an international German player? Are you having a laugh?! It soon became a laughable tall tale, typical of the new cheeky publican looking to boost his Saturday nights. Days went by and the Saturday soon arrived.

Arsenal had played at home in the Premier League. Come 5pm, the game won, Cian and his team were raring to go. True to their word, an hour or so after the game, a fancy coach with German number plates pulled up in front of the pub. One by one, forty excited German fans decked in Koln and Arsenal colours stepped off the coach and into the East End.

In pigeon German, Cian ushered them into the back room and started serving pints of cold lager and ale, however not before some locals clocked their accent and started humming the "Battle of Britain" theme tune, just to spice up the night. Thankfully, this was taken with good humour by the visitors, who were soon seated with a pint and plate of fish and chips, with lashings of salt and vinegar. Even now, with a room full of Koln fans, and TV equipment set up, no one could quite believe what we were about to experience.

An hour later, an excited ripple came through the now packed pub. Up pulled a rather expensive blacked out Range Rover. The passenger door opened and out popped Lukas Podolski. What struck you, was how causally it occurred.

The German international had got a lift from his professional team mate, Mesut Ozil, from the stadium. He was wearing a hoodie, jeans and trainers, and he arrived with no guards or entourage. Just him, on a night out down the local.

Met at the door by Cian, he was quickly ushered to the back of the pub, where he was greeted with a wave of cheering, applause and then German football chants. The fans obviously adored him, and the sound was initially deafening.

Lukas greeted them all, hand shaking everyone he could, as he was swept up on stage. Cian was delighted; even he had had doubts the night before, dreaming of a no-show and a shattered reputation. He stuck to his new-found footballer friend, shoulder to shoulder with him, as if he was his personal bodyguard. As he went past his family and friends, he noted everyone's open mouthed expression and walking past me, gave a wink and mouthed "I'm the man".

The Q&A session went as planned. All the German fans asked questions and Lukas played the perfect interviewee. Every now and then, Lukas would drop into English to entertain the English-speaking crowd.

After an hour, with the interview nearly finished, Cian went to his young son. He was decked in the latest Arsenal shirt which obviously had Podolski printed on the back and whispered, "do you want your shirt signed?". His son was in awe of his dad and said yes. With a flick of his hands, he swiped the shirt off his back and left his son topless as Cian bounded onto stage, mid interview. With his Celtic charm, he thrust a marker pen into Lukas' hand and gave him a broad beaming smile. Lukas signed the shirt and held it up to the crowd. There was a loud roar from all in the room and Cian gave another wink into the camera.

The event was over too soon. It was time for the Germans to drink up their beers, climb into their coach and return to their central London hotels. There had been no trouble, just an unforgettable night shared between locals and tourists. Two nations coming together to appreciate their luck of a free night with an international Arsenal player. For a few hours we were all one. All it had taken was the chutzpah to propose and execute the idea.

And what became of Lukas? Well, after seeing off the Koln fans, signing more shirts, shaking everyone's hand and taking photos, he delayed his ride home and then went into the front of the pub, and sat with the locals watching the boxing on TV. He was there at the end of the night before Ozil came back to pick him up. It was a flash back to old times. Working class heroes and working-class fans sharing a night together.

Cian was special; that he didn't see this, was part of his charm. His sheer presence created the opportunity for something unbelievable to happen. He would go on to expand his family away from the Vasey Arms. It was never the same when he left. The business went back into steep decline.

A year after Cian departed, the pub was closed for the final time; its doors and windows boarded, the plot sold, and renovators flattened the building with all its memories and events to make way for new flats.

The Vasey had had one last adventure, one last chance to shine and place itself in the heart of the local community - and it took Lukas Podolski and a brilliant young manager to make it happen.

Oliver Sweetman

The Regimental Sergeant Major

My career high point arrived in the late nineties with my appointment to Managing Director at Whitbread Inns (Southwest Region). I had a large and talented team to help me, operations managers, area managers, marketing, finance, HR, auditors and so on.

We were trading well and had quickly become a high performing and trusted group. The size of the region and good team around me meant I was rarely dragged down to deal with the nitty-gritty problems at pub level, what could possibly go wrong?

One morning, I was in the office having a review with Richard my finance manager, when there was a knock on the door. Laura, my secretary popped her head around the door looking a bit embarrassed and said, "I am awfully sorry to interrupt Ian, but I have a truly angry man on the phone complaining about the standards in one of our pubs. He says he is the Regimental Sergeant Major of an army camp."

I thought to myself this is a bit different, and I asked Laura to thank him for calling and that I would call him back when my meeting was over. Laura replied, "I have tried that Ian, but he is absolutely raging and insists on speaking to you personally, he won't take no for an answer."

"Ok Laura, you better put him through, Richard, we will finish the review later; thanks."

Richard left, and I composed myself at my desk.

"Hi Ian, its Regimental Sergeant Major Connors from the camp for you", said Laura putting him through.

"Hello Sergeant Major, what can I do for you?"

"Listen carefully Mr Coote. I am absolutely disgusted by the way you are running your pub on my camp. It falls well short of any minimum standard that I would expect of you and your company."

"I am sorry to hear that sir, have you tried to resolve your complaints directly with the pub manager?"

"I'm sorry to say that avenue has now closed after a recent incident with my guards, and your manager being a little over the limit, to put it mildly. I have to inform you that he had to be restrained until he calmed down after climbing over a fence to get back into the camp."

The pub is inside a secure and guarded MOD camp and the only access is via road and walkway with a gatehouse that is constantly guarded. "What time did this happen Sergeant Major?"

"2.26am; it was pitch dark; the consequences of climbing over a fence could have been much worse in the current state of alert across the country."

"I am sorry Sergeant Major, what was he doing climbing a fence to get back into camp at that time of night?"

"You tell me, Mr Coote, he's your bloody responsibility!" (shouting now)

"Sorry Sergeant Major it's the first I have heard of it. I have no idea, I just wondered if he said anything to the guards who arrested him."

"No, they said he was drunk and didn't know what he was doing but they recognised him as the pub manager. They told him off and made sure he got back into the pub; I have ticked them off for that. The least they should have done is locked him up in the cells for a night."

I got the impression he was angry at his own guards too!

"Well thank you for letting me know Sergeant Major, I will ask relevant operation managers responsible for the pub to investigate the matter. I understand it's not acceptable behaviour on the part of our manager and I apologise for that."

"I don't want your apologies Mr Coote, I want to know what you are going to do about it."

"I am going to investigate the matter Sergeant Major."

"Big deal Mr Coote, I am responsible for the safety and discipline of 800 soldiers and I am not being fobbed off by an investigation. I want to see some action." (shouting again) "You can investigate it all you like and involve all your managers, but I want to know what you, yes, you man, are going to do about it? I take it you are the one in command there?"

I don't think the Sergeant major appreciated the difference between being in charge and being in command. He continued, "do you understand the den of iniquity you are presiding over? It's a disgrace man!"

"Well, I appreciate you are upset with the actions of the manager, Sergeant Major, but I am not sure it's fair to describe the pub as a den of iniquity."

"Good Lord man, when was the last time you saw the pub? It's a stain on the landscape."

"Sergeant Major, I moved from Maidstone to Cheltenham to take this job three months ago. I am responsible for 431 pubs from Portsmouth to Lands' End and North to Birmingham, including all South Wales. I haven't made it to this particular pub yet so no, I have not seen the pub recently."

"Well take my advice you need to; pronto!" It didn't sound like advice to me; it sounded like an order.

"Yes, Sergeant Major."

"I've seen khazi's in the back of beyond cleaner than your pub. The place stinks, there is also disgusting sexual graffiti all over the walls in the toilets, and posters of naked women on the walls next to the sinks. It's a morally corrupt and disgusting place, and an insult to the standards I hold my soldiers to in the camp. Am I making myself clear to you Mr Coote?"

"Yes, Sir, Sergeant Major. I am very disturbed by what you are telling me sir, I will look into it personally and ring you back in forty-eight hours."

"How long? A battle can be won and lost in a few hours Mr Coote."

"Yes Sir, Sergeant Major. I will have a report and actions for you in twenty-four hours.

"Twenty-four hours it is then. I look forward to your report tomorrow."

"Once again, I am sorry that you have had to bring these matters to my attention Sergeant Major. Thank you for ringing me."

Click- the phone went dead; I had been dismissed!

I replaced the phone on the hook and went off to find Laura. Can you get me the Ops Manager and Area Manager on the phone? I need to speak to them and see what's going on, and how much they know about it all.

Get Richard for me too will you, I need an auditor down to the pub tomorrow morning. My sixth sense, (and the Regimental Sergeant Major) was telling me all was not right down there, and I wanted to check if we were dealing with anything more than an ill-disciplined manager with lousy standards.

The day after my conversation with the Sergeant Major saw the auditor at the door of the pub accompanied by Chris, the AM (Area Manager). Within an hour of our arrival, everything that was suggested to be wrong with the pub was witnessed, and the manager chose to resign his position for personal reasons. He accepted that he had taken his eye off the ball in relation to running the pub, in the professional manner he had done previously.

I made my phone call to the Sergeant Major. "Hello Sergeant Major, we have looked into the matters you raised yesterday, and I confirm that a change of manager has been agreed upon. The pub is being temporarily run by different management until a suitable new person can be found."

"Very good Mr Coote; "What about the other stuff like the state of the place?"

"Orders have been given to thoroughly clean the place and remove any offensive posters and graffiti. That will be completed in a week. We will inspect it and decide whether anything else needs to be done then." Crikey, listening to myself, I was starting to sound like an enlisted junior officer.

"Very well Mr Coote, I will personally inspect the pub myself in a week and expect to see it looking spick and span. I do not want my soldiers and their families socialising in squalor; it's bad for discipline."

"Yes, quite so Sergeant Major. Now we have established contact, I will keep in touch to ensure the new manager gets a proper introduction."

Within a week, everything we promised had been delivered.

Reports came back that the RSM had visited and seemed happy that things were moving in the right direction. After a fortnight, my HR manager came in with news that they had a cracking couple in training that were keen on taking the pub as their first appointment - Allen and June Jackson. Allen had served in the army for many years before settling down with June in civilian life. June had supervisory experience in working men's clubs in the North.

You could see the benefits within three months of their appointment. Allen could relate to the "squaddies" as he had been one himself and could talk to them about where he served in the army. He nipped issues in the bud; if he saw things getting out of hand, he stopped serving and sent them home.

June would step in and act like a mum sorting out quarrelling brothers if it all got a big macho and fists started flying. The young army lads loved them and showed respect like they were indeed 'Mum & Dad' to all on the camp. The RSM approved.

"At last, a proper mature married couple running the pub and setting a good example to the boys on discipline and standards," he commented one day, when Chris caught up with him to talk about a forthcoming investment in the pub. He approved of that too. "About time you lot stumped up the cash and spent some money here. My soldiers and that couple deserve more than you have been giving them Mr Homer."

In the preparations for the pub refurbishment in mid-summer, Chris wanted to invite the Senior Officer to officially reopen the pub with us. They suggested supporting the opening as part of a wider event that was dear to their hearts: the annual maintenance of the huge (130m) Kiwi carved out of the chalk on the hills above the camp.

This Kiwi had originally been carved out by NZ soldiers stationed in the area shortly after WW1, in memory of the New Zealanders that served and died during the war. So, this particular year we were invited to get involved, as it coincided with the reopening. We had also decided that we would rename the pub "THE KHAKI ARMS" which fitted the bill perfectly, as it honoured the local army history.

My colleagues from SW Region and I marched from the camp armed with picks, shovels and rakes, up the hillside to the Kiwi carving. There we hacked, scraped and raked the chalk to restore it to its pristine white condition.

Afterwards, and during the celebration of the reopening, the Commodore of the NZ Navy cut the ribbon and thanked us for our work restoring the chalk Kiwi. We even got a fly-past from an RAF jet over the pub and the camp.

Before we left, I sought out the RSM to say goodbye and to thank him for his part in the improving communications between the army and the pub. He smiled. "Pleased to be of service Mr Coote. I watched your boys trying to march up that hill from camp today; not a pretty sight; if you need a drill sergeant, you know where I am".

"Yes Sir, Sergeant Major!"

Ian Coote

A Lamb with your Pint?

When I was first a Regional Manager with John Smith's back in the mid '80's I saw a most surreal episode in a pub involving the customers and a lamb.

I was doing a standard tenancy change at a pub near Peterborough one day in a rural village. Everything was going smoothly, and the day included having a valuer there to check the inventory alongside me. Towards the end of the process, the valuer called me to one side and said that the outgoing tenant had a rather unusual request to add something to the inventory at short notice. To my astonishment they then brought a live donkey into the bar and said that they couldn't find a home for it, and could they leave it in the field behind the pub and add it to the valuation!

I explained that such an 'item' would be considered 'optional,' which meant the incoming tenant could take it or leave it. Fortunately, the new publicans took pity on the donkey, and me, and agreed to keep it as an attraction for the kids in the summer. Panic over. That was a first but not quite the last surprise in my fledgling years in my new position.

Around the same time, I was looking after several pubs in Corby, Northants. Almost all the pubs in the town back then were being run by ex-Glaswegian steelworkers (British Steel set up the Corby plant with hundreds of Scots, but the site ended up closing apart from producing specialist steels).

Many former employees took over pub tenancies with their redundancy money. Many of the customers were Scottish of course, (there were even Rangers and Celtic supporters' clubs in the town).

I was in a pub holding a business review one day in the winter. There were about a dozen guys in the bar quaffing lager. Suddenly, the doors were thrown open and a live sheep was tossed into the bar. To my astonishment no-one even blinked! They all just carried on drinking and chatting and even the publican didn't break stride as he discussed his Christmas plans! As if to add to the weird situation, the sheep calmly walked over to the open fire and laid down in front of it like a dog!

When I left it was still there; I don't know to this day whether it was a pet, destined to be Sunday dinner or a stunt from another landlord with a grudge!

The unpredictability of such events helps you to accept that there is nothing that will surprise you in the great institution that is "Our Local Pub."

Mike Harrison

Is it a Pub or a Petting Zoo?

My older sister and I had always thought that our childhood was normal. We loved every second of it and wouldn't have changed it for the world. However, it wasn't until we were teenagers and several raised eyebrows later that we realised that our upbringing had potentially been just a little bit different.

The story started ordinarily enough. My parents moved out of London in the early 70's, to run a friendly little pub on the seafront of Hayling Island. This little pub was called The Olive Leaf. The Olive Leaf had only six to seven tables, matched by roughly the same amount of bar stools, but for what it lacked on the inside, it made up for with the biggest beer garden in town.

My sister and I absolutely loved to ride ponies from a very early age, and I have such fond memories of my dad hiring ponies for us from the local riding school and leading us along the beach for hours at a time.

On my third Christmas, we wandered into the back garden looking for what we had both thought was going to be an ordinary gift – two gorgeous ponies, one each for me and my sister. My amazing dad had even built a pen and put a stable up for them. We called them Muffat and Gemini.

It had barely turned summer, when dad had already extended the pen and we now had three goats too: Stanley, Biscuit and Audrey – just some more regular childhood pets! The garden had become somewhat of a petting zoo, and the tourists absolutely loved it! Together, me and my sister would ride the ponies and lead the goats along the beach thinking this was normal – of course all kids rode their ponies and led their goats along the beach, *didn't they?*

As time went on, the petting zoo continued to grow: two ponies, three goats, a few rabbits, a selection of guinea pigs, oh and not forgetting mum's pond with the fish and the lovely rockery… although my sister and I would usually be using said rockery to jump onto the ponies, whilst the customers in the beer garden watched with horror.

One day my dad was driving us to school when we saw a cheeky bird divebombing a poor unexpecting old lady, and then proceeding to terrorise her

125

by chasing her down the street. My dad jumped out of the car to the rescue, and successfully caught the bird in my sister's school coat.

Dad took the pesky little fella to the vets, who said they would have to put him down as he was not a wild bird and wouldn't survive in the outdoors. This animal lover was clearly not going to let this happen, so he brought him back to the pub to be a part of the family. Dad got straight to work on an aviary for the bird and we named him Charlie.

After a few weeks Charlie had really settled into the family and the pub, and eventually we would let him out so that he could fly around for a bit before happily returning to his aviary. A month later, we were out riding on the ponies when we looked up to see Charlie flying above us, so now our rides had another animal: two ponies, three goats and a bird – just another regular day in the life of a child!

Charlie was a Jackdaw and a special one at that – he could speak! Yes, that's right, a talking Jackdaw. The only problem was that most of the words which he knew happened to be naughty ones (we're not too sure where he learnt them but living in a pub probably didn't help!)

He would peck at the window of the pub squawking "let me in" to the customers, but when they went to open the window, Charlie would have a rather rude two-word response.

Over the years, Charlie became a little celebrity in his own right and people travelled for miles just to see the talking Jackdaw. Whilst he was a hit with the tourists, he wasn't such a hit with the local butcher or fisherman. They would deliver on a bike, only to have him divebomb them and steal the meat and fish - he was so naughty, but it was hilarious to witness.

We stayed at The Olive Leaf until I was seven years-old and our days were filled with endless fun riding on the beach with the animals. Pub life was great as a kid – me and my sister would pretend we were performing a big horse show in our garden with spectators, who were really just customers wanting a drink and a bite to eat.

So, was growing up in a pub normal? Well, it was to us… and our ponies, goats, rabbits, guinea pigs, fish and our talking Jackdaw… and if you wanted to tell us otherwise, then Charlie might just have a two-word response for you too.

Joanne Probert

The Power of the Pub

There is beauty in the knowledge that you can walk into almost any pub in the country, perhaps in the world, on a weekday afternoon and you will find the same things. There may be different beers on tap, a different smile behind each bar, but what you will find consistent is the peace, the calm, and anonymity. Somewhere to hide; like existing in an alternate universe for however long you choose to live your double life.

It was one mid-week afternoon, with the regular hum of traffic filtering in and out of the bar, shoppers stopping for an alcoholic refreshment, and workers coming and going from long lunches. It was in the heart of this atmosphere that the real power of the pub was revealed to me.

Among the blur of faces, one stood out; a friendly smile propped at the bar, gently bringing in the afternoon with beer and conversation. As the afternoon passed, we tackled all the usual subjects of everyday chat, the weather, work, last night's footy scores. We set the world to rights; two strangers passing time in the heart of a Great British Pub.

It is a scene painted daily all over the world, a picture so thoroughly embedded in everyday normality that what he told me next has remained with me ever since.

As he prepared to leave, I asked if he would be a regular and if we'd be seeing him again. He then explained that ten days earlier his wife and child had died suddenly in an accident. I was completely taken aback, and I felt choked by his response. Before I managed to reply, he simply thanked me, and the staff, for our lack of judgement.

He told us that for the last ten days all he'd had was pity and people apologising; he had felt like he had not belonged anymore, his world had been turned upside down. He just wanted to feel normal, just for a couple of hours, so he came to the pub. He thanked us for welcoming and treating him just the same as everyone else that came in that day.

Since that day I have always cherished our pubs, they offer a place of refuge, a place where you will not be judged, where everyone is treated equally. You can vent your issues with strangers, or you can simply leave them at the door, go in and be whatever you wish to be. The pub has the ability to humble, the ever-present leveller that brings all who visit to an equal standing.

For that period of time he was at our bar, he was not a widower; he was not the focus of anyone's pity or puppy-dog eyes.

In his moment of anonymity, he was simply a man capable of being whomever he wanted to be. And that, is the power of the pub.

You cannot get rid of me that easily!

You would describe the pub I work in as being predictable. It is managed by Bea, who is very matriarchal and treats her team like her own family. Cross her at your peril, as she insists on meticulous standards. Our shift patterns are remarkably similar, with our regulars arriving at their usual times throughout the day and rarely deviating from their drinks and food of choice. The younger crowd then join us, as the day turns into night and the atmosphere is dialled up. The football and sporting events are when we are at our busiest.

We normally spend Tuesday lunchtime catching up on cleaning jobs as it is a quiet shift, with only two of us working. On this Tuesday, however, it had been surprisingly busy and myself and my colleague Joe had been rushed off our feet. Thankfully, Joe, with ten years' experience, never gets flustered, and between us we successfully coped with the extra trade.

Joe is also extremely useful at keeping customers in line, mostly due to his height, muscular-physique, and booming voice, but really, Joe could not hurt a fly.

A group of girls had finished lunch and were getting their bags in readiness to leave. Before I could set off to clear their table, Joe was already on his way over. I scanned the rest of the pub; my regulars were still comfortable, chatting away, but a group of lads in the corner were looking ready for refills. Two tables of builders from across the street, still in their work gear. They had been coming in for a couple of weeks, but normally after 5pm. I took a wander over to see if I could squeeze another round out of them.

"I'm treating them to lunch and a couple of pints, after they finished the job early. They'll be getting their own beers after that." The tallest one explained when I took their order.

They were expecting the job to take another day, so he let them have the afternoon off. He seemed like a kind boss, like Bea. When he paid, I noticed his hands were not rough as most of the builders, they were soft and unblemished, except for some paint stains. His scruffy hair was not going grey, as I first thought, the speckles just matched the paint on his hands. His eyes were wide and dark, with a cheeky glint in them, and he had distinguishing smile lines around the edges.

Everyone who works in pubs sees the detail in people, especially when you are single, and this one was quite handsome. Another one of the lads got a round at the bar, he was more rugged than the boss. He thanked me gruffly as he paid, then scooped up all four beers in his massive builder's hands and headed back to his booth.

As he went back to his mates, I saw Ian coming in the front door. Ian is one of our oldest regulars, coming in every day for lunch for thirty years. He used to visit with his old work friends, and they would be a raucous bunch when they came in for a Sunday pint. Retirement had made them rowdy with freedom! They were never any trouble, but they could get very loud, especially when their hearing started to go. That is when I would intervene.

As the years went on, the group grew smaller until eventually it was just Ian who came to lunch. He used to enjoy sampling the menu with his friends, and still did so after they could no longer join him. Recently, however, he has only wanted sausage and mash with a pint of Guinness. I waved over to him, and he grinned happily, shuffling towards me at the bar.

"Having the usual?" I asked, more rhetorically than anything else.

"Please," he says, settling into a free bar stool. "You do look after me!"

I sent his order to the kitchen and started pouring his Guinness. He meant it when he said we looked after him. His wife passed away in the 1980's, before they had children, and he had never remarried.

"True love," he'd told me plenty of times, "is a rare phenomenon."

He felt like he had had his. He rarely seemed woeful of his loneliness, although I expect coming here was most of his social interactions each day. I always had time for a chat with Ian, and so did everyone else that knew him.

131

"Alright Ian?" Joe joined us at the end of the bar, the lull in service a perfect opportunity to have a catch up.

"Not bad, not bad. How's the family?" Ian asked, taking off his hat and revealing his thin white hair. He ran his bony hand through it, the skin is wrinkled and paper-thin.

"Yeah, they're good thanks," Joe replied, "joining us for lunch on Saturday?"

Joe often came in on his days off for a bite to eat and a drink with his wife, Carol, and their older son. After Ian's friends passed away, Joe started inviting Ian to eat with them. Feeling like they already knew him from Joe's stories, his family got on great with Ian, and he slotted right in with them.

"You know I'll be here!" Ian winked at me, then fumbled for his wallet and handed me a crumpled ten-pound note.

As I reached to accept his money, I heard a glass smash, then the whole pub erupted in jeers. Joe and I exchanged a look. It was the lads in the back, one too many for a Tuesday, it seemed. Joe moved to get the dustpan and brush, but as he did, Ian grabbed his arm and wheezed. Before Joe could react, Ian crumpled like his money, and slithered down to the floor.

I was momentarily rooted to the spot. I couldn't think what to do, but then my first aid training set in and I was the other side of the bar checking Ian's airways. Joe was already on the phone for an ambulance. The tall builder from earlier ran over and helped to get him into the recovery position.

Ian's eyes were open, but it was like he couldn't see me or understand what I was saying. His face looked tight and different. Time moved slowly, but before long I was being eased aside so that the paramedics could get in. Joe was giving them information and the builder started to say something to me, but a tap on my shoulder turned my head. It was Bea.

"What happened?" She asked, the worry quite apparent in her voice.

I told her he was fine, chatting to us as usual, and then he just collapsed. I felt I might collapse too, but Bea held out her arms and gave me a much-needed hug.

The ambulance crew had Ian on a stretcher. Joe's strong hands were cupping Ian's weak ones. It wasn't up for debate; Joe was getting in that ambulance with him. Bea would not stop him, I could tell. She did not want Ian to be alone either.

"Take a break," Bea ordered me, and I turned to head towards the staff room.

I hoped Ian would be okay. I knew he was old, and this shouldn't have shocked me, but it still had. I had spent so much time with him over the years, he was like an uncle to me now. I was glad Joe was with him. I could not bear it if he was left alone. Before too long Bea came in to see me.

"I've got cover if you want to go home?" Bea said suggestively. It was not really a question, but she would have let me stay if I wanted to.

Wednesday saw me back at work. I was thankful for the time off the day before, but now I was glad to be back where I belonged. Working in the pub is like having a second family. Last night, Joe sent us a group message to say Ian had suffered a mini stroke and would be in hospital for a while. I had not realised a stroke could look like that, but it was great to know he would be fine.

As a team we tried to carry on as normal, but the whole atmosphere of the pub had been altered. We'd all been affected by Ian's unfortunate incident, but at least he had been here and not at home alone. As lunchtime neared, I caught myself and others watching the door, expecting him to wander in with that big grin.

"He'll be okay." I said to one of the bar girls, but I don't think I sounded convincing.

She smiled back to me, and the front door opened, there was a second of hope but, instead of Ian, it was the good-looking builder from yesterday. The job was finished so he had ditched the work overalls in favour of jeans and a smart jacket, and there was a bouquet of flowers in his arms. He wandered over to the bar and those smile lines wrinkled up as he saw me.

"I was hoping you'd be here!" he said enthusiastically, "How's the man from yesterday?" His dark eyes full of genuine concern.

"He's had a stroke, but he's going to be okay." I replied, "Thank you for your help!"

"No, please, not a problem, I'm glad he's going to be okay." He said, then a nervous look came over him and he thrust the flowers towards me "I bought these for you, I was hoping you would let me take you out for dinner?"

Wednesday was so much better than Tuesday!

It had been a few weeks since the incident and I was sat in the pub with my new man, Ben the builder, with Joe and a couple of the bar girls. The atmosphere was still a little tense and conversations pause every time the door opened. Today, it opened, we paused, and we quickly fixed our gaze on the door.

Ian! He was being wheeled in by his carer. He looked nervous, almost apologetic, but he relaxed when emotional greetings began to hit him. There were tears, mine not his, and then out came that big, beautiful grin that we've all missed,

"I'm back!" he said, almost wickedly, "You can't get rid of me that easily!"

Benny Hill Karma

Quite a few years ago, I was the manager at a lovely, cosy little pub sitting on the canal towpath in Clapton, East London. There was a park on one side and Hackney Marshes on the other. We had our friendly locals, our more than regular regulars, and then those that would pop in to break up their daily walks. The views were great, and many would sit or stand outside with a beer or wine whilst watching the world go by.

One sunny (but cold) winter's day, I was chatting to a couple of regulars outside, when we suddenly heard a scream. On the park over the canal, we saw an elderly lady getting mugged by a middle-aged guy who looked a little worse-for-wear. We started shouting, and were hurrying back inside to call the police, when we noticed two police officers already on the case.

It turned out that they had happened to be on foot patrol, and in the right place at the right time – so had witnessed everything. The guy ditched what he had taken and made a run for it, leaving the lady shaken, but still standing and luckily unharmed. Now we could sit back, and watch the arrest unfold, or so we thought... it turned out to not be quite that simple.

This man had some stamina! He was younger than we had originally thought, but he had given the two police officers the run-around for well over ten minutes by this point. He was frantically searching for his means of escape whilst he continued to circle the park. The two police officers continued to chase him, throwing their arms around and shouting from quite some distance behind him.

The lady had by now composed herself and stood in the centre of the ever-widening circle of people, shaking her bags, and hurling abuse at the would-be robber – I best not repeat what she was shouting, but this was comedy gold for us observers.

It honestly looked like a scene from Benny Hill, less the scantily clad young women that would also be giving chase by now. Round and round he went, as my customers cheered on the police who were now looking red-faced. We had no idea how long this could go on for, he could outlast them – I felt tired just watching them.

Then, suddenly, a moment of epiphany – we could see our perpetrator's face change as he sized up the canal and finally, saw the escape route which he had so desperately desired. All that was missing was the ding of a lightbulb appearing above his head. If he could make it over the canal, past the pub, and onto the marshes, he might have a chance of freedom. But there was no bridge nearby; he would have to swim if he were to make it over.

So that was it – amid the shouting and cheering, he broke the circle and bee-lined straight for the canal – he was really going to do this! Without a moment's thought, he leapt into the greyish-brown murky water with an almighty splash, now just a few yards from liberty. Like a racehorse refusing a fence, the chasing officers pulled up short of the jump. The villain surfaced to see the two sweaty red-faced police officers panting and staring angrily down at him; he was off to finish his escape with a self-satisfied smirk.

He turned to head for the far bank, but the shock realisation on his face was priceless. Two new police officers had arrived on the scene from our side of the waterway, full of grins. He was like a baseball player trapped between bases. He was treading the freezing cold wintery water and had no way out. The police officers obviously had all the time in the world to watch this unfold, they were warm and dry.

They tried to coax him out, while the customers carried on cheering and laughing, and the extremely animated elderly lady hurled some of the foulest language I have ever heard to this day. He dipped under the water a couple of times, before eventually giving up and begging to be pulled back onto land. He was dragged out, dripping, and freezing, and led away to the sound of applause.

And that is what you call karma!

Simon Pac-Pomarnacki

Pubs aren't Haunted... are they?

Public Houses and ghost stories are a combination which present themselves time and again the world over. I'm not sure whether it's the fact that pubs are often old buildings with creepy layouts, or perhaps we are more open-minded to the possibility of the supernatural after a night of double rum and cokes.

Maybe it is comforting to know that our pubs are a common place for such souls to attach themselves should they indeed exist; I know myself having spent more of my life inside a pub than outside, it would certainly be my place of choice in the afterlife! The haunted pub is a traditional trope of the industry, although from my own experience which I write about now, there may be a good reason why.

When I first started running pubs many moons ago, I moved into and managed a pub called the White Swan. I was told by the locals that this pub was haunted and unnerving. However, I didn't believe this one bit; I thought they was just trying to scare me. But after just one day in my new job my opinions changed.

After a busy first shift I locked up and had finally sat down to have something to eat before making my way upstairs to bed, when I thought I heard someone saying hello. The voice sounded male and appeared to be coming from the gent's toilets. Initially I rolled my eyes at the idea of a drunken stray who had failed to leave after last orders, although accidentally locking a guest in was not a great look for the first day on the job, so I searched high and low through every room to see if I could see anyone. Alas, there was nobody around except me and I put it down to being extremely exhausted from my first day in charge. I had been awfully nervous all day and I thought I was just being paranoid about locking someone in, so I went to bed that evening and thought no more of it.

Nevertheless, two weeks later I was sat at the bar reading my newspaper at 8.30am before opening, happily paging through the football news, when I saw a face. The face popped their head around the corner, as if it were trying to get my attention. I was so shocked that I flew off the stool and dashed through the bar to see if I could find this person. I was due to open-up at 9am for the cleaner and yet when it appeared it was still only me in the building. Worryingly, I had to admit that like last time there was no one to be found!

A few months later, I had made my way up to bed after a steady stream of customers had been in and out of the pub. I was feeling very content with the day, when I realised, I had left the landing light on. Knowing I wouldn't be able to sleep without it being completely pitch black I grumbled and reluctantly swung my legs out of bed. As soon as I got up, I witnessed a shadow swiftly moving towards the door that I was about to open. I panicked and immediately ran back to bed with a scream, knowing even if I did turn that light off, I wouldn't sleep that night.

I decided to speak to the previous landlord to see if he had witnessed this figure or whether it was all in my imagination. Looking back, I wish I had never asked! Barry came over and told me that he was getting ready to open-up the bar one morning when he heard the door to the kitchen swing open and spotted the old cleaner walking around. He said he had shouted out a jolly hello, but that she hadn't responded back and at the time he had just thought she may have her earphones in and didn't hear him. Twenty minutes later when all the staff arrived to begin their morning shift, supervisor Janice came bounding in and asked Barry if he had heard the news about the cleaner. Barry was confused and responded "No, but I just saw her in the kitchen?" Janice went white as a sheet and informed him that the cleaner had passed away the night before in her sleep!

Can the haunting begin so soon we wondered? We made sure to enter the kitchen in twos for some time after!

Gareth Lane

One Short Step for Man

One of my uncles worked for a large American engineering company based in Detroit. My uncle managed a factory in Wales on behalf of the company for a period in the early 1970's.

There was great excitement about the place when it was announced that Neil Armstrong, (yes that one) was to pay a visit to the Welsh factory in his role as company president, and my uncle was to show him around and then host him for the evening.

My uncle was delighted with this news and shared this in his local pub, where he was arranging to take his VIP visitor for dinner after the visit.

The day of the visit duly arrived and the visit to the factory had been a great success, with everyone enjoying the day and great feedback from the celebrity visitor.

Later that evening in the pub, my uncle introduced Neil to the pub manager, who made polite conversation, as you do. Once the wet Welsh weather had been discussed the landlord asked him 'if he had to travel a lot for his work'? To which Neil replied

"Not as much as I used to!''

This got the biggest laugh from everyone, when the penny eventually dropped for the landlord.

An amazing visit from such a great celebrity to our small Welsh town.

I often daydreamt that Neil Armstrong might come back to our town one day in the future. Having been so captured by the friendliness of our local pub, perhaps he would come back for a holiday? And if he did, being that he was a busy man and we were on the other side of the North Atlantic; what would he be driving?

From Egg to Internet Legend

The Emu can grow up to two metres tall, making it the second largest bird in the world, and one of the fastest on foot having been recorded at speeds over 30 mph. We can only assume these were some of the facts that convinced our pub regular, Bill, to impulsively buy two emu eggs from the online bidding site eBay, in an attempt to raise his very own flightless bird.

Bill was a familiar face at the bar in the Bay Horse, Euxton, and he made sure to keep us up to date every step of the way throughout the incubation process which followed; supplying us with drink fuelled accounts of how expensive the equipment was and how one day, he thought he may have seen a crack emerging, but that it turned out to be just an eyelash.

All had gone quiet one week, and Bill had taken a few days hiatus from the pub, which was an irregular occurrence indeed. Yet all was explained one quiet afternoon, when he trounced back through the door triumphantly clutching an old shoebox.

Tentatively, with onlookers gathering around, he held his hand over the box with a suspenseful pause that even the X-Factor would have been envious of. An audible gasp rippled around the beer-fuelled circle as the lid was removed and we all locked eyes on what was sure enough, a baby emu.

As time passed, Bill's emu, whom he had named Rodders, continued to grow. After a few months Bill skilfully crafted Rodders a harness. As was fitting of Bill's character, he now walked the cartoonish sidekick daily to the pub.

Rodders understandably became a favourite down the pub, often being a source of great amusement, particularly in instances where non-regular customers would glance up from their steak and chips, to see a 6-ft tall unattended emu blocking the light from the door, while Bill fetched him a bowl of water. Bill and Rodders' notoriety, however, was not destined to stay local.

In 2017 a video appeared online posted by comedy platform LadBible. This video displayed, what had become to us at the Bay Horse, an almost mundane sight, although admittedly for an outsider this would have been a bizarre mix of hilarity and confusion.

Shot out of the window of a passing car, a passenger seems to heckle poor Bill for taking an ostrich for a walk, prompting the now famous reply: "It's a fucking emu not an ostrich!" To date this video has over 22 million views. 22 million people who have watched our pub regular Bill walking his pet emu!

Rodders was an internet sensation, and his celebrity status did not crash and burn like so many stars before him. After a pub refurbishment later that year, the Mayor of Chorley was kind enough to lend the afternoon to reopen our business but did make a special request that Bill and Rodders would be in attendance. The pictures from that encounter are entrenched into the legend of our community forever, the mayor in all his regalia being shadowed by the looming neck of our Rodders.

Bill and Rodders still continue to visit us regularly as they enter the twilight of their fame, yet they do not live alone – Bill now has another emu named Maya!

Turkey is not just for Christmas

I used to work in a lovely, quaint, old pub in Norfolk. It was a proper regulars pub; I knew everyone very well and can honestly say I got on amazingly with everyone. It was an old, converted barn with luxury boutique hotel rooms and beautiful gourmet meals. It really was an idyllic picture postcard type of pub.

The food was amazing and locally sourced, so we had a great relationship with our local butcher. He would supply us with the best fresh meat you could imagine all year round and he would always supply the produce for our Christmas Dinners, including all the trimmings. His business was a farm shop where they would grow all their own vegetables, as well as breeding animals for slaughter. Now, I need to mention here that I was a devout vegetarian at the time, so receiving the goods for Christmas didn't always fill me with joy.

The festive season was approaching, and I knew that we would be expecting a delivery soon. I had mentioned to Michael, the butcher, several times, that I wished he didn't have to kill the turkeys and I'd prefer to save them all as pets. This was usually met with a roll of the eyes and a shrug, but I would not give up so once again, I tried in vain to save a Turkeys life.

We laughed at the idea of them sleeping in my bed and sitting on the sofa. I could just picture them running around free and gobbling on the farm and hated knowing their fate. Not wanting to think about it anymore, I carried on with my days just a little sad, at the thought of the poor Turkeys who would not have known what was in store for them.

Then one afternoon, I got the shock of my life.

In strolled Michael through the pub doors, holding one of his lovely turkeys in his arms and struggling to keep it under control as it found itself in this alien landscape. The noise was unbelievable. You can imagine the reactions from the customers, they were laughing their heads off, adding to the general sense of chaos that had descended upon our sleepy little country pub. People were crying with laughter. As tears streamed down the faces of our regulars, he plonked the huge bird on the bar top and told me that he'd granted my wish and saved one for me. He then turned and walked out leaving the pitiful thing looking totally confused.

Although I was taken completely by surprise, I knew this was going to end well. My pet turkey was going to be so happy to move in with me and live out her days. The butcher had chosen her because she'd been picked on by the other birds and deserved a break.

I was over the moon! We named her "Lucky," as she'd truly managed to escape death. The world's luckiest feathered friend.

I was so excited! So, we managed to convert a shed for her in the bottom of my garden, with her own run. She became a bit of a local celebrity and is alive to this very day.

It was truly a Christmas miracle and the best present I could have ever asked for!

Cakegate

"Stan, where is the Jackson party's cake?" Amelia queried, her hands fumbling around the loose boxes.

Stan popped his head into the cellar. "What was that?"

"The cake!" She snapped. "The blue cake! It was here!"

"There - erm, there was a cake there, but-"

"But what?" She rounded on him, her eyes narrowing.

"But Chris said it was from last night's party, and they weren't collecting it?" She clambered past the towers of stock and appeared with a loosely secured box of flimsy white card.

"You mean this?"

"Oh hell," Stan muttered, his eyes widening and his knees beginning to tremble.

Amelia thrust the insubstantial package onto a pile of bottled beer boxes and made her way back toward the door.

"Stan," She drew his name out, tidying her dishevelled hair from her face, and wincing a smile. "Where is the cake?"

"We ate it."

The noise that followed was so harrowing, that it summoned Tommy, the General Manager.

"What is going on?" He said in a whispered growl.

"He ate the cake!" She cried. "He ate the Jackson booking's cake!"

Tommy's face fell from scepticism to dismay. "You what?"

"It wasn't just me!" Stan pleaded; his hands raised.

"Oh, bloody hell, you've got to be kidding me! Why?!"

"Chris said we could!"

"Wait, what? Why would he-"

"Well, I mean he said we could eat *that* one," His hand gesturing limply to the frail white box that housed another cake. "But we thought he meant, you know, the one she is looking for."

"Stop, please just. . . Amelia. Fix this. Fix it now."

His hard leather shoes echoed in the room as Tommy charged back into the rigmarole of customer service. Amelia shot Stan a stern glance and followed. Back on the bar, the conversion continued.

"Well? This *is* your fault!"

"My fault?" Chris said, grinning down into the limes he was cutting. "I don't see how it's my fault."

Amelia snatched the knife from his hand and slammed it onto the bar top, burying it within the splintered wood. "You're the one that let them eat it. Now, you're going to be the one to help me fix this."

His fingers passing through his hair, he stepped back and sighed heavily. "Okay, okay. Let me think." He looked sharply up to her, clapping his hands together. "Tony used to work at that bakery, didn't he? Maybe he can replace it?"

Her lips pursed, and her scowling eyes widened. "That could work. Yeah, that could work!"

With that Amelia stomped off to hunt down Tony. She found him in his usual hideout spot. The smoke billowed from Tony's lips, breaking on Amelia's desperate expression as water against a sharp cliff face.

"Sorry, darling." He said. "This sounds like a *you* problem."

"Come on, Tony. Please!"

He bowed his head, his voice turning to a whisper. "Look, I'm busy right now, it's not-"

"You'll be saving me here, please. Please." She quickly jumped in, not allowing him to finish.

Grin fading, his eyes dropped to the ground. "Well, maybe. It would b-"

Music blared from his pocket, interrupting him. He clawed out his phone and answered it without hesitation.

"Tallulah, baby! How's things?" Tony smiled at Amelia, mouthing 'sorry' before returning to his call. From what she could hear, it sounded like Tony was in hot water with his girlfriend. Again. After a few more brief words, the call ended abruptly.

Glancing at the phone screen, he turned to face Amelia, brow curdled, and his mouth slightly parted. He spoke lightly, "It's not going to work for me right now, Ame. I'm sorry."

"Tony, are you okay?"

"It's over with Tallulah, I think she's seeing someone else"

"Do you want to talk about it?"

"Not now!" he replied, deep in his own world.

Amelia drew a deep breath. "Okay." She said. "I'm- I'm sorry for bothering you." With that, she stepped briskly away, pushing back through the doors of the corridor.

"Hey? Hey! Everything alright?" Chris called out, stumbling around the bar as she skimmed in front of it.

"I'm going cake shopping!" She screamed, not looking back. "Don't ever try to help me again!"

The steel framed, full-wall windows rattled in their entirety from the force with which she shut the front door behind her as she left the building.

Amelia flicked through the pages of the catalogue from the seventh cake shop she had visited that day. The sun had dipped beyond the city rooftops, and emptying stores began to lower their shutters. She wandered out to the roadside, planting herself on one of the pavement benches situated alongside the canal. Her fingers traced the edges of her phone.

Glancing up, she searched the bustling crowds as if the answer to her dilemma was concealed in amongst their ranks. As Amelia looked blankly across the water, into the distance, beyond what she could see, her glazed eyes focused, broadening as her mouth fell open. She looked back to her phone and, shaking over the screen, her fingers fell onto the unlock button.

She opened her contacts list, and scrolled down to 'Tony', selecting him and hovering her thumb over the luminescent, green handset.
No, no I shouldn't, she thought to herself. *Can I? I mean, maybe I should?*
Amelia exhaled firmly and clawed the hair out of her face, scowling again across the canal.
"I'd want him to do it if it was me, it's the right thing to do."
She pressed hard on the screen and the phone began to ring.

"Tony, I know you have more pressing issues at this time, and I hate to pressure you, but I really need your help………

A little while later, her hand rested on his trembling knee.
"I'm sorry, Tony," she said. "I didn't know whether to call you."
He adjusted his position on the bench, turning to face her. "No. No, Ame. I'm glad you did. I'll make you the cake." He whispered; his eyes fixed beyond the water.
She replied gently, "You don't have to do th-"
"I said I'll do it," He grunted, quickly retracting his tone, and looking up to her with amiable eyes and a forehead wrinkled by the raise of his inner brow. "I'm sorry. I just… I want to, okay?"
"Thank you," she said, smiling and leaning forward to join him in staring out across the canal.

Tony then shared a message on his phone that told him that Tallulah was now seeing Stan.

"Oh, Tony I'm really sorry to hear that."

It was the day of the party. Amelia burst into the customer area ahead of a flourishing trail of balloons. They fanned out behind her, flouncing upon their strings as feathers of a peacock's tail. The walls and windows were lined with rather outdated banners at the behest of the customer. Gaudy, perhaps, though suitable really for the birthday party of an eighty-five-year-old. Amelia stepped back, admiring her labours.

Down by the bar she saw a lady idling forward. "Mrs Jackson! Lovely to see you again!"
"You too, my dear," she responded, scanning the room. "Oh, darling, it looks absolutely splendid. Thank you so much."
"You're welcome!"
Mrs Jackson took her hand. "I am serious, my dear. You have looked after everything for us, and we are so grateful. I'll bet nothing ever goes wrong under your expert supervision."
Amelia forced a smile.

Meanwhile, in the kitchens, Tony fastened his piping bag around his balled fist and began painting the intricate decoration onto his copycat cake. Amelia burst in through the door, stopping with a radiant smirk.
"Oh my god, Tony. It's perfect!" She said.
He did not reply, maintaining his focus.
She softened her voice. "Do you think it'll be ready in time?" when he didn't respond, she pressed. "Tony?"
"It'll be ready!" He barked.
Amelia took the hint and stepped quietly out of the kitchen, her face glowing.

A familiar ringtone burst from his pocket, startling him. "Hello?"

Back at the party Amelia directed the floor team to clear all the plates. The wonderfully cooked food had been served with perfect timing, and the guests had bottles of prosecco being distributed along the length of both tables. Bubbles rushed frantically through their glasses, and the time had finally come

for the cake. Amelia rapped the door of the kitchen gingerly, peering inside
when there wasn't an immediate reply.

The room was empty. No Tony. No cake. She pushed the door fully open and
stepped in, calling out for him. When silence fell, save for the gentle hum of
the extraction fans, she barrelled back out into the corridor and kicked her way
into each room in the staff area, blaring his name.
"He left," Chris said.
"What? No, no, no. Where?"
He stepped closer to her. "I don't know, Ame. He just bolted. I'm sorry."
Pacing the hallway, tears began to slip from the corners of her eyes.
"No, no. This isn't happening," she repeated, over and over.
Suddenly, the door of the corridor swung open. Amelia spun with hopeful
eyes, only to find Raeni.
"That Jackson booking woman? She's looking for you, hun."
Amelia filled her lungs and composed herself. She strode out into the party as
one marching to war.
"Amelia! There you are!" The panicked woman gasped. "Can we have the
cake? Everyone is ready for the toast!"
"I-I don't have it."
"What do you mean you don't have it?"
"It…" Amelia looked away from the woman's desperate stare. "It was ruined
in an accident out back. I'm sorry."
"You have got to be kidding me. Do you know how much that cost, how much
work went into this party? Have you any-"

The lights in the back half of the bar abruptly dropped to a dim glow.
Pouring into the room, accompanied by the flickers of auburn and crimson
dancing on the walls, and the smell of sweet, freshly piped frosting, came a
song that flowed into Amelia like life-a-new.
"Happy Birthday to you! Happy Birthday to you!"

Chris carried the cake, welcomed by a chorus of singing, up into the function
area. Mrs Jackson, her eyes burning with both relief and distress, turned back
to Amelia.
"That was not a funny joke, my dear," she whimpered. Unable to hide her
growing smile, she rushed back up the steps to join the end of the song.
Tony followed the procession out.
"How is this possible?" Amelia said, her eyes still flushed with emotion.

148

He beamed. "You didn't think I'd come through for you, did you?"

"But, the kitchen," she said, stumbling on her words. "You were gone, the cake too. I thought…"

"I didn't have the stuff here to finish the decoration. That thing on top? That's not easy to do." He chuckled to himself. "Stan helped me rush it back to mine to add the finishing touches."

Her face dropped into a grimace.

"Stan?" The man who had just that afternoon been snogging his missus. *That Stan?*

"Apparently, she said we'd broken up. But still, the dude wouldn't stop apologising. I figure there's plenty more favours where that one came from. I might forgive him, one day."

"What about Tallulah?"

With a wink, he replied, "Tallulah who?"

The Spirit of Friendship

Christmas 2006, I wondered what it would be like this year. On the face of it, it should be the same as last year, and the year before that, but this year was going to be different - we had a new General Manager at Spirit, and events may not unfold as they had done in previous years.

I was already working at Spirit, when the new General Manager Craig joined. After a challenging beginning and within the few months I had been his deputy, my workplace had rediscovered its purpose and appeal, seeing the team reshape and emerge better than ever.

But; Christmas was fast approaching.

I was nervous about what myself and other members of the team would do for Christmas Day, where would we go? My first ever General Manager did this wonderful thing, where he'd invite team members with no family or friends to visit, to join him and his partner for Christmas lunch. It was always good fun. We'd arrive before noon, have some food, drinks, clear up and then head back to work for the evening.

The day itself was always enjoyable, perhaps not for the traditional festive reasons, but for those of us that were there, it was important. It is the day of the year everyone talks about; filled with joy, happiness and family get togethers. It was nice to know that you were not alone, and more importantly, have someone that understood, and to share it with. It became our tradition.

I guess this is where the anxiety kicked in, should I ask Craig if we were able to continue with this tradition? Would he know how important Christmas is to those that are away from their families and alone? I didn't know Craig that well and from what had been discussed in conversation, he was truly into Christmas himself. So, would he want to head home and see his family? My mind was muddled.

After a few weeks of dithering, I eventually brought it up in a passing conversation, hoping I wouldn't sound an idiot for asking. I could see Craig thinking about it, the answer wasn't a yes or a no. I continued to explain how a few of the other team had nowhere to go on Christmas Day, which is why they were available to work, so it would be nice to involve them.

I even offered to cook and organise it all, but in what I'd soon discover as a brilliant trait in Craig, was the upmost enthusiasm and excitement for this. *"No, no, I'll do it, it sounds fun"*.

Within moments my fears had been replaced with a fascinating in-depth plan, which sounded more like feeding the five thousand, with all the pomp, the turkey and all the trimmings rather than a simple Christmas dinner for 6/7 of us!

This was going to be the best Christmas spread any of us could ever had imagined; this was it, it was happening. It would be a festive extravaganza and anyone that wanted to join in was more than welcome. The anticipation spread, and excitement began to fill the air.

How did I get to be alone at Christmas?

Most of us were on our own because we had fallen out with our families for various reasons, however being a homosexual was a common theme.

For me, I had half run away from home then fully run away, first to Liverpool, the nearest big city. I was vaguely in touch with some family still, but spontaneously I quit my job, moved to Manchester with this idea of becoming a hairdresser, yes, I know, how very stereotypical.

I became the apprentice hairdresser, but I needed another income, as anyone who's done an apprenticeship would tell you, the pay is poor.

Off I trundled to various bars to see if I could find a job. Canal Street was my main hope as I looked to cement my newly embraced gay status and freedom in one of the UK's most diverse cities.

After a few weeks of applying I got a trial shift at Spirit. I entered a great period in my life and I loved every minute of it. It was fast paced, super busy and Spirit was THE place to be. I was balancing two jobs, apprentice hairdressing and Spirit but an event was approaching that I wanted to enjoy and be a part of, the local Pride event.

However, the hairdressing wasn't allowing me time off for this event. After being denied the time off work (hairdressing) I decided I would go anyway.

Off I went with my new Pride haircut, expertly done by my friend, half bleach blonde, the other side a rainbow of the six colours of the Pride flag, I felt great.

That was until my hairdressing bosses came into Spirit and fired me across the bar. They knew where to find me, let's face it where else would I be on a Saturday evening especially as Pride was in full swing. That moment was pivotal, I decided, to dedicate myself to Spirit. The money was good, and I was loving every minute of working at the pub.

As the months passed, I worked hard and progressed into management. First becoming a supervisor, then duty manager, and assistant to the GM before they left for pastures new. In the week that followed the GM's departure, my name would go above the door, as licensee, where it would remain for over 3 years before I then departed for my first GM role.

You learn from the good times and most certainly the bad times, and over the next few months I would experience it all. There was uncertainty in the air with a new GM appointment that unfortunately just didn't work out. Spirit had fallen from being at the top of its game to almost out of sight.

My managerial career continued through this phase, perhaps a little unhinged and lacking in structure, with plenty of my own mistakes emerging. I was promoted to deputy and now found myself completing stocks, cellar management, rotas, recruitment and cash handling. It almost felt like running my own mini empire before the next manager came along. It was hard work and stressful at times, and for the briefest of moments I wondered if I was made for this.

Managers certainly set the tone and a good manager knows how to set the right one. Craig was refreshing. He had direction, vigour and a resounding and unwavering belief that Spirit would once again deliver.

His previous experience meant he could lead a team and a business in the right direction, even if they had become a little stubborn and set in their ways over the previous few months.

The days and weeks passed and suddenly it was Christmas, yes that one from earlier. Having Craig come into my life and what he did for me on that

Christmas Day can never be forgotten. He did something that changed my life forever. In Craig I found a friend and more importantly something I knew I'd been missing.

The day itself, everything was as it always was. People enjoying the dinner, a few games and laughs; but your mind wanders, and you can't help thinking of the times you used to have. You think back to the laughs with family, opening the presents under the tree and family traditions. It was nice to be with people and not alone, but it wasn't the Christmas I longed for.

I sneaked off to just have a bit of alone time, I was feeling a bit gloomy, but I kept my feelings to myself and wanted to have a cry out of sight. I wondered what my brothers and sister were up to, my parents, aunts, uncles and cousins. I smiled at the thought of my aunt falling asleep on the sofa, then the arguments over Trivial Pursuit. It was always a big traditional family event with up to twenty of us celebrating together.

It was five years since I spent a Christmas with any of them, perhaps longer since I'd spoken to many, certainly my mum, but this year it got to me. After having a rough few months, I was feeling low and very much alone, so much so I wasn't sure if I was cut out for hospitality or if I wanted to stay in Manchester any longer. Perhaps I could move to London instead, start afresh and find what I'd been missing and making me feel this way?

After about half an hour, Craig came and found me, at this stage he didn't know my history, but I talked, and he listened. Craig didn't say much but quietly asked *"Do you know the number to call them still?"* I laughed nervously, but he politely insisted, *"What's the worst that could happen? They don't answer? I bet your mum is dying to hear from you, call her."* And he just held the phone out. So, that's what I did.

That was 15 years ago. A brilliant friendship developed between myself and Craig which is still strong to this day, but I also am closer to my family than ever before due to that moment in my life where someone gave me a gentle nudge in the right direction, and the assurance that they support me and would be there for me whatever the outcome.

I had always been a bit of a loner, the strange kid on his own in the corner, the friend of a friend at parties. I knew how to have fun, I've been all over the UK partying until dawn, but I was always doing my own thing, in my own way, never one for following the crowd. Life takes you on a journey and for me working in hospitality connected me with people in a way I had never managed before. I've created lasting friendships, reconnected myself with my family and I've been forced to face my fears.

Hospitality has brought out the best in me without making me something I'm not. The industry has taught me to work hard but also play hard. I'm immensely proud and passionate about what I do and if other people saw what it means and feels like to work in hospitality, they'd all want to be here too.

G. Davies

Did You Remember the Baby?

Pubs have always been important in my family's life. Despite it being the 'Public House' they are usually also a private home, with the Landlord or Landlady living above or somewhere on the premises with their families.

This got me thinking about where my love of pubs began, so I asked my parents who shared the following anecdote from when my brother and I were little…

When I was a baby in the late 70's, my mum, accompanied by me, often helped at my aunt and uncle's pub. Whenever I was asleep, I would be left in the back room with the crisps and snacks close to the bar, in ear shot, but out of the way. The staff would check on me whenever they passed by the room. So, if the pub was busy and snack sales were good, I was often checked on.

When awake, I would be placed on the bar, giving the regulars a reason to stay in the pub, who would say they were babysitting me!

A few years later, my brother was born, and my parents decided to take him on our first family outing to the local pub to show him off to all their friends. All went well until they got home. This is when they had a sudden realisation that they had left something, or rather someone, behind! The new addition to the family. They dashed back to the pub to find all was well. He was fast asleep and being well looked after by the staff and regulars. How the 70's were a different time!

The experience certainly had a lasting effect on my brother, as he has been last to leave the pub ever since!

Kate Vicary.

Creepy Crofton Carry On

My first Assistant Manager position was in a lovely community pub in Hampshire. I took the job on, not knowing what fun I would have.

On an early start, apart from setting up the bar and tills, myself and the manager would do a walk round and check the pub was ready to trade and welcome our guests.

Every day we would go to the restaurant and find that all the cutlery had been moved around, even after we had checked that it was all laid out correctly.

The first few times we thought it was a staff member playing a prank. We made it clear to the staff that although hilarious, it was to stop. But it kept happening. The manager had now decided it was the cleaner meddling. Words would be had with her too.

To my dismay this still did not solve the problem, but the manager was convinced it was the cleaner. We did not have CCTV back in the day and the manager told the cleaner that she was not to go anywhere near the restaurant. Still no result and the all the cutlery had still been moved every morning when we arrived.

Eventually the cleaner, fed up with the accusations, left the business. Next morning, same thing happened. We could not work it out!

On and on the mysterious moving cutlery continued.

Then came my first lock up, on my own. The staff had cleared down. I had counted the tills and just one customer remained, finishing his Guinness. So, I told the staff they could go. I proceeded to do my walk-round and final checks, the last check being the restaurant.

As I walked through the hatch I felt a tap on my shoulder and turned around to tell the customer to not joke about. But there no one was there! Completely freaking out, I quickly went through to the public bar where Joe was sat finishing his pint. I told him what I had felt. He then laughed and said, "Oh that's only John, he used to sit at the hatch and wind the staff up until he sadly died."

Feeling very cold and nervous I told Joe, "Well, that's it you can't go until I have finished and locked up!"

That was the last lock up I ever did. Later, after talking to a couple of staff, they told me that they had experienced the same tap on the shoulder on many occasions and been freaked out when no one was there.

So, the only explanation for the moving of the cutlery was our departed regular still haunting the pub!

I must say, although the locals were lovely, it was a pub I was glad to leave behind!

E.V. West

The Largest Large

It was a chilly winter night, and I was sitting in my steamed-up car outside the local Masonic Hall, waiting for my elderly dad to emerge from a meeting.

Masonic meetings often ended with drinks and a social catch up after the various secret formalities and ceremonies had been completed. I'd agreed to pick him up around 10pm to save him a taxi fare. The whole secret society thing had never really appealed to me, but he seemed to enjoy it.

The door to the hall opened, followed by a rabble of various grey-haired gentlemen, full of chatter and high spirits, exchanging ancient handshakes and heading towards their respective taxis and lifts to escape the cold February air. Somewhere out of the crowd, my dad appeared towards my car and opened the door.

"Did you know, they've turned the old Sainsbury's into a Spoons?" He asked.

"Evening Dad!" I sarcastically replied, noting his lack of pleasantries. It didn't bother me; he was always short on words and was clearly excited by the news that a new pub had opened in town.

"Shall we have a look then?" I asked, as he buckled himself up.

The new venue in question was literally one minute's drive away, and I thought it would be interesting for him as an ex-publican. He was always full of stories and anecdotes about his forty years in "The Trade," and unless I offered to take him, he would have been too polite to ask me.

"Yeah ok" he replied. "If you have time?" He knew I did.

"Yeah, let's grab a quick one then and see what it's like." It didn't take long to drive the short distance over to where the old supermarket once stood, now replaced by quite a large and shiny new boozer.

We parked opposite using my dad's disabled badge, which always amused him and prompted the expected, "that badge is really useful" comment from him.

We made our way over to the entrance, past two security guys who appeared bored, looking odd and out of place in an otherwise dead high street on a Tuesday evening.

"I'm busting for a wee" my dad said. "Get me a large brandy please," as he sought the assistance of a Sherpa to accompany him on the trek to the distant toilet!

I made my way across to the empty bar. A few metres behind the counter, it appeared that someone was showing a new female recruit how to pour a beer. She looked nervous and a little overwhelmed, as she intently watched the bar manager skilfully tipping the glass against the flow of liquid coming from the tap. It didn't look that complicated to me, but I remember my first job and had some sympathy.

Seeing that I'd been standing at the bar for a while, the bar manager ushered the new girl over in my direction and she gave me a cautious half smile as she walked towards me.

"Can I help you?" She asked. "A large brandy and a pint of Diet Coke" I replied. "Ok" she replied and walked back towards the other end of the bar and around the corner, seemingly to prepare her first nervy order away from our gaze.

It seemed like about ten minutes had passed, and in the meantime my dad had returned from his unreasonably long journey to the toilet and was waiting patiently beside me for our quick drink. Another couple of minutes passed by, and finally, the new recruit appeared from around the corner carrying two pint glasses. She placed them on the bar. "£4:30 please" she said.

I looked at the drinks. One was clearly a Diet Coke, the other looked like a pint of ale or some other light brown liquid. "Where's the large brandy?" I asked.

"There!" replied the girl, pointing at the suspect pint. She quickly gave me my change and retreated to the other end of the bar.

My dad and I looked at each other in disbelief. Picking up the dubious glass, my dad took a sip. Smiled and put the glass back down. "Is it brandy?" I asked.

"Yep, it bloody is you know!" He replied, laughing in surprise.

No wonder our drinks had taken a while to prepare. It must have taken the poor girl twenty or so fills from the optic - almost an entire bottle of Napoleon; but she had clearly thought a large spirit was a whole pint!

My dad took an enormous swig and then conceded. "I'm not going to be able to drink that. It's a shame to leave it. What a waste!" I downed my Coke and we quickly left.

I never saw that barmaid again in that pub. Possibly, the manager later discovered she was serving £50 of spirits at a time for the price of a double and let her go. Maybe the girl realised her mistake and didn't return for another session. Whatever the case, it was the largest large my dad had ever had, and the talk of the Masonic Hall for many weeks to come.

Many ventured down there in the hope of being served the 'legendary large brandy,' but it was never repeated. My dad now always carries an empty hip flask when he goes to 'Spoons,' just in case!

Clive Hawkins

Turning a Blind Eye

Jamie was one of those customers you could rely on to turn up at the same time every day, sit at the same table, have his four or six pints (depending on the day of the week). The kind of customer that if he didn't show up, you would definitely question where Jamie was. A couple of times a week his daughter would join him for a catch up and a meal (this would be his six-pint day).

It was a busy Friday evening, customers were starting to come in ready for their weekend catch up with friends, laughing and wanting to unwind.

Summer, the barmaid, noticed Jamie on the floor intently searching for something under his table. She made her way over to Jamie, a little perplexed at what he could have possibly lost. "Have you lost something?" Summer asked confused, but more than willing to help Jamie find whatever he was looking for.

"Yes, my glass eye. I took it out to rinse it in my glass like I always do before going home, but it slipped from my hand and now I can't find it." Jamie explained without looking up at Summer, while he frantically searched the floor for the missing orb.

Although a little disturbed that Jamie was routinely rinsing his glass eye in his pint, Summer got down on the floor to help search for the 'eye'. Summer couldn't help but think in all her years of serving customers, they have left behind coats, phones, cards, but never had she had to search for a glass eye.

Several minutes later, and with another member of staff in the search, there was still no sign of the elusive eye. They had check under the table, chairs and around the general area. As Jamie had a taxi waiting, he was assured the cleaners would be asked to pull out the fixed seating in the morning to look for it. Jamie smiled; he was grateful.

"Ok, thanks guys, I will see you tomorrow" he replied with a wave as he left.

The next morning the seating was pulled out from the wall. Alongside the dust, a few spiders, countless ball point pens and a few beer mats; there in the corner staring back, was the 'glass eye.' Staff were ecstatic. They had found the elusive glass eye. Jamie would be so thankful to have his eye back.

Rinsed off, in water not lager, then polished, the glass eye was wrapped carefully in a tissue and placed safely in the office, ready for Jamie when he would turn up at his usual time of 4pm. There was something oddly comforting about having regulars who turn up at the same time every day; they became family.

"Got something for you!" Summer called out to Jamie from across the bar as he entered dead on 4pm. She scuttled off to the office to retrieve the prized possession. There was a smile on his face as Summer put the tissue wrapped eye down in front of him. Jamie eagerly opened it up, turned it around carefully in his hand, clearly inspecting the eye, placed it back down onto the tissue and pushed it back towards Summer.

Summer looked on as confused as she was yesterday. Why was he sliding his eye back to her? "That's not mine," he announced and walked off to his table. Stunned gazes followed him, completely bewildered. What were the chances of finding someone else's glass eye in the same pub, at the same table Jamie loved to sit at every day?

His eye was never found, and no one came forward to claim the one that was! To this day the staff are still bewildered. Perhaps one day the eye will show up. Jamie did get a new one, that he continues to wash in his pint before he leaves!

Sue Quinn

Lost Teeth

At the start of my shift, I was clearing glasses by the pool table, when I noticed a lump of something pink towards the back of one of the tables. It was the colour of used chewing gum, but the lump was far too big for it to be that. Intrigued, I went to investigate. The lump was biting the table! It was a set of false teeth!

I figured this must be the handiwork of my manager, Tim, as he often liked to pull pranks on us. Only a few weeks ago, he had asked me to do a toilet check just before we opened. When I pushed open the stall door, there was a skeleton sat on the toilet!

I picked up the dentures in a napkin and went to speak to him.

"Very funny!" I said, as I held out the napkin to him.

"Oh!" Tim exclaimed, "I didn't know you wore falsies!"

"They're not mine," I protested, "Did you not put them on the table?"

"Not this time, but thanks for the idea! You'd better find out who they belong to, I bet they're missing them!" he laughed.

I went back to the pool room and asked the few customers in there, if they had lost their dentures, but none of them had.

Tim suggested that we put them in a plastic bag in case the owner returned, so we placed them on a shelf behind the bar. It was quite funny when an unsuspecting member of staff would come across them! I started to see why Tim got such a kick out of his pranks.

Early one morning, I put a lemon slice in between the teeth and moved them to the glass wash room. Tim wasn't expecting that! This became a new prank for a few weeks, and the teeth would be discovered in various parts of the pub before opening, with a slice of fruit between them; before making their way back to the plastic bag on the shelf on the back bar.

Shifts were now spent tactfully checking customers mouths when they came to the bar. We were desperate to know who had left them, but no one was claiming the teeth. For three weeks they sat on their shelf, looking lonely and hungry, awaiting the return of their owner. We were about to give up on finding their rightful owner, when an old man came in. As he ordered a pint, we saw he had a set of his own teeth, but after he paid, he looked a bit sheepish.

"I don't suppose I left my choppers in here a few weeks ago?" he asked. "I think I took them out when I got a pork scratching stuck in my throat. I'd had a few and I think I went home without them!"

The dentures were quickly retrieved from the back bar. He was very grateful to find that we had kept them safe, secure and well fed with lemon and lime slices, even though he had already bought a new set!

60th Anniversary Celebrations

Dennis and Beryl, both from Norwich, met at a bus stop in 1956. The meeting was clearly meant to be, and the couple soon fell in love. Two years later, Dennis and Beryl tied the knot at Tudor Hall registry office and had their wedding reception at The Lamb Inn. The couple, since then, have always had a special place in their hearts for The Lamb Inn and they like to visit as regularly as possible.

In the six decades since their marriage, they have had four children and now boast ten beautiful grandchildren. Dennis and Beryl still live in Norwich, where they have created a blissful life together and like to spend time with their large and loving family and can often be found gardening in their spare time.

It was coming up to the couple's 60th wedding anniversary and they were trying to decide what to do to celebrate. A priority for the couple was spending the special occasion with their ever-growing family.

Knowing the love story between Dennis and Beryl, the local newspaper wanted to interview them and write an article about their story to mark the occasion and help them to celebrate the milestone. The story would cover their lives, from how the couple met to the present day.

Dennis and Beryl agreed to the story being written and saw it as an opportunity to mark the occasion, whilst having something to be able to keep and pass down the family for generations to come. The story alone was a great gesture for the couple, they simply did not expect anything more to come from it. That is, until the story was published.

The CEO of The Stonegate Group (owner of the Lamb Inn) had seen the article in the local paper (via the company press office) and wanted to offer his congratulations. Having read the article, he realised that the very pub the couple had held their wedding reception sixty years ago, was in fact a Stonegate pub, so he decided to track down Dennis and Beryl and offer to help them celebrate their diamond anniversary.

A week later Dennis and Beryl, surrounded by their close family, enjoyed a complimentary dinner at The Lamb Inn, in the same spot they had been sixty years earlier. The room had been decorated especially for them, with balloons and flowers adorning the walls, and the table was set the same as it had been sixty years ago for their wedding reception. It was all planned out perfectly and the family celebrated with an exceptional meal, served by an incredibly attentive and friendly team. Nothing could have made the day more perfect.

After the celebrations, Dennis spoke with Oliver, the manager of The Lamb Inn, and he could not thank Oliver and his team enough for making this special day. Oliver accepted their compliments and thanked Dennis, then went on to explain to the couple that the pub may be special to them, but they should realise that they are very special to the pub too.

Bob's Seat

It was a glorious midday in August, and the sun was shining brightly. The regulars were at their usual seats and the bustle of the lunchtime rush was just beginning, but something was not quite right. A conspicuous empty seat. This was not just any empty seat, this seat had been occupied at the same time, 11.50am on the dot every day, since as far as any of us could remember. This was Bob's seat.

My colleague Amanda was the first person to notice Bob's absence. She had a quick look around the pub to see if he had broken his routine and sat somewhere else; but there was no sign of Bob.

Amanda asked the rest of the team if they had seen him, or if he had told anyone he would not be in. They had not heard nor seen anything. This was puzzling as Bob was regular as clockwork, he even frequented the pub the day his grandkids were born, the day his wife passed away, Christmas day, in fact every day without fail. If for any reason Bob wasn't coming in, he made certain that somebody knew. For instance, when he went on his jaunts to the Cotswolds with his daughter.

As time progressed, at half past one in the afternoon, there was still no sign of Bob. Alarm bells were beginning to ring. A concerned Amanda asked if she could go to his house to check all was okay. I said I would go with her.

He didn't live that far from the pub, a five-minute walk if that, although that wasn't the case for Bob anymore, he had told us it seemed to take a little longer each day, and by then it was taking him the best part of half an hour.

We arrived at Bob's house. Even though neither of us knew his house number we instantly identified it as the one with the famous blue door, the only blue door on the street. The one that had been blue since 1952, when he had first moved in. The first house in the street to have a different coloured door than black. A blue that he had liberated from the bus depot where he had worked. A blue which matched the dress that his wife had worn on the day they moved in. It's amazing how these details stick with you when you hear them over and over again.

I guess this is one of the untold requirements of a great bartender - the ability to listen to the same story repeatedly and always receive it with the same welcome as the first time that you heard it.

We knocked on the door and waited, but there was no answer. We knocked again, this time louder, there was still no answer. As I remember Amanda asked, "Shall we go around the back?" I replied that we should look through the window and see if we could spot anything first. As I moved towards the glass, the glare from the sun and the reflection of the road were all that I could see, so I pressed my face harder to the window and peered in. It felt like my heart had skipped a beat and that time had stood still.

Staring through the glass I could see what looked like a foot with a shoe on lying on the ground, it was partially hidden by the living room door.

Anyone that has had one of these moments will understand what comes next, a jolt of what feels like a thousand volts charging through your body, a heightened sense of focus, vision blinkered so all that can be seen is what's straight in front of you - as though looking down a tunnel, or maybe you're charged like a bullet, looking down the barrel waiting to explode. Adrenaline had kicked in!

"The door's going in!" I said as I bolted towards it like a freight train. "Wait!" Amanda yelled, but it was too late as she had not seen what I had. I was past the point of no return. "They don't make things like they used to!" an internal voice reminded me, as I impacted the door with as much power as I could muster. The blue door stood firm as the full force of my shoulder hit it, in fact, not only did it stand firm, but it felt like it hit me right back as I bounced off the door, landing full plant on the seat of my pants.

By now, Amanda had also looked through the window and had realised what I was trying to achieve. She grabbed the handle of the door and... "Hey presto!" it swung open.

The sight that greeted us was a very pale Bob on the hallway floor, with a gash to his forehead and a blackened wrist. Immediately we were at his side asking if he was okay and what had happened. A semi-conscious Bob said he was fine and was more concerned about what all the racket was, he had heard a bang and thought the door was going to come in! I couldn't help but laugh as I dusted the gravel from my trousers.

Within minutes, an ambulance was on the scene and Bob was safely in the back of it. We secured the house and returned to work to complete the lunchtime rush, recounting the tale to all concerned.

The pub staff and many of the regulars visited Bob during his week in hospital, we learnt that he had suffered a concussion and a broken wrist. The story goes that he had fallen at the start of Coronation Street the night before and had remained in the same position for over eighteen hours until we had found him the following day. Who knows how long he may have been there had he not been missed from his regular seat in the pub.

Within a fortnight, a bruised and bandaged Bob was back in his seat at the expected time. The only difference now is that the walk takes him a little longer and there is a new story to tell about the blue door.

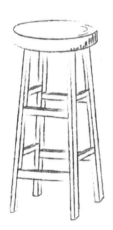

One Wedding and a Funeral

During the summer of 2016, I was General Manager of a lovely country pub in Essex. We had a roaring log fire in the autumn/winter, busy gardens in the summer and five quaint letting rooms. We hosted private events of all kinds, and we would quite often have wedding parties staying the night before the joyful day.

This was a Friday wedding. The bride and bridesmaids had arrived at various times on the Thursday afternoon, had a meal, a few drinks and then retired upstairs to their rooms.

They had had a very sensible evening and were up with the larks the following morning, buzzing with excitement. This manifested itself into a lovely chorus of chatting and laughter at the breakfast table. The hairdresser and beautician arrived to complete the final additions, whilst the excited ladies enjoyed a flute or two of champagne.

Everything had gone to plan and there was a little time left before the group was due to depart at 12.30. This tiny bit of downtime left room to ponder. Nerves and emotions kicked in and the bride took herself off to the bathroom.

The bridesmaids fondly discussed their friend and left her alone to her thoughts. The minutes slowly ticked by, and it was now the mood of the bridesmaids that was becoming a little edgy. Where is she? Has she gone? Has she changed her mind? The Maid of Honour accepted her duty and went in search of the missing bride, but she returned at twice the pace.

"She's locked in the toilet!"

There was not a pause, not a breath taken, no "OMG's," they were just gone, without a sound. Either they were a well-oiled military unit that had trained for this all their lives, or it is just something built into the female psyche for such an occasion, but they were gone. The handle on the inside of the toilet door was no more, and no amount of shoulder barging or combined kicking at the door would make it open.

We were going to have to go in through the roof. The chef grabbed the ladder and up we both went onto the roof. The imprisoned bride had managed to climb onto the toilet and open the skylight, so we dragged the ladder up and carefully lowered it.

The bridesmaids were anxiously pacing around, knowing that the wedding cars were due to arrive, and they could only watch, wait, and hope. The ladder was now down in the cubicle, and it was the chef that whispered to me the words the three of us knew to be true,

"She's going to have to take the dress off!"

There was no way she would fit through the makeshift exit with it on. To be fair to the bride, she showed the same spirit as the bridesmaids. Without a word the dress was frantically removed, cautiously passed up to us, and then she followed. It must have seemed like a Carry-On film! Passers-by could see the bridesmaids pacing around, two men clutching a wedding dress, only for a half-naked, blushing bride to emerge from below. Whilst there had been passers-by, we had beaten the cars, so we took that as a win.

Once down, the bride had a few minutes to get back into her dress, fix her veil, and get into the arriving car. She then headed to the church, her future husband, and the waiting guests. By mid-afternoon, the wedding party had returned for the reception.

With one lady's cubicle out of order, the queue began to build, and the story of 'the incarcerated bride' soon spread. Luckily, the groom saw the funny side and laughed as he said to me, "I thought I would have been the first person to get her out of her wedding dress!"

It was just over a week later, the naked bride story was still fresh, and embellished, when we had a funeral party arrive for the wake. We were expecting around fifty guests, with a few in wheelchairs, and so the organiser had checked that we had an accessible bathroom and easy access into the building.

The day had gone well. They spent around three hours reminiscing about their recently departed relative and friend, picking their way through the buffet, and consuming plenty of alcohol.

It soon became dusk, and the guests began to leave, each saying their goodbyes, and all being thanked by the organiser for attending. This took some time and eventually, once most guests had left, the organiser approached me to pay the bill. Whilst doing so, her father visited the accessible toilet in his wheelchair. When he returned, he and his daughter thanked me for our commitment and making them feel welcome.

It had been a busy day, and it was late when we finished clearing everything away. We were about to take the weight off our feet when we were told the organiser from the funeral was on the phone.

"This is rather embarrassing," she said, "but my dad has somehow misplaced his prosthetic leg. Could you please have a look for it?"

Off we went in all different directions. It did not take long.

"We've found it!" I gasped down the phone with a sigh of relief. I explained how it was discovered propped up in the corner of the accessible toilet. There were a few more words of thanks, we said our goodbyes again, and as I was about to end the call, I heard:

"For Pete's sake dad, I told you not to leave the pub legless!"

High Five!

Weekends in a busy pub can be hectic!

Hight street boozers can be packed, with drinkers in for a quick pint mid shop, or to catch the sports results. Destination pubs that are renowned for their food have a whole different pace to them.

As the Deputy Manager of one such pub, who at a moment's notice must be able to jump in with both feet, willing to help in any situation and in any department of the business, I knew it was going to be a day of variety.

The pub I worked in was well known for its quality of food, and on this day, we were extremely busy. The weather was unusually warm for the time of year, and we had more walk-in guests than booked as people decided to go out and enjoy the unexpectedly pleasant weather.

As the tables filled up with customers ordering lunch, I decided I would be better placed running food from the kitchen to the diners rather than behind the bar.

Entering the kitchen, two plates of mouth-watering fish and chips with mushy peas were sat on the hot plate waiting to be dispatched to the guests.

"Table four away please" hollered Chef from behind the pass.

The clear command that the food was ready to go. "Four away" I replied.

Always eager I picked up the two plates, turned and exited the kitchen in the direction of table four.

Without warning, in those few seconds from picking up the plates and making my way to the customer, I felt my fingers getting extremely hot and uncomfortable. I had failed in my haste to feel the plates and dived in with both feet, and in this case both hands.

Having rushed in from the bar I had neglected to pick up a serving towel. The plates in the kitchen were always kept quite hot so that the food remains hot on the way to the guest, and whilst they eat it. My fingers were screaming at me, and the pub was so busy I could not see an empty table on which to rest the plates and get some relief.

Only a few more steps. The question to myself now was, could I make it to the table? Off I dashed at a pace worthy of an Olympic sprinter. Upon reaching the table, I got them down as quickly as I could and informed the guests that the plates were extremely hot, and that I was only a couple of seconds from losing a finger, so please be careful.

"Thanks for the warning, but it could have been worse" said the gentleman at the table and whilst my immediate thought was, 'I don't think so,' I wanted the ground to open and swallow me when he smiled and raised his hand.

With a huge grin on his face, he had raised his hand for a 'High Five,' and that is when I noticed a hand with only a thumb and no fingers on it. The customer was laughing, whilst I stood there, my face glowing brighter than the surface of the sun.

He explained how he lost his fingers in an industrial accident and was not in the least offended by what I had said. We had a laugh about my reaction and from that day whenever he came in, I always received the customary wave and a warm smile.

There are so many nice people in this world. He could have reacted differently but was quick to see my embarrassment and put me at my ease.

You cannot be too careful about the things you say!

Is that you Dave?

According to the regulars of The Red Lion; Bushey had once had the most pubs per capita than anywhere else in the country. With The Red Lion being the oldest site in the small town, originally built in 1648 and rebuilt after a fire in 1895, it's no wonder it's rumoured to be haunted by many ghosts.

The Red Lion has a long history as a coaching inn during the age of the Highwayman; outside buildings that were used as a makeshift morgue during the war, and a previous landlord that shot himself in the pub while it was open! No wonder there's a plethora of ghost stories!

Hilda, who works at the pub, first realised the staff weren't the only occupants of the pub, when some inexplicable things started happening. After seventeen years of working there she has had many experiences, especially after the loss of Dave, one of the regulars.

The news came in that Dave had sadly passed. It wouldn't be the same without him and his gruff ways, sitting at his usual spot at the bar with his newspaper.

This is when Hilda, a veteran of the pub for the last seventeen years, started to notice some strange things going on. Nothing major, a glass being smashed when no one was near, things breaking and then suddenly working again with no interference; that kind of thing. But this was enough for Dave's presence to be felt once again, or so it was thought.

One day, Tony, the regional auditor, popped in to do his usual stock check. "Want a cup of tea, Tony?" asked Hilda. One always had to keep the auditor sweet with a cuppa!

"Oh yes, that would be lovely, thanks," he replied. "Milk and two sugars, please."

"How's things with the wife and kids?" Hilda made small talk while she prepared the hot drink.

"Yeah, they're fine. Just got back from holid…" Tony was cut off mid-sentence as a cup flew from the coffee machine at him. It was quite frankly, a rude interruption, in Hilda's opinion.

"Oh, don't mind that!" Hilda laughed. "That's just Dave, he's up to no good again!"

Tony dusted himself off, taking the moment to compose himself. "Well," he cleared his throat. "Better get on with this then. Mind taking me down to the cellar?"

Hilda led the way down the stairs and started to head back to the bar when Tony called out to her. "Erm, Hilda? Why isn't the fan on?" he asked.

Hilda had stopped midway up the stairs. "It is, Tony," she replied, certain it had been on earlier. At the shake of his head, she moved down to him again, muttering. "Well, it was when I changed a barrel."

As they investigated, Hilda was proved correct. The light on the machine said it was indeed on, the fuse was clearly on, but there was no movement in the fan itself. "Hmm. Strange!" she muttered to herself.

"I think I know what might fire it up," Hilda said as she smiled to herself. "Come on Dave, put the bleedin' fan back on!" she shouted. Her voice filled the downstairs room, and as if by magic the fan kicked into action.

Tony wrapped up his count after that, and scarpered, but not before awarding them a Gold Audit. Hilda chuckled to herself, suspecting he was a little too wary to mark them down. Dave clearly wasn't a fan of auditors!

Hilda thought nothing further of the day's events. She was looking forward to a relaxing bath with a large G&T to soak away the aches and pains of being on her feet all day. Feeling a bit more human after her bath, whiling away the time online looking for the perfect cat to rescue, a noise caught her attention.

Someone was running themselves a bath – clearly jealous of how relaxed Hilda felt. However, she was the only one at home. This caused her to pause a

176

moment. Garnering her courage, she went back up to the bathroom only to find the taps running at full blast.

"I must be losing it," Hilda said to herself as she quickly turned them off. Trying not to let the interruption disturb her relaxation, chalking it up to old buildings and its other ghostly inhabitants, she thought no more of it, and switched off for the night.

A couple of days later, after a well-deserved break, Hilda was back and opening the pub on a lovely quiet Tuesday morning. Whilst doing the usual jobs allocated for that day, Hilda brought Lucy, one of the other bar members, up to date on the strange encounters with Dave over the last few days.

"Excuse me," a woman interrupted the pair. "May I have a quiet word?"

"Yes of course," Hilda replied, inwardly grimacing, assuming the lady wanted to speak to a manager with a complaint.

"I'm sorry to interrupt," she said softly. "My name is Patrice, and you might think I'm crazy, but I'm actually a Psychic."

Completely taken aback, Hilda said nothing for a moment. Not what she had expected her to say. "*Riiiight…*" she drew the word out, unsure and just a tad sceptical.

At this point, Patrice the Psychic continued, seemingly unaware, or perhaps deliberately ignoring Hilda's doubt. "I wonder, do you ever feel as though this pub is haunted?"

"Well, maybe sometimes. Maybe?" Hilda said, not really wanting to reveal too much to this random woman.

"It's just that I need to tell you that his name is Paul, not Dave," Patrice the Psychic said, sending Hilda's brows to her hairline, and dissolving all doubt.

She joined in with the other woman's laughter when she continued. "And he doesn't like being called Dave!"

From then on, Hilda made sure to greet the otherworldly presence with a cheerful 'Hi Paul!' and all tea cups have remained firmly in their place on top of the coffee machine ever since.

Well, that is, until Tony the Auditor comes back…

(Names have been changed to protect the innocent. Except for Paul. We are not making that mistake again!)

Dawn Hall & Lisa Jeffs

The Carling Guy and The Blaze

The unexpected pandemic, and three subsequent lockdowns, were undoubtedly catastrophic, the world over. These bombshells, however, weren't as shocking to me as my indelible tale from my pub!

Running a peaceful, quiet venue, I knew most of my regulars by name. Well, except the Carling guy. The blue-eyed rascal was neither scary nor intimidating, quite the opposite in fact. He seemed polite, charming and untroubled. I knew this from my secret observations.

I took careful precautions, of course, not to interact with him, whether by urgently leaving the bar area upon his approach, or by gently pushing a member of my team in front of me to obscure his view. Without beating around the bush, I believed him to be the most attractive guy alive. Yes; direct competition for Mr Tom Hardy. I was adamant my ears would set on fire if the simplest exchange of sentences occurred, even something as trivial as a drink order.

One day during a quiet shift, after he had been served his customary pint of Carling by my colleague, I asked her to go on her break, safe in the knowledge that I wouldn't need to serve Carling guy in her absence.

Then, horror of horrors, my cunning plan didn't work, as the object of my affection suddenly approached the bar. There was no-one to save me, and I had nowhere to hide! He asked, quite calmly, for a piece of paper and, as I felt my pale carnation turning burgundy (almost certainly the image of an exploding tomato), I grabbed him that damned piece of paper from the communal printer and frantically pointed at it, mumbling that there is more, should he wish to grab another piece later.

I didn't see Carling guy for several months and began to think I never would when, unbelievably, we matched on a dating app. A little after that, we became official and, before I knew it, he had moved in to my cosy flat above the pub.

It is quite fascinating to think that, in one moment you can't serve someone a pint because the rapid heart palpitations make you look insane, and in the next, that same person is popping a question and planning their future with you. To this day, I can't believe how funny life can be. But of course, this is not the end of the tale.

During one hot August weekend in 2020, I received a phone call from my line manager. It was good news. I was going back to work on Monday, to prepare my pub for re-opening after the first Covid lockdown. Certainly, after months of work-free, surreal idyll, returning to a more normal life was exciting indeed.

Naturally, I wanted to ensure that my last weekend of "freedom" was as pleasant as possible. Carling guy and I spent the first half of the day outside, enjoying the beautiful weather, and wandering, at a leisurely pace, around the town centre. However, you can only take so much sun, so we agreed to return home and settle down on our new sofa with a couple of ice-cold beers.

Soon after taking my first and glorious sip of our favourite poison, Carling guy observed; 'There's smoke coming out of next door,' and pointed a finger toward the neighbouring roof.

Whilst, at this stage, the situation did not appear too serious, our attention quickly moved to a small group of people standing outside the front of the building. Curious passers-by perhaps?

'Let's go and investigate and see if the fire brigade needs to be called,' I responded.

Shortly after leaving my pub, the fire brigade arrived and promptly commanded us all to vacate the area. Reluctantly, we trudged across the street, and sat at the bus stop, regretting the abandonment of our beers. Within just a couple of minutes though, the smoke had spread dramatically and taken on a far more sinister form. We became acutely aware that the fire was spreading towards our flat.

We caught the attention of a police officer, who had suddenly appeared on the scene, and asked for permission to return to our flat to rescue Gherkin, our beloved cat. This request was refused and instead, the police officer took my pub keys and handed them to a firefighter. Once the firefighter understood the reason for our increasing concern, he went in to the pub and our accommodation but couldn't find Gherkin.

After an hour watching the fire spread and fight its deadly battle with the firefighters, we heard the fire alarm in my pub finally being triggered. Sweating with stress (and unbearable heat), it was impossible not to torture ourselves further with questions regarding Gherkin – is she okay? Is the awful alarm sound unbearable for her? Why didn't we think to take her with us?

Our helplessness and hopelessness were almost palpable, and fear emanated from our inner beings. The staff from a nearby venue very kindly invited us to join them for a drink. Just a few buildings down, they also suffered the consequences of the fire - as the length of the street was now closed off.

Well, I guess 'suffered' is a strong word – I'm sure that most of them were more than happy to finish work for the day! Their enthusiasm, however, was completely taken over by their sincere sympathy and care of the two of us. The kindness of those strangers was heart-warming and even somewhat lifted our spirits although, of course, a pint on the house also worked its wonders!

Our infantile hope of returning home within a couple of hours, was crushed by a police officer who approached us with updates. Upon taking our names and details, I was bracing myself to be told that we wouldn't be able to return home until the following day. This would have sounded like a sweet melody in comparison to the cacophony that came out of the officer's mouth, "I have just come back from your pub, and unfortunately, the situation isn't good. The floors have collapsed… everything's gone."

The pain we felt in that moment was indescribable and every second after was even more agonising. Guilt was undoubtedly the worst we felt, followed by excruciating self-blame. To put this simply, every single thought hurt. We had lost our pet, our belongings, sentimental treasures, our documents, and with this, our identities. We lost a place to live and possibly, my job.

How does life dare to do this to us in the middle of the chaos that already is 2020, like it wasn't hard enough already? And how ironic, that we had just spent a substantial chunk of our salaries on a new sofa a few days ago. This thought almost had me in stitches, perhaps in a moment of insanity.

Thankfully, however, we had each other. We also had our phones and smoke smelling clothes as well as two bags of necessities obtained from the local supermarket and presented to us by our newly made friends. They included water, underwear, toothbrushes, socks and cosmetics. We could not thank them enough. My faith and love for humanity had been fully restored.

We grabbed all that we had and bade our goodbyes. We were off to stay the night at our friend's house. Before leaving however, we wanted to see the catastrophe with our own eyes. Tightly holding each other's hands and our new and only belongings, we were joined by my Line Manager who had responded to my desperate calls for help and attempted to get as close to our pub as possible.

From a distance, we could clearly see that my pub was not on fire – this of course ignited a ray of hope which almost got us running. Finally, standing directly in front of the building, we could clearly see that my kitchen chairs and table had survived. I began to question not only my sanity, but also my eyesight. Is it possible that the police officer confused us with our neighbours? Or, had the floors only partially collapsed?

The uncertainty that night was horrendous. Morning could not come quickly enough. With barely any sleep, we got up exceedingly early and immediately headed back to our pub. Some firefighters were still (or already) present, investigating the area. They didn't allow us back in the building, but they were happy to go inside to look for Gherkin. I desperately described her possible whereabouts, and the location of her carrying bag, in case she was found.

They came out after a couple of short minutes, with her! The tears poured down my face yet again – this time from relieved happiness.

When eventually allowed to, I will never forget entering the pub for the first time; everything was still uncertain right until this point. So, my pub did not catch fire - it did however suffer major water and smoke damage. The back of the venue was completely trashed, and the smell of smoke was over powering. Parts of the floor had risen making it challenging to walk. The front of the building, however, was fine, which included our flat! Despite a horrible experience, we considered ourselves incredibly lucky – not one of our belongings was damaged.

Of course, this is life, not a fairy tale. Severe water damage meant no electricity, which resulted in us living in a hotel. Being stuck in a dated room with no air conditioning was far from fun. After five long weeks of fantasising over the luxury of cooking a homemade meal, we officially moved out to a privately-owned apartment in a fantastic location. Making our first breakfast after a whole month of eating out was the most amazing meal I'd had – and this is irrespective of my cooking skills!

Gherkin needed an urgent visit and overnight stay at an emergency vet before returning to us. She loves our new flat and, apart from the occasional sign of PTSD, she's back to being herself – a little demon, that is!

I don't know how many people can say this, but my pub, my very first pub, taught me a couple of lessons. Everything is possible (I am still referring to my love life), don't take anything for granted, appreciate what you have and for Pete's sake, invest in contents insurance!

Roxy Zym

Mobile Phone

In the late 80's, I was a regular at a pub close to Brighton Station, for the purpose of this story let's call it The Carriage. The place was run by a bit of a character going by the name of Jimmy.

Jimmy was a typical old school pub landlord, a big personality with even bigger tall tales and wind-ups. One evening, a local came in by the name of Fred, who worked in the communication industry. Fred had the latest gadgets and let everybody know about it. Brighton's answer to Bill Gates if you will.

On this particular evening he came into the pub bragging about something he called a 'mobile phone.' Now, in the late 80's, I knew more people who had landed on the moon than had a mobile phone, and here was Fred saying he had one in his car!

Jimmy wasn't the most trusting landlord, having heard more than his fair share of exaggerated stories, so he called Fred's bluff and asked to see it. Fred explained the mobile phone was charging, and after he finished his pint, he would nip out to his car to get it.

What followed was the tensest half an hour you could imagine. Everyone watching as Fred slowly sipped his pint, willing and wishing for him to neck it and get on with showing us his gadget.

Final sip done, and off Fred wandered. Ten minutes later he returned with the mobile phone, which everyone in the pub that night all agreed looked more like an army field radio from World War One. The phone had an aerial the size of a telephone mast and was contained within a briefcase which would be too large for an aircraft cabin bag! With every customer laughing at Fred's not so high-tech looking toy, Jimmy called out, "You'd have a better chance of calling in an airstrike than making a phone call with that thing. Prove it works, ring the pub phone then!"

In anticipation the whole pub went quiet, everyone was intrigued to see if it worked. A minute went by while Fred entered the phone number and then *ring-ring, ring-ring*. The pub phone was actually ringing! Off Jimmy went out the back to answer it and to his surprise he heard Fred's voice on the other end! While this was going on, Fred had reached over the bar to the optics and poured himself a large scotch. The whole pub burst into fits of laughter, then a few seconds later Jimmy returned with a bemused look on his face, asking what the joke was.

Assuming he was somehow the butt of a joke, he'd asked Fred to ring the phone again. Another minute went by, and *ring-ring, ring-ring,* the pub phone went off again. "You better answer it," Fred said. Jimmy returned to the back to answer the phone, and again Fred leant over the bar to pour himself a second scotch, to the great amusement of the other customers.

Jimmy returned with the same bewildered look on his face still not understanding why everyone was laughing. Shaking it off, he asked Fred what the phone was called.

"It's a *Motorola,* series *WF*," Fred replied.

"What's the WF stand for?" asked Jimmy.

"It stands for Whisky Foxtrot," he said. And went on, much to everyone's continued enjoyment,

"There are no foxes involved, but the whisky certainly trots!"

You Can Buy My Shoes

On a chilly winter evening, I was at the entrance to the pub supporting two members of my door team. It was absolutely freezing. I could see my breath in front of my face and, not surprisingly, everyone in the considerable queue was desperate to get inside and start their party.

Unfortunately, at this point, a member of the team had to inform a customer that, due to the dress code on Friday and Saturday evenings, his footwear was not acceptable. "Sorry sir, no trainers tonight, shoes only."

I kept an eye on the situation. While the customer was disappointed at his rebuff, a big grin started to appear as he was clearly hatching a cunning plan. "No worries, I'll put my socks over my trainers and hey presto, they'll look like black shoes!"

Somehow, I kept a straight face, as I fondly remembered the time that I had attempted the same ploy many years ago. Unfortunately, I had been unsuccessful too and decided that I would quit while I was ahead and waved goodbye to my friends. Now the boot (or rather sock) was on the other foot, although I could already tell that this customer had far more resolve and determination than I had previously shown.

While he continued to engage with the door team in a non-threatening manner, a very loud voice piped up from the middle of the queue. "I'll sell you my shoes for £20 quid mate." This caused much mirth and merriment in the queue, and I was intrigued as to what was going to happen next.

Unbelievably, the rejected customer left his position at the front of the queue to start negotiations with the man with the very loud voice. To everyone's disbelief, he firstly tries on the right foot, followed by the left foot, and starts to strut up and down, alongside the queue. It was as if he was trying on the latest fashions in his local shoe shop! He turned, satisfied, and promptly returned to the shoe seller. Negotiations were completed and with a shake of hands the customer made his way back down the queue to the applause and cheers of his waiting friends.

I laughingly said to the proud owner of new shoes: "I can't believe you've just paid a stranger twenty quid for his shoes."

His reply was almost indignant, "I didn't, I swapped my trainers, I need cash for tonight."

"How much were your trainers?" I asked. "Much more than twenty quid," came the cheerful reply, and off he went with his friends to have the party they had been looking forward to all week.

What value can you place on having fun and being with your friends? It just goes to show that with a little determination and ingenuity, nothing will stop someone enjoying a night out with their mates!

Darren Earl

Should have gone to Specsavers

There are lots of aspects of running a pub that I find exciting. The weird & wonderful people you meet, and the buzz created during a big football match, are just a couple of my favourites. But today, I want to tell you about one aspect the whole pub team enjoy. On a regular basis, we are sent sample drinks from our suppliers. We all look forward to tasting the drinks prior to putting them on sale, although this often comes with a logistical challenge as the drinks will often arrive without warning.

One Friday morning, I was really feeling the pressure. One of our team had called in sick and there was so much that needed doing. Counting cash for the tills, ensuring the fridges were fully stocked, firing up the grill, to name just a fraction of the daily tasks needed to keep a pub running smoothly. However, I still managed to get the doors open bang on time. Unlike most mornings, we had a flurry of guests, on opening, that added to my stress.

So, there I am running around, trying to ensure everyone is happy, when in walked a delivery man struggling with a heavy looking box. Sweat was pouring from his brow and he looked as stressed as I felt!

"Can you sign this? I'm in a hurry!" he gasped, plonking the box in the middle of the pub floor, and shoving a form in my face. One thing you learn while running a pub is to multitask. I signed his form with a grimace while simultaneously pouring a round of five pints. I then dragged the box behind the bar and continued serving through one of the busiest shifts of my career; single-handedly.

Fortunately, Georgie and Tom arrived early for their evening shift, and both jumped behind the bar having realised how busy it was. Despite only having joined the pub recently, they were both a huge help and remained unflustered. With their support, we managed to get the shift back under control.

I then remembered the surprise package.

188

Excitedly, I ripped open the box and saw that it was a new cider, with quite an unusual name. I figured I would get it out on display before taking a hard-earned break.

"Right guys" I called out, loading up a fridge shelf with the new cider. "We've got a new cider to sell, first one to sell a 'Rek..your..dick' gets a prize."

For some reason, Georgie greeted this announcement with a barely restrained snort of laughter. But I was too exhausted at that moment to wonder why, and instead of asking what the joke was, I went off to take my break.

Come nightfall, I was back on the bar, feeling fresh, and eager to go for the chaos of a busy Friday night. The morning was forgotten, and the guests were once again flocking in. I was just getting stuck back into things when Tom called over to me.

"Hey, boss! What's the name of that new cider you want us to sell?"

Calling out the name to him across the bar, I noticed he was obviously struggling to hold back a laugh. This happened a couple more times with Georgie and Tom each asking to be reminded what the name of the new cider was.

Every time I replied, they were either grinning like Cheshire cats, or quickly turning away from me with their shoulders hunched, as they clearly struggled not to burst out laughing. Something clearly was not right, but I could not put my finger on it.

I had just finished another round when I felt a tap on my shoulder. I turned to see Georgie standing behind me with a very self-satisfied grin. "Boss, can you serve this lady? She wants to know about our new cider."

Well, that was it, I had had enough! Why couldn't they be bothered to remember the name of the new cider? I stomped over thinking I will show them how a professional would sell a new drink.

With a bright smile, I greeted the lady, and began to talk about our delicious new cider, suggesting that she should try a sample. Wide eyed with horror, she began glaring at me and, in a loud voice tinged with barely suppressed rage, declared: "I'm not going anywhere near that. Just get me a glass of wine!"

At this point, both my team were in tears. Tom had his head in his hands, leaning across the bar and unable to stand as he was choking so hard on his own laughter.

"What's the joke guys?"

I asked feeling very confused. Georgie grabbed a bottle from the fridge and asked me to read out the name.

"Rek..your..dick"

I said, only to be greeted by another gale of laughter from them both.

"Read it again…... slowly" she said.

Squinting carefully, I slowly re read the label.

"Rek...order..lig."

At this point, she very gently suggested that it might be time I considered an eye test. I had always hated the idea, thinking they would just make me look old, but realised with a heavy heart it was time.

An optician's appointment was made and, thanks to my new glasses, and the fact I now read everything twice, this has thankfully never happened again. However, Georgie and Tom, going against my noticeably clear instructions, make sure to tell the story to every fresh staff member who joins our team, ensuring I can never forget that embarrassing night!

Sue Quinn

Jack the Lad

Jack is stereotypically one of the lads. Jeans, basic t-shirts. Smokes roll ups. Usually (most nights) he's quietly glued to any football (it doesn't matter who is playing) and sits at the table nearest the bar, drinking pints in endless rounds with his loyal group of local mates.

So, we were all a bit taken aback when he rocked up to the pub in fancy shirt and smart trousers, and then joined an unknown young lady in a booth in the corner away from everyone else.

After a brief time, Jack approached me at the bar, triggering a loud burst of jeers and wolf whistles from his mates. Jack takes it all in the good humour that it's meant, casting back a submissive smile. As I take his carefully explained food and drinks order, Jack reveals that he is on a date with a girl who works with his sister. Her name is Sarah.

She spotted Jack one evening when he gave his sister a lift home, and asked Jack's sister to pass on her number. I questioned his reasoning for bringing her to the bar as he knew his mates would be in, and as the laughs and jeers continued, I think he realised it may have been a mistake, but replied with a wink "where else would I bring her, but to the best pub around!" I took the compliment.

It was a midweek night, there was an exciting Champions League game on the TV, so we were quite busy for a time. The football ended, people had finished their meals, and bit by bit the tables and booths were clearing. Jack had been back to the bar a couple of times and said things were going very well. Sarah had been to the bar also and we chatted briefly, she seemed a nice young lady.

We close at 11pm during the week, so at 10.30pm there were only few customers left, including Jack's mates who were finishing their drinks, and Jack and Sarah who had moved from their booth to the comfy sofas at the front of the bar.

The boys said their goodbyes and after a few more jibes at Jack, they were gone. By now the cosy couple were all that remained, it was almost 11pm. I approached the sofas and asked them politely to finish up their drinks. "No problem," replied Jack.

The other remaining team member Chris, and I continued to do our routine nightly clear up. 11.15pm, Jack and Sarah are busy chatting away, staring into each other's eyes, but have still not finished their drinks. I approached once more, and as diplomatically as I possibly can be, I ask them to finish up and leave. Again, Jack replies "No problem," but as I turn around, I hear Sarah say, "What's her f*****g problem?!"

Facing them, I notice Jack's look of shock and sudden embarrassment. "I don't have a problem, but it is time to finish up and go. You're the last customers here."

"Alright, alright, keep your knickers on, we're going!! Is it ok if I go for a piss first!" Snarled Sarah.

"Of course," I replied, and she stomped away. I noticed that instead of climbing the stairs to the ladies she had chosen to use the disabled toilet; and for the sake of peace and harmony, I let it go (I like to try and keep this toilet available for our elderly customers etc).

Jack and I continued chatting, ignoring the mood swing that had changed the atmosphere. He finished his drink and some of Sarah's, but suddenly, from nowhere a barrage of insults and slurred foul language cut the air. I span around quickly and coming straight at me like a missile was Sarah. Within a split second, she was millimetres from my face, poking me sharply in the chest, and screaming like a banshee.

Jack and Chris jumped in between us, looking as confused as I was feeling. They had to hold her back with her arms flailing, nostrils flaring, and bulging eyes crazed, like a rabid dog. I stood still watching in shock. Jack grabbed their coats and her handbag, and firmly ushered her outside, apologising as he went, and with Sarah continuing to turn back and shout even more manic abuse.

I wondered what else she would have done if the boys hadn't got between us. Outside we could see Jack talking sternly to Sarah, pointing at her and back at the pub; then just as suddenly as it all started, she squatted down and started crying like a baby. We continued to watch as Jack stood outside with her in the rain, waiting anxiously for her taxi to arrive to take her home.

Chris and I burst out laughing, "what was that all about?" I said.

The last job of the evening was the toilet check. Chris headed upstairs to do the ladies and gents while I checked the disabled toilet. Lo and behold what did I find on the floor, but Sarah's bank card. It was covered with traces of white powder, so now we knew what that was all about!

Jack came in the following evening. The jeans were back on, as was his usual simple white T shirt. He was full of shy embarrassment. He regretted bringing someone he didn't know very well to his local. "I won't be seeing that f*****g mad cow again" he stated nervously, hoping the whole pub could hear his apology and that he wasn't barred.

He was aware that the story had already reached the other locals, who peered over their pints from their usual places. And, he had warned his sister not to bring her back in the future either, just so it was clear!

So, after buying a round of drinks (including one for me and Chris) and more sincere apologies which I accepted with motherly grace; he was settled back in his usual spot, tin of tobacco out and roll ups on the go, quietly glued to the football with the lads. Just like normal.

Susan Smyth

Would We Get Away with That Now?

In the 90's I ran a pub called The Duke, located in the heart of a small and infamous village in the south of Leicester. For me, the unpopular area lived up to its bad reputation during one unforgettable morning, when the burglar alarm went off. Along with my partner, I lived in accommodation above The Duke; so, when I heard noises from downstairs, I checked the alarm clock at the side of the bed; it was 3:45am, so I knew this was authentic, and not a false alarm.

I am sure you are familiar with the saying 'fight or flight.' All I can tell you is that I went into auto pilot, and instantly programmed myself into 'FIGHT' mode. It's hard to explain the horrible feeling you get when this happens if you have not experienced it. Your heart is pumping fast and hard, it feels like you have just had twenty cans of a well-known energy drink, the one that gives you wings. My partner must have sensed this, as she shouted at me: "Just call the police!" I chose to ignore her advice, however some thirty years later, I would 100% take her words on board.

It may help you understand my mood and my actions by thinking of it as your own home. You see a pub is a business but for those who live above the premises it is also an extension of their home, so any attack on the premises is an attack on 'your home' not just your business.

I kept a 'friend' halfway down the stairs leading to the bar area. I'd had this 'friend,' a small pickaxe handle, for many years, and never had to use it – until that morning. My heart was thumping out of my chest, and with my friend in tow, I ran into the bar area like a man possessed. There, I saw two burglars wearing old fashioned balaclavas; it was obvious that they were not there for a bite to eat or a quick drink. I remember thinking to myself, 'Just two of them, okay, let's have it!'

I started shouting and swinging my old friend like a baseball player would swing his bat, which thankfully scared one of them off – the skittish burglar ran like a whippet. He dived through an open window, which I assumed was

194

the way they had got in, as I hadn't heard any glass break. This left just me and his braver friend.

At this point, I thought my odds were pretty good. With my old friend, there were unofficially two of us. I noticed my opponent had a 'little' tool of some sort in his hand as well, and on this occasion, I could definitely say "mine is bigger than his!"

Everything happened quickly – with his pocketknife, he made a couple of lunges at me. He wasn't very handy with his little friend, and I was fast enough to jump backwards to avoid his efforts to harm me. Then, I managed to defend myself by catching his collarbone in a downward motion; I knew I had hurt him by the yell he let out.

He dropped the knife, either by accident or by not being able to hold it anymore, because of my shattering blow to his person. I chucked my mate to the side, and we began a boxing match. Luckily, he wasn't that good at boxing either, or maybe this could have had something to do with him holding his arm up.

After round one, I picked him up and dragged him to my cellar. I locked him in there, knowing the police were on the way as my other half had told me she had called them.

She had also made it clear how she felt about the situation, if this were to happen again, I was not allowed to come downstairs! I think she wanted me to handle it slightly differently! She went back upstairs, and I thought she really had the hump with me for dealing with it the way I had. Then, I heard her coming back down the stairs, and thinking all was forgiven, she threw a pair of boxer shorts at me and angrily said: "You'd better put something on before the police get here!".

Throughout the whole event I had not even registered that I was completely naked!

The police seemed to take ages, but if you are reading this and suspect where the ominous village is geographically, you'd know that the police did well to get there in the time they did. When the first crew arrived, they heard the perpetrator banging on my cellar door and shouting. I briefly explained the situation to the officers whilst they followed me to the cellar. One of the officers grabbed his cuffs and the other got her baton ready to arrest him.

The burglar didn't put up any struggle physically, but he sure did protest vocally: "Look at what this bastard has done to me he protested!". The brilliant police officer with the cuffs calmly replied:

"What are you on about? I just saw you fall down the cellar stairs."

I wonder would we get away with that now?

Ant Surtees

The Best Pound Ever Spent

It was a quiet midweek afternoon in the bar. It was the middle of the school term. Parents, and children were busy, either at school or at work. That all changed, however, when Andrew and Martin walked through the door. As housemates, it was unusual for them to have a Tuesday off together, so they had decided to have a few beers in their local where I was behind the bar with just my colleague Jane for company.

Drinks were bought and poured, pleasantries exchanged, and they took seats at a table by a window overlooking the street. I thought that was strange as Andrew and Martin were normally 'bar flies," who liked chatting and exchanging banter with staff and other customers.

The boys were not long into their drinks when the giggling started, which then escalated into outbursts of uncontrollable laughter.

Curiosity got the better of me, and under the guise of clearing tables, I went over and asked what was so funny. Another fit of giggles commenced with Andrew gesturing towards the window. Looking out, I saw a lady trying to pick something off the ground. She stopped, looked around sheepishly, and hurried off. Unbeknown to anyone, while Martin had popped out for a smoke, he had glued a pound coin to the pavement! Hence the entertainment began.

As the day progressed, and more customers arrived in the bar, they all became transfixed with what was going on outside. Apart from the usual background music and chatter, the room was full of giggles and laughter. Like Andrew and Martin, many of those who routinely propped up the bar were now seated elsewhere, primed like meerkats, to get a decent view. This made for an incredibly quiet and lonely shift for Jane and me, although we too kept an eye on the shenanigans going on outside.

Being a busy street there were many passers-by, some oblivious, while others spotted the coin. A few tried picking it up quickly without being seen, several used the 'swift kick' approach, trying not to look foolish, while others casually loitered while on their phone before diving in for the kill! Whatever methods they used, the results were both futile and hysterical.

Then, this bloke in blue dungarees comes along and spots the coin. He kicks it, kicks it again, and again, and again, each time with a little more force. Suddenly he is aware of the spectators, and the frustration, followed by embarrassment, is apparent with a crimson glow slowly rising on his face. There is a fast flurry of kicks and several expletives, then he storms off.

"We won't see him again!" someone remarks over a chorus of laughter.

Fifteen minutes pass and a few more passers-by have unsuccessfully tried to dislodge the coin. Our customers, having enjoyed an afternoon of merriment, were now beginning to return to their usual seats as they realised that the pound coin was well and truly stuck to the pavement.

"He's coming back!" Andrew suddenly roars. Lo and behold, there he is. The blue dungarees man striding purposefully towards the pub, hammer and chisel in hand. Oh no, is he going to attack the window? He stops outside and addresses the coin with his tools.

After many heavy-handed attempts, the coin breaks free. Standing up, the by now, perspiring, blue dungarees man, with a great flourish, puts the coin in his pocket and slowly turns to the now silent crowd at the window. He smiles and takes immense pleasure in providing us all with a two fingered salute before swaggering away victorious.

Martin stands up with great aplomb and announces proudly, "That's the best pound I've ever spent!"

Susan Smyth

Desperate Dan

I joined one of the large breweries in the late 80's as a management trainee, and part of that work involved a considerable amount of training in different pubs. The first pub I was sent to was in Enfield, to work under a real stickler, let us call him Jimmy, in case he reads this.

To say he was obsessive is an understatement. Every day I had to pull every bottle off every shelf to clean them (there were three bars), every day I had to get a toothbrush to the backs of the toilets in each cubicle (there were two sets of toilets and twelve cubicles), and every day I had to peel a large sack of potatoes and prepare the home-made chips for the day's food trade. I hasten to add that I always washed my hands between the latter two tasks.

These tasks were completed before the pub opened at 11am and Jimmy would sit on a bar stool directing the mornings activity. He loved having a trainee as it allowed him to save the cost of his usual team in the morning. It also allowed him to make even more money out of his franchise catering business as I was peeling the potatoes rather than his own staff.

Jimmy believed that by me completing all the tasks that he didn't want to, I would learn to be a great manager. Maybe he was right as it taught me not to expect people to do things that I wouldn't do myself.

Jimmy believed that every penny counted and in turn, controls of stock, consumables and equipment were of paramount importance, *even* if that affected the customer experience.

Each morning we were allocated how many pint glasses we could use, we were trained to take off any uneaten garnish from plates for re-use, any drip trays were poured into the House Bitter (let's call it TW Bitter) and customers would often comment on the changing flavour of said pint especially if a drop of lime cordial got in to it! We were also allocated twelve loo rolls a day, one for each cubicle!

One day I was stood behind the lounge bar in the middle of a busy Friday lunchtime session, when a rather flustered regular, walking strangely and looking a bit red faced, approached me and asked for a quiet word. I went over to him, and he informed me that the Gent's had run out of loo roll and asked if I could get him another one as he was mid flow.

Panic struck me, not least as we had only been open for two hours and Jimmy would likely be livid that once again, in his words, "customers had stolen the bloody bog roll." I didn't have access to the said loo roll store and so had to find Jimmy to give me the sacred key. Meanwhile Dan, our regular, stood looking slightly pained as I went to find the boss.

I popped my head into the office and Jimmy, as expected, went up like the proverbial bottle of pop when I asked him for the store cupboard key. He stormed out of the office to behind the bar and started to berate poor old Dan for using too much loo roll in front of all of the other customers. Asking, did he think that Jimmy was made of money, and could he not go at home before he came out to the pub. Dan, getting redder and more agitated, suddenly grabbed a Castlemaine XXXX bar towel off the bar (they were yellow with red writing) and walked away from Jimmy back into the Gents.

Jimmy stood waiting for Dan to reappear to continue the telling off. When Dan did come back into the pub, clutching a no longer yellow and red Castlemaine XXXX bar towel, you could hear a pin drop. Customers put down their pints of lime flavoured ale, and then lit cigarettes ready to watch the next instalment.

Oblivious to the bar towel, Jimmy continued to berate poor Dan as he came back from the Gents. From my position behind the bar, I could see from his face that Dan had decided he'd drunk his last pint in Jimmy's! I could see that as a paying and loyal customer he had finally been pushed too far.

Approaching the bar in anger, the soiled bar towel suddenly rose from Dan's side and was calmly pushed into Jimmy's unexpecting face. The astonished, onlooking customers broke into a spontaneous round of applause. Jimmy, who as I mentioned was just a little bit obsessive about standards and hygiene, did not know what to do or where to look, and shot behind the bar and up to the flat.

The other staff and I knew he had it coming, and we laughed our heads off, obviously until he reappeared in a new clean shirt, and we immediately agreed with his decision to bar poor old Dan.

For those of you who look back fondly at pubs in the old days, be thankful that today's pubs are run both professionally and by people that put customers first.

As the saying goes; some people couldn't give a Castlemaine XXXX for anybody else.

Matt Brown

FATE - How I met my Wife

If you are a fatalist like me, you will appreciate that fate leads you on a journey in both your personal and work life and that these lives are often intertwined. There are many ups and downs on your path, but if you remember your glass is always half full and stay positive, as a close friend once told me, then that journey will be fruitful.

In the early nineties, fate took me from managing the busiest pub in Northampton to open a nightclub complex in the quiet reaches of the southwest coast, the den of Michael Cannon`s Devenish Pub Company. A new adventure I could sink my teeth into, I was nervous and excited at the same time, however, I grabbed life to the fullest and jumped in with both feet, excited to get stuck in.

We were converting a harbourside venue into a glitzy two floored nightclub upstairs, whilst the downstairs area was to retain a more traditional real ale pub, somewhere regulars could come and feel at home. Beavis and Grant helped run the nightclub team, while Declan looked after the downstairs pubs in his own very Irish way. Bring on the Guinness and Caffrey's.

Monday nights were quiet, as is the case in many pubs and nightclubs, so I introduced a 999 night in the club, where the emergency service's staff could come and enjoy an evening of discounted drinks and let their hair down on an evening that would be quiet for many emergency services staff. Oh, and party they did!

One Monday evening, the lower floor was full of customers having a ball, the music was playing, and people were dancing. The upstairs bar was not in use and alarmed, this alarm would alert us to any person who may have accidentally wandered upstairs to the top floor for mischievous acts. This particular night the alarm sounded and caught my attention, and as I turned my head to search the cameras for the source of what had caused the alarm to sound, I saw a lady helping herself to the top shelf spirits.

I headed up to confront her and encountered a nurse, who was disorientated and tipsy, so I escorted her down to her colleagues to try to retrieve any money owing for the drinks, and to get her looked after. So, who should take over the negotiations but a Sister in the local Hospice in Dorchester.

They kindly covered all the wandering nurse's drinks, and I got all twenty nurses and doctors in her group to sign up to the nightclub's privilege card at £10 a go, so I was happy. I also remember thinking that the Sister had caught my eye and wondered when I would see her again.

June hit, and I spied the Sister again, this time in the downstairs pub, which was packed to the rafters with drinkers watching the World Cup. The pub was bustling, and the atmosphere was lively. I had DJ Squeaker playing in between matches to keep them all drinking and got him to do a shout out to all the nurses in the house. I still didn't know her name, but I hoped that I would eventually, and if I was lucky; get a date.

A couple of months later after an incredibly hectic summer, I was on duty on a busy Friday night. Declan had closed and alarmed downstairs as usual by 11.30pm. The club was full, and the dancefloor was packed, with the party crowd busting the choreography to 'Saturday Night,' a firm favourite in any nightclub setting. Suddenly, I had a message from security saying the police were at the front door, so I headed to see what they wanted.

On arrival, I met a police officer who said the alarm was going off in the pub, so I went with her to turn it off and investigate. I got to the door of O'Malley's as we had called it, and realised that I was unfamiliar with the keys, as Declan was the prime manager for the pub, and I spent most of my time managing the night club. I struggled with three or four and even dropped my whole bunch before I finally managed to gain access and turn off the deafening alarm.

I checked around the pub, sometimes the alarm could trip for no reason.

Outside, the police officer had been replaced by a stern looking colleague. He introduced himself as Sergeant Bradoch and proceeded to accuse me of being drunk, and he was going to report me to the licensing officer on Monday morning for being "Drunk in charge of a nightclub."

I was gobsmacked!! Clearly he had interpreted the dropping of the keys and my fumbling of them as being drink related.

Well, for someone that has never had a drink on duty throughout my whole career, I saw red. "Look, Sergeant Baldrick" I seethed. I realised my error too late but stammered on. It probably confirmed his suspicions. My only defence was to demand a breath test at once, I was not going to be accused of something I had not done and risk losing my license and my job.

He initially refused saying, "One needs to be driving a car for that," so I said, "Ok which car do you want me to drive?" That got his attention and he got on his radio and demanded a breath test be dispatched to the pub immediately, and within five minutes the meat wagon turned up and the kit was dropped off.

The original police officer took over from Sergeant Bradoch and asked me to blow in the white tube. I did and, frustratingly for her boss, the reading was zero.

I was made to blow again, again with the same result. "Clear," she said. "Do you want to keep the white tube as a souvenir?" she asked me. "No, but I want an apology from him," I replied, pointing at Baldrick. None was forthcoming, so I headed back into the club.

High, not with drugs or alcohol, but with adrenalin and outrage.

As I walked up the stairs to the office, fate led me to bump into the Sister from the 999 nights. I offloaded the whole silly story to her and, at the end I blurted out that I would like to take her on a date.

Where that came from, I will never know! My adrenalin had boosted my confidence to a high that night. I got her to write her name and phone number down and finally, I had a name for that beautiful face - Tracy.

I rang her Sunday, dated her on the Monday at the Sun Inn in Dorchester and we married just over a year later.

Twenty-five years and three beautiful children later, **fate** and obviously love, have kept us together. So, thank you, Sergeant Baldrick!

Iain Turnbull

One week of Dating

The week that nearly ended my dating life forever. I found myself single, again! It was going to be hard finding someone else after walking out of a two-year relationship to take on my first pub as a General Manager. Not working the normal nine to five could be quite off putting for some people. That followed walking out of an almost ten-year relationship to take on my first Deputy Manager position.

So anyway, this is the basis of this story. I found myself in a brand-new big city, and the only people I sort of knew, and that were close by, were my team. I'm alone, with only a few (busy) distant friends to talk to on the phone, and a nomadic lifestyle. It was a profoundly lonely time. Ironic how I was surrounded by people day in day out, but I had no one.

So devoid of inspiration and the confidence to go out alone I tried online dating. It was hit and miss, mostly miss as online dating usually goes. I went on a few dates; I would arrange to meet them in a local cat café as I had to rehome 'my girls' when I moved, so any excuse to see animals was a bonus.

At this point I was putting in a few extra shifts, and I was extremely busy. Why not invite prospective dates in for a quick pint?! If we got along, I could then catch last orders with them elsewhere. Perfect. Especially as the pub has CCTV. If I was murdered, then at least there was evidence of who had done it. You could never be too careful these days….

After this genius brainwave I arranged a new date. The guy seemed lovely, really my type. After talking for a couple of weeks it was time to meet. He claimed he was five foot six, chocolate brown hair, dreamy blue eyes, and a builder by trade. 9.30pm rolled around and in walked, well let's call him 'Idiot one.'

He had clearly exaggerated his height as he could not see over the bar. But that was fine. Some men are touchy about their height; I'm small anyway so it's not an issue and I wasn't going to judge the guy on his height. He ordered a pint of lager. Five minutes later he orders a second. Again, it's fine, maybe he's nervous. Builder culture, they like a pint or two with their workmates.

So, in between me bumbling about putting glasses through the washer and generally preparing to close the bar for the evening, we do manage to have a few exchanges. We kept the conversations light; they had to be as I bustled about. I wanted to get finished as quickly as possible plus I wasn't really feeling the date vibe. I had soon come to realise that 'Idiot one' was not my type. There was just something odd about him.

That's when it happened. My friend Adrian, who was a regular at the bar came rushing in from the smoking area, muttering to himself. It wasn't unusual, he does it a lot. He nips to the loo. On his return 'Idiot one' grabs his arm and says, "What did you just say to me?"

Adrian replies with "Erm nothing mate, I was out front for a smoke and realised I needed a wee and came into the toilet." This discussion goes back and forth for a minute or so, until we realise that Adrian had remarked "schoolboy error" as he wandered through, referring to himself for not realising he needed a wee. 'Idiot one' on hearing this had felt his little man syndrome kick in and thought he had been called a schoolboy.

Adrian went back out to enjoy his smoke and 'Idiot one' came back to the bar. I had now reconsidered going anywhere with him and was thinking about how to let him down. Adrian and his friends came back to their seats. This inspired 'Idiot one' to begin asking me at the top of his voice "Why did you tell them you didn't like me before you told me?" I had been nowhere near their table, so I asked when he had seen me talking to them. He replied that he hadn't!

It was at this point that I asked him to leave. He then coined a classic phrase which for many months became everyone's parting words as they left the venue "You're all pussies!!!" Yes, a grown man almost in his forties was escorted out of a pub by his collar by me whilst screaming "You're all pussies." It took a while to live that one down. Especially because he rang me ten minutes after he left to inform me that he had never hated anyone he had dated, until now.

Although, even this was slightly overshadowed by 'Idiot two.' In the same week, I agreed to another date. Surely it couldn't be terrible twice? I was so wrong, I invited him on the Sunday as I was planning a few games of pool with my team. One extra would even the teams out. He could get to know me and have a great time.

He arrived, six foot two, I was winning. (Did I say I didn't care about height?). He then proceeded to get absolutely slaughtered and inform me he was going to drive home. Sorry, no you are not. I was temporarily staying in a local hotel and luckily it was a twin. Considering he had driven from a nearby town and had nowhere else to go I offered him the bed. He accepted, and I laid down the strict rules. Number one; don't even think about coming near me.

He abided by the rules and fell asleep almost instantly. What followed can only be described as the sound of the world ending. This man was the loudest snorer I had ever encountered in my life.

Considering Monday was delivery day and I needed to be at work for 7am I tried to wake him up and get him to turn over or something. That's when it happened, he told me he loved me. That's it for me. "Its 5am you're sober enough to go find your car and drive as far from me as possible. Get out!" I wasn't going to spend another moment with 'Idiot two.'

I sent him away and fully planned on never seeing him again. I left the hotel to do the early delivery. Then I got a text about 9am informing me he had left his wallet somewhere in my room. Great! I went back and found his wallet shoved right down the back of the bed in a position that could only have happened with human intervention. Informing him I had his wallet, and he could collect it the following day from the bar, I then sent a text to my chef, to make sure he wasn't going to be late the next day. I wasn't going to be the one to give his wallet back to him. I never wanted to see Mr 'I love you' ever again.

Yes, I got my chef to hand the wallet back whilst I hid in the back room. And no, I'm not ashamed. It was necessary! Later that day I got sent a picture of lots of ingredients and the offer of making me dinner. I graciously declined and that was the last I heard from him!

So, folks, that's the week in the life of a mid-thirties General Manager. Tragic is one word that comes to mind.

Luckily, I've now met someone lovely and have my happy ever after. The moral of the story when online dating, make sure you meet them in a safe location with plenty of CCTV, and oh yes, idiots come in all sizes!

N.M

The Wheelchair and the Winky

I feel like this story should start with a disclaimer. This is in no way derogatory towards any disability. Full stop. I am fully aware how this story comes across; however, I must stress you really do have to make it to the end of the story before passing judgement – but it's worth it!

I should also point out that this is my life. My actual life. It happened to me, and I lived it. Not quite live, laugh, love. More like cry, scrub your skin with Dettol, and assume the foetal position.

So, let me set the scene. It's a gaspingly hot day heading into the back end of summer. 'How did I know' you ask? - well every customer had told me. If it wasn't for them then I would never have known!

My venue is in a market town. It's a lovely big venue. The main room is set out for sports viewing in the middle, and it has booths and tables elsewhere around the room. Now here's the thing, we have a ground floor disabled toilet but it's up three steps! Yes, you read that correctly, the disabled toilet is accessible via steps. These steps lead to our top section which has larger family sized tables for dining, and a huge double door leading onto our outside area.

I have failed to mention a key element to this tale, in that we do have a disabled lift. It gives access to the top section, however since our refurb something had gone terribly wrong with it, and we were waiting for a new part. Most patrons were happy to leave via the front entrance and make their way down the side passage to use the rear entrance and access the facilities. Was it ideal? Hell no. Was it the best choice? Yes. Or so I thought.

A little about me… at the time I was a Deputy Manager and handled most of the evening shifts barring Saturday, which was our biggest session and run by both myself and my General Manager. For this story, his name will be Alan. Purely because he reminds me of Alan Partridge and this small revenge will help to heal the hurt, that two years on I still feel from this incident.

Alan would take care of the morning sessions. If for some reason I had to cover his shift, he would take the time to warn me about certain characters that I may not have come across in the evening. For example, 'Carlsberg Man' who isn't allowed more than 3 pints (not after the epic 4 pint fuelled smash and grab he went on!).

Here we are then at the proper beginning of the tale; Wednesday morning. I was covering for Alan who was at a meeting. He had left me a lovely note in the office which told me to have a nice day and make sure one of our regulars got his ten-pound note back that had been stuck in the till.

That was it. No warnings, no mentions, no characters explained. You can see how underprepared I was for what happened and how it's all Alan's fault.

The morning was typically slow, the usual monotony of the latte and John Smith's crowd. I had my favourite team member on shift with me, a former waiter who could carry at least a dozen plates and still pour a pint with his free hand. We were a close team, and I knew with him on shift I didn't have to worry. It got to around 12.30 and we had a slow trickle of sandwich hunters in.

It was then that 'he' arrived.

I'll call him Richard. Once you have finished this tale you can conclude why. Richard was wheeled into the venue by his carer, who promptly popped his bags on the table and left.

He sat for a few minutes just gazing out of the window and I kept my eye on him should he need table service, which as time would tell he did, when a few moments later he beckoned me over.

I walked to his table, greeted him, and asked how I could help. He said he wanted to use the bathroom. Now, I must have the horrible conversation explaining the lift is broken, but I would help him around the side and through the back to the toilet. He immediately said no and wanted to be bumped up the stairs. I protested as much as I could and tried to persuade him otherwise, but he was very insistent.

So, I did indeed wheel him to the stairs and bump him up what felt like Mount Everest. He wasn't a small man. At least 6-foot-tall and 14 stone. I am not that lofty or weighty a lady, so it was a struggle. But we made it with as much dignity as we could muster. Slightly out of breath, I wheeled him into the bathroom and shut the door.

The whole exchange had taken roughly 15 minutes but, in that time, things had backed up slightly. We had a few customers awaiting coffees, and the team member was cleaning up after a couple of departures. So, I got on with making those coffees.

Our glass wash room shares a wall with the disabled toilet and it was through that wall that I could hear a faint 'help me, help me'. I went into what could only be described as 'Casualty' mode. I legged it out of the room, leapt over the bar and practically flew up the stairs before forcing my way in.

I gazed upon utter carnage. Richard was lying on the floor with his trousers and pants round his ankles, his limp penis winking at me. I felt awful for him! What do you do? Pick him up first, put it away first? There is no training for this. I put my panicking aside and tried to think of how I could handle this matter in a way which would be most dignifying for the customer; I chose to put it away first.

After some reassuring words, I finally managed to secure the beast and was trying to help him into his wheelchair when he began to become uncooperative. I wasn't sure if it was something I was doing but I was clearly out of my depth physically. I couldn't hold him but didn't want to drop him onto the floor again. So, I called my friend who had popped in for a quick drink "mate, I need you to come to the disabled toilet now". The response I got was "no way, I'm not unblocking the shitter for you."

After I conveyed the situation, he too sprang into action. The scene when he arrived however was even more horrific. During the struggle, poor Richard's trousers had again fallen down. The weird position I was in, trying to hold him up, meant that now his arms were wrapped around my neck, and I was semi squatting, with his winky resting on my leg.

Did I mention it was hot? I was wearing shorts!

My friend got over his shock and helped me put a now fully dressed Richard back into his wheelchair. We were now all three of us slightly dishevelled, me especially with a stain on my soul, and we were now positioned at the top of the stairs.

I was just about to insist on taking Richard round to the front entrance via the side passage, when he casually wheeled himself backwards down the stairs. It all happened in slow motion. Both myself and my friend ran forward to save him at the exact same time my team member was passing the bottom of the stairs; he had a second to react and managed to catch Richard in mid-air and place him safely on the floor. To do so, he had to drop at least twenty plates that were stacked in his hands. He dropped all of them. About a third of our entire plate stock; wiped out.

But it was okay. The main thing was that Richard was safe and well and currently wheeling himself back to his table. I bent down to console my barman, who now was almost in tears at the mess he would have to clean up. I reminded him that he had done an amazing thing and had cat-like reflexes and should be proud. As I was getting up and going to fetch the broom, I saw Richard at the bar. I said, "let me serve, and I will be back to clean it up together".

Going behind the bar I made my way to Richard and asked if I could help. "A bottle of Merlot" was requested. We keep our full bottles in the spirit cupboard under lock and key, so I went to fetch a bottle of our finest and grabbed a glass.

After sending the payment through to the card machine, I then said I would take them over to his table for him. "No, no it's fine I'll do it". And with that he got out of his chair picked up the bottle and the glass and walked to his table, came back sat in his chair and wheeled himself away.

I looked over at my barman and he had obviously seen the whole thing because his face looked how I imagined mine did. Mouth open, brow lined and confused. We couldn't believe what had just happened. But it did happen. My friend who had helped me put the penis away had seen it too. I don't think he stopped laughing for at least three weeks. Especially when he did some digging and found out Richard had been barred from several venues in the town for similar willy activities!

So, thank you Alan. Thank you for not telling me in your handover note that the regular who comes in every Wednesday morning in a wheelchair can actually walk and likes to be naked!

My friend hasn't looked at me the same since. To be honest I can't look at myself in the mirror either, some days.

N.M

Not Quite CSI

It was 2011, on a typical rainy February day. I was halfway through my very first 'holiday hold' for another manager who was off sunning himself on a beach somewhere. It was a different city; new people and I would be lying if I said I wasn't nervous. So, the last thing I needed, or indeed expected, was a dead body found in the gutter outside.

I was prepared for reluctant staff members, the occasional fight between customers and even the need to give first aid, but I was only expecting a bloody nose or sprained ankle! No one had ever discussed the protocol for a corpse found within proximity to my venue.

There was a slight thrill that buzzed through the staff, including myself. For an instant, I was transported from dull grey England into my favourite crime fighting TV shows.

Brief images of CSI type labs and forensic teams dusting for prints and even myself in an interrogation room, not guilty but giving that vital piece of evidence, that one clue that would lead to a mob boss or long-time serial killer being caught. This was better than Line of Duty.

So, imagine the exhilaration when a police officer, complete with a badge, came into the pub and said he had a few questions for me. I was in a whirl of combined worry and enthusiasm to do whatever I could to help; this was my chance to be involved in the most exciting thing to happen to this pub, well; ever!

We went through to the office and the police officer started the questioning. They were attempting to get an ID on the dead man. I was shown a picture on a card, I tried and tried, I racked my brain; could it be the man who drank a Carlsberg at 10 o'clock every morning?

What about the guy who forgot to pay for his fish and chips last week? My brain was whirring but, unfortunately, I had to tell the officer that I could not help him, and that I could not recognise the man in the photo. He didn't seem disappointed but turned to me with a small grin and said, "Well ma'am I expect not, you see that's my warrant card."

All CSI fantasies fled at that moment, of course he was just showing me his ID, it also turned out that the murder or mob boss killing was in fact just a man who had fallen and hit his head in such a way that he had sadly died. Any dreams I might have had of a best-selling book or movie rights from my story were promptly dispelled.

This wasn't the last time I dealt with the police in my career, but it was the most memorable, and not quite the CSI I had hoped for!

When WWE Came to Town

Sport has been popular in pubs since the dawn of time, and no more elsewhere than in Glasgow. In more recent years the upgrade to satellite technology and increasing screen size has made the sporting experience in pubs a much better prospect, than everyone crowding around an old 22 inch. Satellite has also widened the variety of sports available to watch, and the high-quality audio-visual equipment, coupled with a packed venue provides an atmosphere you just can't get at home, even with a big TV from Amazon. Football always was, and I guess always will be, the main sport that people show in pubs and bars, but for the true sports bar, you had to be all over the full sport viewing spectrum and our bar was no exception.

For several years, we had been showing wrestling (WWE) live in our massive 'Walkabout' venue. We were among the very first to trial this as an option for live sport, and it had grown to become a major event for us across the four main pay per views that the WWE show each year. The Royal Rumble, Wrestle Mania, Summer Slam and the Survivor Series.

What had started out as a normal Royal Rumble event in January 2020 soon changed, after a video from the venue went viral.

Drew McIntyre, a Scottish wrestler, won the Royal Rumble match by hurling Roman Reigns over the top rope to win. The pub had erupted in hysteria. As it turned out one of the customers had recorded the moment on his phone and the video was an internet sensation. It was covered on social media accounts of the likes of BT Sport and ESPN, and it soon spread around that the venue it had taken place in was *my pub*.

A few weeks later, we received a phone call from the WWE on a midweek evening saying they had seen the video and they wanted to interview someone the next day live on the WWE Network! Realising I was about to have the chance to be on the WWE Network, I sheepishly volunteered. It was then arranged that I would be on WWE the Bump, live, the next day via a video call!

After an early dial in to make sure it was all good to go, I was passed through live to the studio where Royal Rumble winner Drew was a guest. It was so surreal seeing myself on the screen. They even gave me my own name bar, which I must admit was very cool. They chatted to us, and we managed plug our Wrestling promoters along with all the other venues in our company before talking about our Wrestlemania plans.

So, in the space of a few weeks we had gone from a very busy, Wrestling pay per view screening, to me being live on the WWE Network, which at the time had around four million subscribers! What a plug for the bar and the Walkabout chain!

Absolutely mind blowing. So, you're looking to watch loads of different sports in a true sports bar? I guess the bar has been reset in Glasgow!

Ever So Slightly Out of Focus

This is the story of how a pub visit both delivered and then deleted the learning of a musical instrument. While I should probably be sheepish about it, for reasons best known to whatever demon was in the drink, all my feelings about the occasion are fuzzy and warm. Mind you, there is a good chance that this itself has been rather idealised by the presence of excessive amounts of alcohol…

In the very early 2000's, for some mad reason Prog Rock legends Focus (see Hocus Pocus, Sylvia) would kick off their UK tours at The Hawkley Inn, a little pub nestled in the Hampshire countryside.

Tours consisting of vast venues and many thousands of attendees would begin under the thoughtful gaze of the front bar's wall-mounted moose head where the band would play long into the night, to small but thrilled audiences of young Heavy Metal nerds (wild beards, indecipherable band shirts, rolling tobacco) and middle-aged Prog fans (denim, Aramis, divorce). We were spoilt rotten by this special treatment and we jealously guarded any news of these events as strictly secret.

One such date fell on the weekend of my friend's 25th birthday celebration. A fun-loving creature, he had decided it was to be a dressing up party with the brief of 'Characters from 1980's Kids Television.' As he not only frequented, but also worked at the pub, the party was to follow the end of one of his daytime shifts. Details were sent around, and our friendship group was elated with silly suggestions, excitement and high anticipation.

The afternoon of his birthday fun arrived, and finishing his work at the bar, a collection of close friends followed him upstairs to one of the pub's bedrooms. Burly young men, we crammed into the modest bathroom and (consensually) spray-painted the lad a deep 'Wotsit' orange in the sort of tone usually only available to daytime television stars or plastic cheese slices. It proved a very messy job indeed. With his long hair sprayed upright like a flame, a dab of make-up and donning an eye-wateringly tight leotard he had nailed the look of

Liono (Thundercats). It remains one of the finest party efforts I have ever seen, albeit one of the most distressing and confusing for the domestic cleaning team.

It must have been a surreal sight as we made our way back down to the bar, for, as well as the neon birthday boy, at least two of us had come as Grotbags: a heavily be-wigged, bright green witch draped in bin bags. It was like walking around in a personal oven and only a matter of minutes before the green paint was stinging my eyes, and the dense headgear had to be binned. My body politely insisted that I took in at least as much liquid as was escaping from of my armpits, and so it was that the evening launched at some considerable pace.

We were Real Ale enthusiasts at that stage, and The Hawkley Inn kept at least ten strong lines on at any one time. These were mostly faintly, mossy-tasting pints with names like Nanny's Belchwater or Old Dick's Stagnant Rinse. These were hastily funnelled-in and were quickly reborn in the steamy vapour under my bin bag-cladding without an enormous amount of improvement.

Focus had launched into their second set of the night and vocalist/keyboard player, Thijs van Leer, was teasing and cajoling the crowd like an old friend. Booze just tipped into us and the room, from the bouncing fans to the ruddy-jowled barflies, felt united in that strange and unique way that live music seems singularly to conjure.

I am unsure quite when the music stopped but the band were then plied with alcohol and swamped by admirers, of which I was one of the most fervent (see tedious). Van Leer and the band were beyond generous and chatted and drank with us all, fielding questions and slugging-down beer. At one point he grabbed a pint glass and, placing his mouth over a section of the open rim whilst covering the top with his hand, produced a series of clear blown notes which he altered by changes in positions of the hand and lips. It was spellbinding! How many pint glasses had passed my lips in a rather wasted youth and never once had they been weaponised for music!

I was extremely drunk, but the simple brilliance of it cut through and I watched in a stunned way as the larger-than-life pensioner before me fairly jigged-out a ditty, his eyes gleaming with the fun of it. Overheated from performing, he resembled a cheeky Santa from an old Christmas card - all twinkle and perhaps a few too many brandies.

I insisted he teach me the method and the next few minutes were spent mastering the basics of the pint glass. Eventually he extracted himself back to the party whilst I continued to sway and poot softly into my pint glass in the middle of the pub. At this stage, the pub had boiled down to only the most committed partygoers and was almost certainly a lock-in (then again, I was just a hairy witch in a bin bag, standing in a swirling room and maybe not on top of all the facts) And that is about where I log off, only to log back in again at 5am.

Early morning light is a cunning predator to the bruised brain of a reveller. It crept through the windowpanes, slunk across the floorboards, and then viciously jumped up and down on my eyeballs shrieking hysterically into my ears until I caved in and sat up. I mean eventually I managed to sit up, albeit at the second time of asking, because the first attempt had met, at speed, with the underside of the table and returned me to a prone position.

The pub looked like a film set - the fallout from something violent and involving quite a lot of choreographed punching. Bodies were dotted about, groaning weakly or softly snoring. Beyond the fog of hangover all I could sense was the loss of something: a wallet, keys, perhaps my phone?

Hunched under the table in my bin bags and under the gaze of the moose, memory leaked back into my pulsating skull and it felt shadowy and hollow. I had been given the gift of music only to have it stripped away by a reservoir of 3.8% ullage.

I had proved unworthy of such permanent wisdom, and the hammering just behind my temples was what happens when a mortal flies that bit too close to the sun, crashes and burns never to fly again. A single hot tear of alcoholic grief sidled down my face, across the black plastic of my bin bags and threw itself at my feet. It was green.

Mark Willson-Pepper

A Legend in the Sacks

Doug worked at the Sacks for twenty-five years and was known universally as the grumpy bugger who would swear and curse everyone. It's a trope that is often associated with the pub landlord, particularly on television soaps, as they banish a troublemaker from the local, or in gangster films as they stand stoically, brow ever-furrowed, and arms folded in uninviting grouchiness. But under the surface, Doug didn't fit this narrative; he was the nicest sweetest man you could ever meet, and everyone knew his grumpy nature was just a front.

The Sacks was his life; he worked there seemingly without pause, and like many in the pub trade, when he wasn't on shift he spent most of his free time there.

In 2016 he started to feel unwell; but as was his character he simply carried on as he always did. At the start of 2017, he did go to the doctors and they started to test him for one thing and another, but still he pushed on unperturbed.

This year, Doug myself and another member of the team, Sheila, were celebrating twenty-five years of service and we decided to have a party to celebrate. This was the end of May and was a brilliant night, the place was packed, and despite the hard man routine, Doug was up dancing and having a wonderful time. It was the perfect example of the man; despite his reputation, he was the life and soul at a party that recognised his dedication to the trade, and endless work in the role.

A couple of weeks later he went to the hospital for the results of the tests he had had and was told the devastating news that he had cancer; even worse than that it was inoperable, and he had six months to live. It was an awful time for him, the team and the customers.

Unfortunately, he didn't last six months and sadly, he died on 18th July. There was a great outpouring of grief with many stories shared on the pub's social media page, and his funeral had a superb turnout, which proved he wasn't the grumpy bugger he pretended to be.

He was a true legend at the Sacks and even now people come in who haven't been in for a while and still ask about him. Although a deeply sad time for his friends and family, and all of us here at the pub, we take great comfort in the knowledge that his life's work, had such a deep and far-reaching effect on the lives of so many.

We often don't realise it in the hospitality sector, but we should be proud that the work we carry out has much more of an impact than simply delivering a service. And for the customers, it is important not to take that for granted, as I believe Doug's passing taught us all.

Vicki Phillips

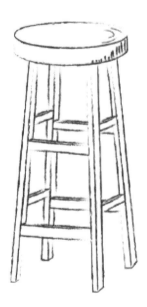

Looking After Our Own

This story starts out on an average Tuesday afternoon. Luciana was working behind the bar of a quaint local pub; the shift was running smoothly, and the bar was filled with the chatter of all the usual regulars, discussing anything and everything whilst enjoying each other's company. Luciana could not help but notice there was something, or rather someone, missing. Nick, one of the pub's regulars, was not sat with his usual group of drinking buddies. Luciana was about to ask them where he was when the pub door swung open, and in walked Nick with his head hung low and a slight heaviness to his step.

As she did with all her regulars, Luciana poured Nick's pint of choice, set it on the front of the bar counter, and waited for him to come and collect it before immersing himself in the company of his friends, for the rest of the afternoon.

Unexpectedly, Nick collected and paid for his pint, before turning and walking straight past his mates and sat down in the furthest corner of his local, without uttering a single word to anyone. This was quite remarkable for everyone to witness, as Nick would usually engage in friendly conversation with the staff, and would always make a few harmlessly flirtatious remarks towards Luciana. She knew something must be wrong.

That first pint barely touched the sides. Normally, Nick would come back up to the bar to order another, but this time Nick sat slumped in his chair and stared into space. Luciana noticed this and poured him another pint. She quickly checked to make sure Alicia would be okay serving the guests on her own for a bit, walked over to where Nick was sitting, set the pint down in front of him and sat down at the table.

"What's up Nick?" Luciana asked with a concerned look on her face. It was at this point that Nick couldn't keep the river of emotions back any longer, and tears began streaming down his face.

Struggling to keep it together, he explained that he had just been given the news that his six-year-old grandson had been diagnosed with Adrendeukodystrophy, commonly known as ALD. He went on to explain that ALD is a rare genetic condition that affects the brain. This rare condition could cause rapid deterioration, including vision impairment and the inability to communicate.

To help his family, Nick had set up a fundraising page in honour of his grandson, to raise the funds needed to take him abroad for the treatment that could potentially treat the condition. Luciana sat and listened attentively, comforted him, asked if there was anything she could do, and asked for him to let her know if there was any help his family needed.

Nick finished the final dregs of his drink and walked out of the pub, just about managing to keep his composure.

As soon as he had left, Luciana grabbed her phone and put an announcement out to her team that they were to have a team meeting that very evening. There was no time to lose. Luciana had a plan.

The meeting was an energetic success. The team, along with a few regulars, sat and brainstormed ideas until they had produced a plan, to hold a fundraising event for Nick's grandson. The event would be held at the pub. Everyone threw their heart and soul into the ideas, and before they all left, they had decided on everything from the advertising, to when it would be held, everything down to the last fine detail.

Before long, posters started appearing all over town to let local people know about the big fundraising event, and the worthy cause. The team and regulars put their collective effort into ensuring this event was the enormous success it needed to be, and to ensure that it was literally the talk of the town! Local businesses were offering raffle prizes and products to sell left, right and centre; and those that couldn't offer products or services simply made monetary donations instead. This really was a community coming together, and fast!

The big night finally came, and the local pub was bursting at the seams with supportive locals from every part of area. There was music booming through the speakers, playing requested favourite tunes, there were bar staff up on top of the bar, dancing like nobody was watching, and others were weaving through the crowds, shaking donation buckets, and encouraging donations at every opportunity. There were activities happening in the four corners of the pub. From one corner, you could hear a constant buzz where the local barber was shaving people's heads for donations, and in another the girls from the local beauty salon were waxing people's body hair.

Raffles tickets were selling thick and fast, with the generously donated prizes boldly displayed on the back bar, all from the local businesses.

At the end of this insane night Luciana found Nick and his family. She told him that during the night they had raised almost £1500! Nick's face beamed. He thanked and hugged her, smiling with grateful tears running down his face.

"Luciana, you have brought this whole community together in such a short time, in support of our little lad. I don't know how you did it, but we thank you from the bottom of our hearts."

The Great Art Robbery

I think it would be fair to say that many of us, at some point in our lives, will have decided that it would be a clever idea to take a memento from a pub. A reminder of a great night out, a drunken badge of honour, a trophy. I for one have been guilty of this minor misdemeanour, that is until I became a Pub Manager.

I was running a pub in the heart of the financial area of London; mostly suits, bankers, brokers and the like frequented it. Having such a premium clientele you would not expect so many items to disappear from the premises. Cutlery, condiments, or branded glassware were the norm, but this pub was in a league of its own. If it wasn't screwed down it went out the door. Candle holders, lamp shades, plants, ornaments, nothing was sacred. On one occasion a very happy customer attempted to get a three-foot, forty-kilo, stone statue, past the door security!

On an evening off I went for a drink with a friend near London Bridge, far enough from my pub to switch off and forget about it for a few hours. The evening progressed, and we were heading to another bar when we noticed two young girls in fits of giggles. They were walking towards us carrying a rather large floral canvas painting. As they got closer the painting seemed strangely familiar, but I wasn't quite sure why? Then it suddenly dawned on me.

Turning to my friend I said, "I'm sure that picture is from my pub!"
I was almost certain, but that one percent of doubt stopped me from approaching them. We needed a plan before I went rushing in to rescue my artwork. My friend stopped the girls and struck up a conversation, keeping them distracted whilst I frantically phoned the pub. Speaking to my deputy I asked if any of our pictures were missing from the wall.

"OMG! Sorry Jen, the picture of the flowers has gone from the wall!" she shrieked. "I've no idea how this happened or how we didn't notice!"

I hastily hung up the phone and approached the girls.

Politely, I introduced myself to them both and informed them of where I worked. Their faces were a picture as their smiles turned to pure shock and embarrassment, and then the apologies followed. It was hilarious, but I did my upmost to remain straight faced and extremely serious. The painting was handed over and the two girls went on their way. As soon as they were out of sight, we both fell about laughing.

The following day, I smugly put the canvas back in its rightful place but with the addition of a highly adhesive nail glue, so it never went walkies again. I said to myself,

"What a result, what a victory! ……………What else is missing?"

The Heart of the Community

The best part of running a local pub is the feeling of camaraderie and togetherness, and there is no better emotion than when you pull together for a common cause. Whether it is to support vulnerable people, celebrate success or to raise money for a wider charitable cause. The people and the community are always there as an unbreakable pillar.

My Area Manager had experienced the fantastic, beyond care support, that was provided by Parkinson's UK. As a result, he decided to launch a fund-raising initiative across his area with an initial target of £500 per pub. When I met up with my fellow Managers we landed on a lot of different and fun idea's, including a pub quiz, guess the number of jellybeans in a jar, raffles, and football cards.

Our quiz night proved to be a tremendous success with record numbers and an additional edge, as our quizzers recognised that this was an extra special night as all monies raised would benefit Parkinson's UK. We introduced additional rounds whereby every team had to buy a raffle ticket, with the opportunity to win half the money raised. The other half was earmarked for Parkinson's UK.

The first team to win the first additional round donated their prize to our charity, and this started a trend for the night with every winning team donating their cash to Parkinson's UK. This even included our overall winning team who won the weekly rollover of £249. What a gesture and what a night! Everyone left feeling that they had contributed to a special event.

Our jellybean guessing competition also hit a chord with our customers, and we uncovered a level of competitiveness that I had not seen before! They would spend hours trying to physically count the jellybeans and pay for multiple guesses to be in with a chance of winning! Well done to Eileen who guessed within one number! The generosity theme that had started with our quiz, continued, as Eileen also contributed her winnings to Parkinson's UK.

The football cards and raffles were some of our most popular events. Football Cards is a game akin to guessing the bonus ball on the lottery, where each player gets to pick a football team, that they think is the winning team in exchange for a donation. Once the card is full, a scratch panel is removed to reveal the winning team and the person who guessed correctly wins 50% of the total cost of the card. We hosted a raffle alongside this, and it is very surprising how excited someone can get over winning a pair of tights! Nevertheless, I am sure he enjoyed them!

While our pub is not in the most affluent of areas, I was hugely proud of the way my team and our customers joined together for a common cause.

Parkinson's UK really resonated within the community, and everyone got involved. Every cash prize that was won over the course of our first fundraising weekend was donated to our chosen charity and, as a result, we smashed our £500 target and decided to continue with our fundraising. Over the next three months, we raised a stunning total of £10,000 and became recognised locally as the "Heart of our Community."

My Area Manager used our pub as an example of best practice, and I was invited to present our fundraising initiatives at his Area Meeting. Unbeknown to me, he also entered our pub into the annual Publican Awards and, one of my greatest achievements, was winning the national Best Community Pub award.

Many years later we are still raising funds for Parkinson's UK, uniting us in a heartfelt cause and further strengthening our bond and spirit with the local community.

Waltz Dyzney

It is London 2012. The capital is at fever pitch as the Games of the 30th Olympiad return to the UK. The Olympics have just kicked off with a spectacular opening ceremony highlighting the 'Best of British' sport, art, performance, and creativity.

I was running a gorgeous little pub just off Leicester Square, in the heart of London's West End, and the Games were not just welcoming athletes from all around the world, but also welcoming an abundance of tourists to the area. So, it came as no great surprise, to welcome a charming American family into the pub on a sunny midweek afternoon.

They opted for our ever-popular Fish and Chips, a large succulent slab of excellent quality white fish encased in a crunchy golden beer batter, served with a generous portion of crispy chips, fresh peas, rich tartare sauce and topped with a lemon wedge for that extra acidic zest where required. They each chose to wash down their meals with a pint of our freshly tapped local pale ale which, with its American style floral and herbal notes, paired perfectly with the traditional pub fare that they had chosen.

Once I noticed they had finished, full stomachs, and plates were so clean that the sun bounced off the surface of them as though they had, by way of thanks, taken the liberty to clean them for us. Being intriged by their thick southern accents I made my way to clear their table, and we immediately struck up a conversation.

The exchange started as expected, how the Fish and Chips did not disappoint, discussing their trip and how they had 'brought the sunshine with them', which was a great coincidence as London had been bogged by gloomy days of cloud laden skies, followed by torrents of rain before the opening ceremony.

However, when the conversation found its way onto the sightseeing antics of the day, I have to say that I was taken a little by surprise.

"Yep, we've already seen some of the London sights and have been taking in a lot of the city's history"- the father glides his hand from the top to the bottom of his pint glass - "My, we even learnt that Walt Disney`s father lived just a few doors up from you, here on Leicester Street"- his eyes widened in amazement - "To think that young Walt grew up just here! And we always assumed that he had American roots!"

"Well, that is surprising," I thought, with a twinge of guilt for not knowing such a great little fact. Over the years you find yourself becoming a part time tour-guide from across the bar, handing over local recommendations and knowledge just as much as you hand over pints, so this was a conversation starter I was baffled to have missed.

"Gosh how did you come across that amazing piece of information?" I asked.

"Oh well, we just happened to be passing and one of the kids spotted the plaque on the wall. You must go and check it out!" he responded, with a look of bewilderment at the fact that this knowledge had evaded me.

Having bade our farewells, and with trade easing in the late afternoon, and as the sun slowly began to dip behind the skyscrapers looming over the city, I decided that I must check out this elusive plaque myself. This is what I found...

"Father of the Waltz Dynasty, not Father of Walt Disney!"

Well, me and the team had a chuckle or two over that, and a new tourist conversation starter was born!

Christopher P. Sturgess

HELL NO, H20!

I used to run a bar, and every month we ran a 'Big Night Out'; a themed party which we always put a lot of effort into. We had a live DJ, we decorated the pub according to the theme, and even the staff got dressed up! We really went all out, think booze-tube backpacks, shot girls wearing ammo straps full of booze, they were some of the best days. We did beach parties, school discos, Halloween and one very memorable St George's Day, but that's a different story for another time! We had so many great party nights but the one that always springs to mind was a 'Coyote Ugly' night, based on the film of the same name.

Customers were not allowed on top of the bar for obvious Health and Safety reasons, and throughout the night, many were also encouraged to get off the top of those tables and chairs that hadn't already been removed to allow for a larger dancefloor. However, as a special privilege, the team used to get up on the bar and dance along to the DJ. The costume theme for this night was 'Western,' with cowboy boots, vest tops and those checked shirts with the popper buttons.

If you have seen the film, you will know there is a ritual, that if someone asks for water then the staff will shower the crowd with water from their post mix (carbonated drink) gun, whilst shouting "Hell no, H20!"

Now, luckily enough, we also happened to have a post mix gun long enough to lift up and over the bar, and on this particular evening I decided I was going to go the whole hog and follow in the footsteps of the film. When someone eventually asked for a drink of water, I started up the chant of "Hell No, H20!" And within seconds the whole bar had joined in. I then got on the bar and proceeded to spray the crowd from left to right.

Whilst I was doing this and riding on a wave of whoops and cheers, I spotted what I initially thought was someone in costume. That costume being one of a Police officer. I didn't remember a Police officer being a character in the film, at least not an English one. It wasn't until he got closer to the bar that I realised it wasn't a costume at all, and I'd just been spraying cold water all over one of our very real boys in blue!

I climbed down, hoping this wouldn't be the start of a soured or rather dampened relationship with our local Police. He was just on his last patrol of the night and thankfully he was very good natured about it, and he could see that everyone was enjoying themselves in a reasonable, (albeit soaking wet at this point) manner.

I gave him a hot drink and he went on his way home. From that day on, I have always kept a much sharper eye on who's in the crowd; I'm not sure a second dousing would go down the same!

The Spitfire

Hi Mum,

I hope your trip is going well? I tried to call you before we left, but you must have been out of range at that time. I got your last email just now. The cruise sounds amazing! I'm so sorry I haven't had a chance to write sooner, but there was no Wi-Fi at the campsite, and Nick being Nick, he forgot to pack the chargers for our ones. So annoying!

It was tough these last three days without our phones, but we really enjoyed our time together. We finally got around to playing Pictionary, and the kids loved it! Mason and Emmy thought it hilarious that I couldn't draw at all. I took some photos of all of us on the beach with my camera, while our phones were dead (I'm so glad I remembered to pack it!), so you'll have to wait until we get to our B&B this weekend to see them when we finally have access to the internet.

Anyways, I hope Dad's feeling better? You gave us a scare when you said it might be that bloody virus. I'm glad it was just a cold. I think every time we sneeze from now on, we're all going to worry! Thankfully, it all seems to be dying down, and hopefully we can still fly over to join you and spend Christmas together in Germany like we planned. I'm really looking forward to the Christmas Market.

The main reason I'm writing today, though, is because I wanted to tell you about this little pub we visited for lunch today.

So, I bought a road map once we packed the campsite up and figured we could just use that to navigate to the next stop on our trip, knowing we would be able to find somewhere along the way to buy a charger – but we got lost! I honestly don't know how you did it before technology, we couldn't figure out where we were!

Somehow, we ended up near Horsham, in a small village called Coolham. We decided to stop and get some lunch and ask for directions, and luckily the hostess lent us her charger, so we managed to get one of our phones charged up while we ate – enough that we were able to use the GPS and make it safely to this next campsite.

The pub we stopped at, The Selsey Arms, has this memorial outside for World War II, and they have a plane sitting there as part of it. It's what caught my eye in the first place, and why I told Nick to pull over. When we went inside though, there was more - they have soldiers' uniforms on the walls, and documents laid out on tables. It looked a little like a museum, but a place you can eat and drink at. I've never seen anything like it!

I asked what the story was, and the couple that owns the place heard me asking the questions, so came over and told us the story. Ken and Belinda, the owners, bought the pub a few years ago, and after realising the historical importance of the area decided to make it a showcase for all things about the war.

Didn't Grampa have an uncle, or a cousin, or know someone that died in the war? On D-day?

This pub is right next to an airfield that was used as a support area for the day the boats landed. It was called an advanced landing ground, or something like that, where the pilots touched down, and where a whole lot of soldiers were based. It's now known as RAF Coolham. If you look it up online, you'll be able to see where it is.

Anyway, so, Ken was telling us that this pub is the very same one that many of those soldiers visited while they were stationed there, because there was nothing else to do really. Belinda went on to tell us that just last year the community actually came together to have the memorial outside put up, listing the names of the fifteen men that died from there. You can see the names in the pictures I attached. They told us all about how they've been collecting the memorabilia for the last few years, arranging the displays throughout the pub, and how they plan to add more to it.

During lockdown when everything was shut, Ken repainted the place himself, and he built the life size plane out front too! He used to be an engineer and decided to build one. It's accurate, apparently, right down to the invasion stripes painted on its sides. I had to write down what it's called so I could remember – a 'Vickers Supermarine Spitfire.' You can see just how big it is in the picture with the kids in it – bless, Jason wanted to sit in the pilot's seat, and threw a fit when we tried to explain it wasn't a real plane and Emily just refused to smile, so we eventually gave up and let them run around on the grass before we set off. It was a long morning after all, what with the pack up at the campsite, and then the four-hour drive.

There was a whole lot of interest behind it too, and quite a few articles written about this place.

When you visit us next, we must take a trip out to see this pub, I think Dad would love it! By then Ken said, the plane should have the signatures on it - they're getting the entire community to sign it, which I think is just lovely.

They were also telling us that they plan to have a dress up party later this year, and have the theme fitting around the World War II era to celebrate the Spitfire. I wish we could come back for it, it sounds like it will be quite fun! But it will most likely be when the kids are at school, and it's a long drive from Manchester to Horsham, just for a party!

Well, that's all for now.
Chat soon!
Love to you and Dad
Marie

Bridge Under Troubled Water

Allow me to set the scene, it was a sunny Sunday morning in November, at The Bridge pub in scenic Shawford. The General Manager and Deputy Manager were sat having an early morning coffee, finalising preparations for a busy festive period.

The Deputy, hearing running water coming from the back of the pub, shouts through to the chefs to turn the tap off and stop wasting water. Hearing no reply, she goes to see what's going on, and finds a steady stream of water coming through the ceiling above a window!

Quickly letting the General Manager know, they go to investigate further. Upon opening the door to the back of house staff area, they hear the ominous sound of falling water. Heading towards the stairs they are faced by what can only be described as an indoor monsoon! The Deputy's first thought is of her booking diary and all the pre-orders for the Christmas parties, that have booked with them, which were residing in the office, on the other side of the monsoon.

Luckily, the chef was a keen golfer, and had left one of his golfing brollies near the bar. Ignoring any bad luck that may befall her, the Deputy grabbed the brolly and made her way up the stairs and down a long hallway, through the freezing torrent of indoor rain to the office, and rescued all the booking information, carefully organised, and stored in her booking folder. On her way back, she woke the staff that lived on site, safe to say the site of their Deputy soaking wet under a brolly was not how they expected to be woken on a Sunday morning!

A weary, and somewhat confused team gathered in the bar area, which was currently dry, whilst the Manager, who kept his cool under pressure, organised an emergency plumber to visit site and rectify the internal water feature.

Whilst the team started to wake up over a much-needed cup of coffee, the water continued to follow the laws of gravity, and a team member, who had gone to check the downstairs cellar was dry, appeared, soaked to the waist.

238

The manager now knew the cellar had flooded as well.

Then the whole team heard a mighty crash come from the kitchen. They ran to see what had happened and were met by the site of water pouring through every available gap, most notably the brand-new gaping hole in the ceiling!

Using more quick thinking, the Deputy grabbed bundles of freshly laundered chef uniforms and table linen and started to try to seal the gap at the bottom of the door to the restaurant, as the Head Chef could do nothing more than look on in horror as his kitchen rapidly filled with water.

Once the team had done their best to minimise further damage, the plumber arrived and thankfully the boiler that had created the internal monsoon was disconnected and dripped its last drip.

By this time the kitchen was two feet under water, the cellar was full to bursting point, and the carpet in the bar area was soaked and damaged beyond repair.

After an electrician said it was safe to do so the local fire brigade attended to pump out the excess water, and the repair works could begin!

With the help of the team, and some of the local community, the pub was ready to re-open by 6pm the following evening. The booking folder was dried out over radiators, and thankfully, though now crinklier than before, no information was lost, and the customers were none the wiser about the early Sunday near disaster!

Darrell Appleby

Security Breach Flushed Out!

Not long before the Covid-19 outbreak, I was the 'Greenhorn', or newly appointed duty manager, of an extremely popular late-night venue. It was the type of place that opened when most customers were going home, and you were going home when others were off to work.

Procedures are paramount in a business such as this. The team are tired, and everything must be military-like, especially security. It is drilled into you from the start. You should never work alone; you look after each other…. and you always check the dark corners and toilets at the end of the night. While training, you are warned of the calamities when procedures are not followed, some may have been urban myths, but you do not want to forget those golden rules!

So, on this night in question, I was running the business with the support of my assistant manager, Karen who, thankfully, was not the type to moan (apologies to all the Karen's out there). We were expecting a good night and, as predicted, the night went without a hitch. The bar-team were performing, there were no issues at the door, and the customers were leaving with a degree of respectfulness. Karen and I were cashing up and cleaning the bar to within an inch of its life.

Derek, our head door supervisor, was your stereotypical man-mountain, old-school bouncer. But, as with a lot of giants, he was the nicest, friendliest guy you could ever meet. I mean, you wouldn't want to walk past him in a dark alley, but to us he was wonderful.

Derek, and his crew of slightly lesser giants, were completing their security checks. Everything was going so smoothly, and it looked as though we would get out at, what we would call, a reasonable time. Tucked up in bed, dreaming sweetly, all before the sun had begun to put his hat on. Happy days!

After around 15 minutes the bar supervisor, Jack, came wearily into the office. The team were finished and ready to go. Derek, who was stood behind Jack, more than filled the door frame and, also looking a little tired, said his team checks were all complete and they were ready for a well-earned early night. Again, like a lot of doormen, this wasn't his only job and he had to be up again in a few short hours.

"Have you checked all the doors?"

"Yes." came the fatigued voice from somewhere just above the door.

"Have you completed all the paperwork?"

"Yes." replied the jaded Derek.

And then the only question I really needed the answer to,

"Have you checked the toilets?"

"Yes." was the final drawn-out reply from a guy that already sounded asleep.

Time to let them all go home.

I walked them down to the rear fire exit where the rest of the team were waiting, thanked them, and wished them a good night. Just a few more bits to do and we were on our way too, so I headed back to the office when the blood froze in my veins. The noise you never want to hear when you are locked in a huge dark club with virtually everyone gone…a flushing toilet. I stood there, heart pounding, hairs on the back of my neck standing on end, and palms dripping with sweat. Brave as a lion, I ran back to the office and locked the door.

"Someone's out there!" I gasped to Karen.

You could visibly see the colour draining from her face. If it were a cartoon, there would be a Karen-coloured puddle rippling around her feet.

"What are we going to do?"

Ever watched a horror film through your fingers? One of those slasher types? Ever screamed at the TV through your hands?

241

"Don't go outside!" you'd chant over and over, "Don't be an idiot, he's out there."

Well, I wasn't going out like that. There was a relieved, clean-handed, crazed madman out there ready to brutally murder the pair of us. There would be a mask and an axe involved, I was convinced, his favourite axe, probably. As the senior person I knew what I had to do…. call Derek!

"Derek! There's someone in here! They're in the toilet! You told me you had checked! …. No, I am NOT hearing things! You better get back here right now!" went my nervous whisper.

I couldn't raise my voice any further, the mad axeman was bound to be listening at the door by now. "I will be there in ten minutes." came the weary, reluctant reply.

Nothing for it now but to hope the lock would withstand the roaring, smoking chainsaw that was about to come through the door. Barker, Craven, Kubrick, this guy would have seen them all. He would know all the tricks. It felt like a lifetime waiting in that windowless, used-bankbook strewn prison. It was so quiet, too quiet. Maybe he was planning to use the ceiling, he couldn't get through the floor, could he? Karen and I sat there shaking, with our hands on the other's arm.

BOOM! The decisive slamming of a door, and the heavy stomp of boots moving around outside. Clearly, he'd grown impatient and was trying to rattle our already shattered nerves. Maybe he'd heard us talking to Derek. He'd been waiting silently in the darkness and was about to go psychotic.

"These marks are where one of the young women escaped. But she was then re captured and brought back to watch the other one die."

That's what the officers would say when we were finally discovered.

Bang! Bang! Bang! The knock on the office door was deafening! Karen and I were now in each other's arms, whimpering, ready to scream.

"Jenny! It's Derek, open the door!"

He had made it, thank The Lord! We opened the door gingerly, after all, this could still be a trick; But staring down at us from a great height was the now irate face of our very own Big Friendly Giant.

"Did you scare them off?" I squealed, trying to peer around him.

"Follow me," he replied and walked purposefully towards the toilets.

What were we going to see? The now dead body of our would-be assailant on the toilet floor? How much blood would there be? It was too much to take. We entered the toilet but there was no crime scene, just a clean, polished, tiled floor. Well done team!

Then it happened, we jumped, we screamed.… our newly installed automatic flush came on, which in a quiet cavernous nightclub rang in our ears like an air-raid siren. I will never forget the look of disgust on Derek's face as he silently turned around, headed back to the exit, and closed the door quietly behind him. He forgave me, and we never mentioned it again, but it will always stay with me.

Always, ALWAYS check the toilets!

The Bar Phone

Back in the early 90's I was running a pub off the beaten track in East Ham, that needed investment and refurbishment to say the least.

It was quite different in the pub game back in the nineties. It was the kind of pub that people used to ring the bar phone and ask to talk to a mate, or find out who was in. Nobody had a mobile phone, and most people had a land line.

I spent so much time telling lies to wives that their husbands were not in, it was practically a full-time job just taking and screening customer calls.

This pub had a great little secret back garden, and I could see it had enormous potential. Sadly, it was used as a dumping ground by the old tenants, full of damaged equipment, beer crates and debris and it had taken many painstaking hours to make it habitable.

I could not get my regulars to use it, and it would sit empty for days at a time. I had begged and borrowed to furnish it and I had managed to get ten lovely branded parasols from Hofmeister.

Hofmeister was my biggest selling draught at the time. The lads would walk in and ask for a pint of Bear Piss. (Hofmeister merchandise always featured a bear called George if you did not know).

Being a back street local, I knew all my regular customers well as we rarely got strangers in.

One summers day a large family came in early one Saturday morning and gravitated to my much under used garden, where they were joined by some friends making about twelve in total. These customers proceeded to get quite rowdy and out of hand after a few rounds. They were a real nuisance, and they would not calm down.

Some of the women from the group left after a couple of hours, and the rest moved on a short while after, much to my relief and that of our well-behaved regulars. I was grateful to see the back of them.

I went to clear up the garden after they left. What greeted me made me so angry; After the effort I had put in to make the area nice for people to use, my flower beds had been uprooted, the area was a mess, and my ten new parasols were missing.

Now you must remember this was a different era, no CCTV, no cheap imported goods from China, merchandise was rare and expensive. At the same time no one else had been in the garden that morning so it was obvious who the culprits were. Sadly, I had never seen any of them before so had no idea who they were or where they were from.

I was fuming!

I tidied up as best I could with help from some of the regulars, who, whilst not fond of drinking outside appreciated what I had done for the pub to make it nicer.

Not too long after coming back into the pub the bar phone rang. It was a lady looking for her husband, (as per usual), she demanded to speak to Tony and went to tell me that he was in the garden wearing a green polo shirt.

Immediately I realised from her description that this was one of the gentlemen who had been in the garden earlier, with the group responsible for the damage, and missing parasols.

I asked the lady politely for her full name and her phone number and that I would get Tony to call her back from the bar phone in five minutes, knowing full well that he had already left of course.

I then called her back five minutes later and told her that Tony had gone, along with my parasols, and that I would be passing her and her husband's names, and phone numbers on to the police so that they could ask her husband and his friends if they had any idea what might have happened to my parasols.

Within a noticeably brief time, the ten parasols were delivered back to the pub, arriving in a mini cab, with a bouquet of flowers!

My regular customers thought it was hilarious. When the parasols were dumped on the bar by the mini cab driver. They congratulated me on my ingenious impulsive plan to get my precious garden kit back.

Once more my secret back garden was looking bright and cheerful again.

Sandy Castle

The Pub Life

It has always been the pub life for me. When I think back upon my fondest memories, from a nervous bright-eyed young girl to the confident married woman I am today, one thing has always remained a constant – a trip down the local! As something that has brought me so much joy over the years, I welcome you to join me as I take a swift trip down memory lane.

The comforting hum of a car's engine always takes me back to memories of lying down on the back seat of my mum's Vauxhall Nova. Driving at night through the never-ending darkness of the country roads, until at last we would reach a group of beautifully lit up pubs.

Thatched roofs, hanging flower baskets in full bloom, and artfully arranged lighting giving the whole building a warm glow. "One day that will be mine," I said, thinking with the innocence only a child can have. I would change the pub's name to 'The Cherry Drop,' like the name of my favourite sweet. A decision, I felt, back then was nothing short of utter genius.

Do you remember walking into a bar back in the day, and seeing the lines of smoke wafting lazily towards the ceiling from everyone's cigarettes? I do, especially when it came to visiting my grandparents at the local cricket club. They had it all! Skittles, a little bowling lane, and those 20p machines with golf ball bubble-gum. I did not think there was anywhere more exciting to spend a weekend.

When I was 5 years old, my brother and I would often spend our Sundays at the pub where my mum worked. If I was feeling hungry, and mum was busy, she would send me to the bar to get some crisps. I only liked Ready Salted, or 'plain' as we all called them back then. "Please may I have a pack of aeroplane crisps?' I would ask politely, resulting in a roar of laughter from the regulars at the bar.

One reason I loved them was the prizes you could often win in a pack. I have so many memories of eating crisps in pubs and then winning more free crisps. In one of the competitions, if you found a blue envelope you could win £5, and with one brand you could even win a Mini-Cooper! I used to say to my mum that I was trying to win one for her; it was the only way to get her to keep buying me crisps!

When I was sixteen, I was living above a pub in Burton. The building was ancient, with wooden beams and dim lighting that gave it a cosy charm when full of guests. But at night, all alone, I often found myself cringing at every creak from the old staircase and jumping as a breeze from a loose window frame stroked my neck. It did not help my nerves that the area was famous for its ghost walks.

One night, I woke with a start as I heard a pool ball dropping and roll across the floor downstairs. Trying to rise from the bed to investigate I discovered, to my horror, that I could not force myself to lift even a single finger. Then I found I could not draw a single breath. It felt as though I was being strangled. Unable to turn my head, my mind began to paint horrific images as a strange feeling crept over my body, as if tiny feet were running all over me. Too terrified to do anything but squeeze my eyes shut in terror, I eventually found the strength to move my hand and give the ghost the middle finger!

Years later I found out about sleep paralysis, where the body simply requires a few minutes longer to properly awaken from a deep sleep, but that night haunts me until this day.

My passion for pubs has been a constant throughout my entire life. Like many bartenders, I have a lot to thank pubs for. The gift they gave me was my voice and confidence. I was once an incredibly quiet & timid girl, and when I took on my first bar-tending job I thought "What have I done?!" Now, years later, you cannot shut me up. I would not even recognise that quiet young girl!

I have worked in all kinds of pubs. Biker pubs, student bars, even some fancy hotels. I have met some great people from all levels of society, and I have pulling pints to thank for it. The funniest thing I ever saw was a slightly overweight middle-aged man, dressed as Britney Spears, getting head-butted by a bald young lad dressed up in a pink Tinkerbell costume! But what else would you expect from a last-minute stag party.

Well, after all that reminiscing, let us fast forward to now. My husband is the manager, and I am his deputy. We live in a quaint little village, above a beautiful pub, with hanging flower baskets and beautiful lights that ensure the place always looks warm and welcoming, even on the chilliest of winter nights. We may not have the thatched roof, and we decided against calling it 'The Cherry Drop,' but some nights I like to imagine that there is a 5-year-old girl passing by in the back of their mother's car, mesmerised by our lighting and flowers, and dreaming of their future.

Who ever said that dreams do not come true?

Ciara Nile

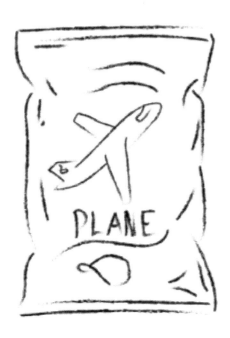

Know Who's belongs to Who!

I was working in Solihull, behind the bar of a popular local pub on an extremely hot and busy summers day. While serving a gentleman his requested drinks, a vulgarly overdressed lady forced her way through the patiently waiting crowd, and rudely commanded me to urgently bring out a bowl of water for her 'very hot and thirsty' dog.

Being quite thirsty myself on this sweltering day, my immediate thoughts of responding with 'please and thank you wouldn't go amiss' were quashed by surprisingly well-mannered self-control and I courteously replied, "no problem, I'll bring it over for you". With that and a quick click of her heels (not too dissimilar to Dorothy in The Wizard of Oz) she sauntered off through the crowd disappearing as quick as she had arrived.

Turning to the gentleman I was busy serving, and placing his drinks in front of him, my aggravated thoughts tumbled out of my mouth loudly; "Only in Solihull do the dogs get table service on command".

I revelled internally at my own wit at this fast-double entendre, hoping this was not lost on everyone who had been waiting and was shoved aside by the arrogant dog lady. Without eye contact or comment he paid, took his drinks and off he went outside. This is going to be 'one of those days for sure' I thought to myself.

Seeking out a dog bowl from the back room I promptly filled it with fresh cool water and off I went out into the packed beer garden to find the mysterious dog lady (hoping she had returned to Kansas). A few seconds later I noticed said lady offering me an upright arm reminding me of my school days when I desperately wanted to answer the teacher's question. Winding my way to her table and focused only on where she was sitting in the crowded garden, I calmly knelt down, placed the bowl on the ground next to the clearly disinterested dog, stood up, and offered my best forced smiling 'There you go madam'.

"There you go ruffles. You are 'SO' thirsty aren't you' said the dog lady in a childish voice to the spoilt and inanimate ball of fluff. As I turned to leave, and to my startled horror, I noticed that sat opposite her, was the gentleman with whom I was busy serving drinks to whilst receiving my command for urgent dog water at the bar. He was fixing me straight in the eye with a squint not too dissimilar to that of gunfighter in a spaghetti western. Not knowing whether to make a hasty retreat or reach down my side, hoping to find my six shooter, I quickly received a wink and a warm smile to which I returned a sigh of relief and a smile mixed with embarrassment, relief and thanks.

I think he got the joke, but in that millisecond exchange, I also sensed both his sympathy for my plight, and also his acknowledgment at the dig at his selfishly pre-occupied wife.

Have I learnt that my thoughts should remain exactly that, and to try hard, whatever the pressure, not to pass them on to a stranger...?

Only time will tell if I can do it, but as my recent history shows, I doubt it!

Three Little Ducks

Dawn was the General Manager of a gastro pub where I worked as the Head Chef for nearly four years. Rarely did we have the same night off, but when we did, we very much enjoyed a night out together. On the odd occasion that we were both partaking in a 'few' drinks, Dawn would always like to obtain a 'souvenir' of our night out.

One evening we were in a country pub when Dawn spotted three ducks on a shelf. There was a baby duck, mummy duck and daddy duck. With an excited smile she set herself a challenge to 'borrow' one of the ducks just for fun.

During the evening. while we were eating, Dawn who was in fits of giggles, very carefully managed to pick up the baby duck without anyone noticing. Dawn had the baby duck sat beside her under the table and when were ready to leave, she made sure no one was looking and slipped baby duck under her coat, then sheepishly took it into the taxi and back home.

The next morning, she woke up, came downstairs, and noticed the baby duck sitting on the kitchen table. Suddenly it came back to her what she had done the night before. She knew she had been rather naughty, but she was quite fond of him and a little too embarrassed to take him back, so she decided to keep him.

Dawn placed the duck in her garden, whenever she looked outside, she would have a little chuckle to herself about how he came to be there. Friends and family that visited the house commented on the duck and how cute he was, they asked where he came from, but she would never admit the truth, instead she would usually say, "Oh I can't remember, I've had him ages."

A few months passed after our night out, and Dawn, whilst hoping no one would pull her up on her naughty deed, took her parents out for a meal to the very same 'duck' pub. Whilst enjoying their meal, her dad Jim was looking around, enjoying the scenery, and looking at the many interesting artefacts around the pub when he then spotted two ducks sitting on the shelf.

"Don't ducks like that normally come in threes?" said Jim, "It looks like they are missing one!"

Jim suddenly paused for a second, trying to work out where he had seen one similar. Then it struck him, so he turned his head to Dawn with a cheeky smile and a strong voice he said, "Those ducks look very much like the one in your garden?" All Dawn could do was laugh like a naughty schoolgirl.

Sadly, my friend Dawn passed away in the February 2021. Dawn was so much fun, a great person with a big character and always a positive outlook on life. She had so many friends and a family that will miss her very much; but I know that she would find it hilarious that her 'Pub Duck' story had made it into the stories of this pub book.

Zoe Hayward

The Surprise Visit

It was the middle of February; the traditional time for hospitality workers to celebrate their Christmas night out. I had suggested to my manager a Saturday in December but given that these are some of the busiest nights of the year, we went with a Tuesday in February instead.

An area of our bar was reserved, and we had pulled out all the stops for our amazing staff. It was time for them to indulge in a well-deserved evening off and enjoy the festivities. Christmas hats, crackers, secret Santa gifts and even some leftover pigs in blankets were on display. What a sight for customers when we were quickly approaching springtime! A glitch in the matrix?

I'll let you in on a little secret… It is a rare occasion when a full team in the hospitality sector can all get together at the same time, so there is a running joke for many, that the morning team make a pact to take it easy and stick to a self-imposed curfew. As you can guess this never goes to plan! All it takes is a promise of bacon rolls from the kitchen in the morning to make you feel invincible. On this occasion, I was unlucky enough to be opening the business the next morning, and it was a delivery day!

It will be of no surprise to you, I had hit snooze on my alarm a few times that morning. But being late on delivery day is not an option so last night's clothes were hurriedly pulled on and off I went. There was a plus side though, I was not needed out front as it is a day of checking off deliveries, stock rotation and stacking our cellars in preparation for the busy weekend. So, for me, it didn't matter too much how I looked or felt.

With only three hours of my shift left to go, I received a call from one of the bar staff "The CEO is in the bar and he's here to see you!".

"Ha ha" I replied, "Not funny". The line went quiet for a few seconds.

"It's not a joke, he's in the bar, waiting" was the reply.

Complete and utter panic set in!

The last person you want to walk through the doors after your Christmas night out, is of course, the CEO of the company. We had no idea he was coming or was even in the country! Ripped jeans paired with a drink-stained top is not how you would usually like to present yourself to the 'Big Boss' of the company.

Luckily for me another manager was on site too and after a frantic two minutes begging for her to greet him for me (with the promise that I owed her one), she did. We went with the story that I was at the bank; I was not at the bank. The used chef whites I found in our staff room did not fit. Running out the fire exit and rushing off to the high street for a whole new outfit was the only option.

I felt like I was a contestant on Supermarket Sweep, I grabbed some trousers from the bargain basket of New Look. I only had time to quickly look at the size and colour of the trousers, not what they actually looked like. The scene became even more ridiculous when I was confronted by security who were questioning why I was running around their store like a woman possessed, wearing a radio and earpiece.

Getting back to the pub after putting on the rushed purchase, it's hard to describe how unfashionable these trousers were, imagine nurses' scrubs, but skinny fit. I couldn't put it off any more it was finally time to introduce myself to our CEO; presentable or not.

To my relief the conversation was flowing; then he asked for the full tour of the building. This is when I felt like our visit may take a turn for the worse. So far it had been a nod and take note exercise; he'd looked round the relatively empty bar and noted that it hadn't been *that* busy of an afternoon for the glass shelves to be empty, that kind of thing.

The next stop on the tour was our first-floor bar, the same first floor bar where our team night out had taken place. No one had stepped foot up there since. As we were walking up the stairs, I felt the need to come clean in preparation for what we were about to walk in to.

If you can use your imagination for one second here, the bar looked how it does on a Saturday night at midnight. All that was missing was Derek being cut off from any more drink, Irene teaching the girls how to get sloshed and Susan complaining that she couldn't taste any vodka in her gin and lemonade.

To my surprise, he said that he expected nothing less and these were the signs of a successful team night out! At this point I'm not sure if it was the inflatable dart board, the giant unicorn, or the paddling pool in the middle of the dancefloor that had swayed his opinion.

The following day our manager received an email to say that he was pleased with the visit and that we were all a credit it to her. If I had been told that whilst running around New Look changing my shoes and trousers, I would never have believed you.

It would bring me immense joy to say that even one part of this story was even slightly fabricated, but unfortunately, welcome to a day in the life of a hospitality worker.

Jamie McCann

The New Suit – Directors Cut

I took a deep breath. I was 21 years old, and it was the most important day of my career so far. Excitement pumped through my veins as I stood in the beautiful beer garden and gazed up at the gleaming white building. The sun was shining, and I had honestly never felt prouder – I had just been appointed as the General Manager of my very own pub.

My internal bliss was suddenly shattered by the shrill ringing of my mobile phone. My heart momentarily vacated my chest as my screen displayed the name of my new boss Richard. What followed was brief and concise:

"Good afternoon, I will be visiting all of the sites in this area in the next two weeks. I will be with my boss and we will be dining with you - don't let me down! See you on the 27th."

In just forty words my mood had been torn apart at the seams. Whilst I was delighted to hear from my new Area Manager, the thought of entertaining our Operations Director in my new pub left me feeling very exposed. I could feel my cheeks burning up as I put down the phone, and I muttered some colourful language under my breath.

Suddenly I felt ripped from my comfort zone; I had never met an Ops Director before. It began dawning on me that I had always had a manager to take the lead, and I quickly realised that this manager was now me. But there was no time for this, I had work to do if I wanted to make a lasting impression, and so I left my worries behind me.

Without being coy, my career progression had been meteoric up until this point. To succeed, I would always remember some basics which I had learned from the managers who had trained me, such as "failing to plan is planning to fail." This was my moment to prove myself, and I set about creating a military plan of action with my team to ensure that no stone was left unturned.

We spent the next two weeks tearing through the jobs: painting and decorating, fixing and renovating, polishing and scrubbing. The pub had never looked sharper, so I needed to look sharp to match. I purchased a new and expensive suit for the special occasion.

D-Day finally arrived. It was a hot summer's day, and I had arrived early to ensure the finishing touches were complete – such as the morning litter-pick of the car park. In my best bib and tucker, and with just fifteen minutes until the estimated arrival time, I obsessively decided to have one final check of our car park.

Disaster struck as my eagle eyes noticed a cigarette butt on the floor. Thank goodness I had checked; I'd heard that our Operations Director was a stickler for detail. I bounded over to the offending debris and bent down promptly to remove it from sight.

What happened next will be etched into my memory forever. As I hastily bent down, I heard an almighty rip, swiftly followed by a fresh breeze in the derriere of my brand-new suit trousers. This unsightly scene was sharply followed by the unmistakable booming tone of Richard's voice:

"Afternoon! Probably a little more of you than I wanted to introduce to my boss!"

Whilst you may feel that this was bad enough, unfortunately due to the extreme heat I had decided to go commando on this historic day!

In hindsight (literally), whilst this was excruciatingly mortifying at the time, at least I could say that I got my most embarrassing moment out of the way early on in my career as a General Manager.

Although I became the 'butt' of many jokes, neither my Area Manager nor Operations Director forgot me in a hurry, as it wasn't just the sun that was shining bright on that fateful day!

Jonathan Seed

Finger Fun

It was a beautiful picturesque looking pub. Huge beer garden to the side, a carpark sprawling from the front to the back and a nice cosy log fire inside. This was the sort of pub that you love to dine in on a cold winters day or sit relaxing in the garden sipping on a cold beer in the summer.

One of the great things about having such a large car park was that there was plenty of room for the team to park their cars whilst they were working their shift. Or so I thought until the dreaded 'finger incident' happened.

The shift had ended and the team and me were enjoying a well-earned drink after a long day. It was usual for the team to get together after a long shift to unwind, it was a chance to get to know the people you worked with.

The sun had been shining so the shift had been a busy one. The sun always brought out people to the beer garden. One of the girls (Hannah) said her goodbyes as she had to be back in early the next day, but after a few minutes she returned. We looked on confused, was everything ok? Maybe she had forgotten something. Unfortunately, her car was parked on a bank (as she had come in late and there was no room to park in the main car park), and would not start, and she was unsure what to do.

One of the young lads on shift was Tony. A local lad, quite a keen rugby player, (and quite keen on Hannah) stood up, offered his assistance, and went out to see if he could help. Now I did think at the time "What the hell does he know about cars?" Yes, he owns and drives one, but he was no mechanic. No, keep your mouth shut Grace…. he has offered to help which is extremely sweet of him. Many staff had hidden talents, perhaps Tony's was being able to fix cars?

So, I was sitting there sipping on my large glass of red wine unwinding when Hannah came bolting through the door as white as a ghost. "OH MY GOD! Tony caught his finger in the fan belt, and it's chopped his finger off!" I was completely stunned! This couldn't possibly be true!

I have heard kitchen staff claim this thousands of times on previous occasions, then when I have gone to look at the wound, I am greeted with a tiny cut that does not even warrant the first aid kit coming down off the shelf. But no, not this time. In walked Tony with a dazed, confused look of horror on his face. Rich red blood squirting from the stump where there once was a finger. "Oh wow" I thought, this is not a drill. This is for real. Remember your training.

As I applied pressure to the wound to stop the fast flow of blood it suddenly dawned on me that Tony's finger was now somewhere in the vast carpark and it might be a good idea to find this and stick it in on ice to try to save it. I turned to one of my team, Junior, who was a lovely young lad from South Africa. Always keen to help, hardworking and willing to do what was asked. Would this request send him over the edge? Could I possibly be asking for too much?

"Umm Junior, you don't mind just nipping to the carpark and finding Tony's finger and then popping it into a bag of frozen peas my lovely?" So casual was my request that it was like an everyday occurrence. Luckily, true to form, Junior stepped up and carried out my request like a trooper. You have got to love teamwork and Junior was a team player.

Unfortunately, the bad news was Tony's finger could not be saved that night; but the good news was that the car did get started, Tony did hook up with Hannah, and Junior did get employee of the month.

If there was ever a time for the classic saying it was now; teamwork really does make dreamwork!

The Decoy Tavern

Who would have thought I would become misty eyed and nostalgic about a pub? Let me explain.

Many years ago, my then girlfriend, now wife, relocated to a village between Lowestoft and Great Yarmouth for work purposes. We bought a house that was the last but one on a dead-end road that turned into a sandy track surrounded by woods. The end house was derelict, and we were soon to discover that the sandy track was the ideal spot for burnt out cars – but that's another story!

Soon after our move, we decided to explore and were keen to understand where the sandy track would take us. After a good hour's ramble which led us through the local golf course and in peril of mis hit golf shots, we finally arrived at a road of residential houses which, in turn, led to a pub called The Decoy Tavern.

On first appearance, the pub was clearly incredibly old, dated, and unappealing but, having built up our appetites and not knowing if there were any other pubs locally, we would have given most pubs the benefit of the doubt!

On entering the pub, we were greeted by a very tall, thin man who walked with a stooped back and rounded shoulders to prevent his head from brushing the low timbered ceiling. While he was carrying plates, he was keen to greet us and point us to the only available table. This table was on its own and positioned on the main walkway without any intimacy or seclusion.

Having witnessed our hesitancy, the very tall man informed us that historically, this was the favourite table of Lord Somerleyton. Not knowing who this was, and without any alternative tables available, we reluctantly sat down and surveyed the scene.

There were only forty covers (chairs) at most; a wall mounted jukebox, and a dart board in the corner. The pub was festooned with colourful Toby jugs, mismatched old crockery and every light fitting had a red lightshade hanging loosely over it.

Everyone was dining, and the very tall man and a charming waitress were running the show between them. On perusing the homecooked menu, I chose the steak and kidney pie with fresh vegetables while my pescatarian wife went for the "catch of the day" cod and chips.

At this stage, our expectations were low, although we had enjoyed the friendly welcome and were aware of how happy our fellow diners appeared to be. Once our meals arrived, we understood why. The quality of food was a triumph while the man and his younger colleague were efficient and attentive. Whilst we would not normally succumb, we couldn't resist the homemade desserts which were equally delicious.

On finishing our meals, I suggested a game of darts to my girlfriend. Again, not something that we would normally do, but it just seemed right at the time. There were plenty of spare darts available with a variety of shapes and weights, with many interesting flights from semi nudes to national flags.

On departing the pub after a magical two hours, the very tall man, while carrying plates, made a point of wishing us a good evening. Our hour return walk flew by as we glowed with quiet satisfaction and contentment at our discovery.

We stayed in this village for several years until work circumstances led to another move. We continued to visit The Decoy Tavern on a regular basis, always sitting at Lord Somerleyton's table (funnily enough it was the only table that was ever available), and invariably enjoying the steak and kidney pie, "catch of the day" fish and chips and homemade seasonal desserts. Our darts capability improved immeasurably as did our fitness with the round two-hour hike!

Without realising it at the time, The Decoy Tavern became our safe place away from the hurly burly of life. It had become our own personal institution. We never did get to know whether Lord Somerleyton had sat at our table, although we did enjoy several memorable visits to the impressive Somerleyton Hall. We never really got to know the very tall man, either, as he was always running around serving and clearing tables, but he never missed a 'hello or goodbye,' and was always available when we needed him.

We have subsequently moved on several occasions, and as much as we have tried, we have yet to find another Decoy Tavern.

Our circumstances have changed, we now have two teenage daughters and, while we regularly eat out as a family, we miss the atmosphere, service and food quality that epitomised The Decoy Tavern.

Life is more hectic, and my wife and I rarely find the time to go out together. If we could only replicate The Decoy Tavern, we would have the incentive to do so. I wonder what the very tall man with the stoop is doing now. Hopefully still doing his stuff at The Decoy Tavern although he must now be in his eighties!

Colin Cassels Brown

Confessions of an Auditor

When one has been a pub auditor for around two decades, one has a list of things they wish they had never seen… here's four memorable ones -

1. After realising I had uncovered a substantial cash shortfall in one of the pubs that I was auditing, I knew it was time to pull the manager to one side and make them aware of my worrying discovery. It soon became clear that the manager knew this conversation was coming…She began to cry pitifully; and as if without a second thought, moved in remarkably close to me and put her arms around my shoulders.

   "Is there anything I can do to make this go away?" she whispered softly into my ear.

   I, being young and gullible at the time, responded innocently. "What do you mean?"

   She looked me dead in the eye with a smouldering and seductive look and said, "I think you *know* what I mean…"

   It is safe to say I leapt out of my seat, grabbed my belongings, and left. I have never exited an office quite that quickly before, nor since!

2. There was one particularly tricky morning where I discovered perhaps the worst kitchen I had ever come across. Everything about it screamed hygiene issues and so, I took the decision to not allow the pub to sell food until it was sorted. About an hour later as I was continuing with the bar and office section of the audit, I was asked if I would like a sandwich or something to eat whist I worked. I was gobsmacked at the offer. I had just deemed their kitchen unfit to sell food! Err… No thanks, *friend.*

3. One day, I was attending a site where the manager had just upped and disappeared without a trace. All that could be found was a note left behind saying he would not be returning. I was there to ensure that the

safe and its contents were still on site (having the safe contents missing would have been a far less shocking discovery!). I found nothing to be out of place and soon received a call from the Area Manager. He informed me that he had arranged for a deputy from another pub to come around that afternoon to hold the business in the short term. He also asked me to have a quick look at the pub flat to ensure that it was in a liveable condition.

I did…It wasn't.

Safe to say, the last door on the left is one I wished I had never opened. Inside it was completely blacked out. The windows were covered, and the walls appeared to be painted black. I was unable to make out anything in the room until I eventually found the light switch and flicked it on.

Full on '*Sex Dungeon.*' It was horrific!!

4. Being an auditor is not always looking at reports and counting stock. Some people always ask what the scariest thing that's ever happened to me on the job is. Well, I was helping a manager to try and light the boiler as he was struggling. I am a helpful chap after all, and I wasn't going to let him struggle as I watched. As I was leaning in and attempting to light the boiler. BANG!

Unfortunately, the boiler BLEW UP in my face, resulting in me requiring some immediate hospital treatment. I was fortunately ok, and it could have been so much worse. I did, however, lose both eyebrows and all my eyelashes because of the boiler explosion. The most embarrassing part?

I was best man at a wedding two weeks later, and for some reason I wasn't asked to be in many pictures…

Live Sex Shows and The Frozen Turkey

Forty-eight years in the licensed trade has provided me with the most eclectic array of experiences. Dealing with people, as we do, means that one should always be prepared to expect the unexpected. In my career I have had to deal with a wide spectrum of experiences, some happy and some sad. The happy memories include births, engagements, marriages and millions of our customers having a great time; but perhaps the most important has been watching talented young people who, like me, never went to college or university, build such successful careers in the leisure industry.

The sad memories include murders, fatal accidents, major disturbances, serious fires and burglaries. Area Managers and anyone in pub operations will sadly all have dealt with one or more of these scenarios during the course of their career.

One situation that they hopefully will not have experienced is waking up on a Sunday morning to find that the front-page headline of the now defunct News of the World read 'live sex shows in Midlands pub'.

It was, unfortunately, a pub for which I was responsible, and the expected call from the Chairman came through at around 10am on Sunday morning. The message was along the lines of "I want this investigated straight away and the tenant responsible fired with immediate effect!"

I duly turned up at the pub in question to interrogate the licensee. His response was to fully accept that the illicit show in his function room had taken place; but said that before we go any further with formal action, would I like to see the list of brewery employees that were present on the night? It is perhaps not surprising to report that the tenant enjoyed many more happy years in the pub albeit with significant changes to his entertainment schedule.

By far the most bizarre event in my career occurred when I was operations director in the East Midlands. I had responsibility for a group of six experienced Area Managers. In early December I took an urgent call from the man responsible for Derby. He had made an unannounced visit to one his pubs

266

only to encounter a once in a lifetime incident. He caught the pub manager in the kitchen making love to a frozen turkey.

The manager was immediately suspended (as was presumably the turkey) and his response was to run upstairs to the private accommodation, locking the door behind him and appearing at an open window with a shotgun. He threatened to kill anybody that tried to enter the premises. This led to a full-scale police operation by the equivalent of a Derby 'SWAT' team including the use of a helicopter.

The drama was eventually resolved peacefully when the manager gave himself up without firing a shot. There were no Christmas lunches served at the pub for some time after.

I have told this story many times and the same question is often asked. Why did he choose a frozen turkey? Having no experience of, or interest in, necrophilia I am not qualified to opine on whether it is more pleasurable to have sexual intercourse with a frozen or fresh turkey. I will leave you to decide dear reader!

Ian Payne

Memories of a Little Pub Company

I joined the Stonegate Pub Company (now the Stonegate Group) early in 2012, seeing it as the perfect chance to combine my HR career, with my life-long passion for pubs from a customer perspective. What soon became apparent to me was that, not only had I joined a great sector, but the unparalleled culture that accompanied it was at the forefront of all the amazing aspects that there are to working in pubs and bars.

This was perhaps best illustrated just three months after I joined, when I gathered my whole team together for a meeting. It was then when we set a precedent that we have followed ever since, which is to meet earlier in the day in a town or city where our company has several pubs and bars, and to then head out in the evening to support and meet our hard-working teams in the businesses.

That initial get-together in 2012 took place in Leicester, which had, and still has, several student sites. The evening was very much my induction into the rituals and traditions of such pubs, as, firstly, I was popped into a giant pig costume which I had to wear as we toured the city, and secondly, I was encouraged to remove as many things as I could from the bars to carry around with us as we headed to our final destination. I must say that nothing in my career thus far had prepared me for the act of stealing from the businesses that we operated!

We ended up in what was the Goose (now the Friary) in the city centre, where the team there had laid on a space hopper race circuit for the HR team, much to the amusement of the other customers in the pub.

So, there I was – a few weeks with the business, dressed as a giant pig mounted on a space hopper, drinking Jägerbombs (responsibly of course), surrounded by pool cues, drip trays and bar stools purloined from pubs across the city of Leicester.

It was then that I remember thinking to myself, 'I think I've found my perfect job' – which is exactly how I still feel nine years later.

I should of course finish by stressing that all the items taken from our other pubs were safely returned the next day! Although, I may still have the legendary pig outfit hung up in my wardrobe somewhere...

Tim Painter

Beating the Bookies

I am a General Manager of a small pub with a little snug bar. I have three Sky TV boxes (so I can show three different channels at once in the pub), and every day of the week horse racing is shown in the snug for the regulars.

Early sessions on a Saturday can be a sleepy affair so the sports enthusiasts and horse racing fans are welcome visitors each week. On a couple of occasions each year the word quiet does not apply, as the pubs fills from before noon in anticipation of the days big racing event ahead.

On the occasions of the Grand National and Cheltenham, I dress as a jockey and run back and forth for the older customers, taking and placing their bets in the bookies across the road. It creates a bit of fun, and I do believe they look forward to seeing me in my colours!

It was the 2019 Grand National, and everything was going great. The pub was packed, the tills were ringing, and our clique of usual regulars had decided to all put a tenner on "Anibe Fly" at odds of 10 to 1. Eighteen of us had joined in the bet and after I collected the money and was just about to leave one of the older regulars stopped me and asked if I could put a tenner on for him for "Tiger Roll" at 4 to 1.

"No problem," I said and continued over to the bookies.

I handed over the slip to the guy behind the counter, he did some typing and gave me the printed slip back. I didn't bother to check it, I just placed it back on the table with the guys who look after the bets back at the pub.

The race started, and we were doing well. It was a quiet affair for the first half of the race, but every single person in the pub was on their feet as it approached the last few fences. Normally quiet and passive customers, young and old, male and female were roaring at the screens and cheering on their chosen horses.

It is an amazing scene to watch. It was no different over at our table where I watched the joy turn to disappointment as eventually Anibe came fifth and Tiger Roll came first.

Disappointment on one table but joy on others around the pub including the little old gent who had asked me to place his bet as I left the pub.

So, we had lost our £180, but the old gent won had £40. £180 sounds like a lot in total but it was only a tenner each, and part of the fun of the day so no great loss for me and the lads.

I took the slip back over to the bookies and he gave me £900! Now obviously some confusion must have shown on my face as I looked at him. He asked me if everything was ok and I didn't want to question it so just said yes, brilliant, thanks.

I couldn't wait to get outside and see what had happened because I was only expecting to pick up the £50 for the old boy in the pub.

On the way back to the pub I checked the betting slip and realized the bookie had got mixed up and put our bet of £180 on "Tiger Roll" at 4 to 1 and the old gents bet of £10 on "Anibe Fly" at 10 to 1!

When I got back and told the boys, they were ecstatic, winning £50 including their stake back!

We all pooled together £50 for the old gent's winnings from our winning pot plus a couple of beers on top, and to this day the bookie never knew he wrote the slip out incorrectly!

It was good to beat the bookies for once!

Keith Owen

A Christmas Tip

This was a Christmas my team and I will never forget! While we all love working at Christmas, the work is challenging, as you can imagine, particularly when you are dealing with several large parties simultaneously. If only we were able to secure a single large booking to fill our six hundred capacity venue in the heart of London!

Imagine my delight, therefore, when our sales team were approached by a client from a local research company, who was keen to secure a venue for their large team. After much negotiation, we were delighted to seal the deal for six hundred guests alongside a guaranteed minimum spend. This was one of our biggest ever bookings and there was much back slapping as a result although, once the excitement had died down, the real work was about to begin!

The success of any large event is in the detail. The organizer, let us call her Lisa, was very particular and kept us on our toes right up until the event itself. We had several meetings, at which a comprehensive event plan was agreed, including drinks on arrival, table plan, timings for food, speeches and even the number of our team in attendance.

Most importantly for them was the style and choice of music. The festive atmosphere and number of guests on the dancefloor would determine the success of the event! Lisa even added that "service charge would be decided at the end of the night." No pressure, then, for my hardworking team!

The big night was on us in no time, and we were religiously following the plan we had agreed with Lisa. Every guest was greeted in turn by my management team and promised the event of a lifetime. The drinks on arrival, and food, were presented with panache and consumed ravenously, while the speeches were spellbinding. My team were doing me, and themselves, proud. What could go wrong?

Catastrophically, our excellent resident DJ, Chris, was taken ill just before the big event but he promised me that Casper, his stand-in, would be just as good and that he had personally briefed him on the agreed playlist. Despite this reassurance, Casper chose to ignore the party classics we agreed with Lisa and, unbelievably, started to perform House Music. I have never moved so fast in my life! I crossed the dance floor like an Olympic athlete and clambered up to the DJ booth. Casper looked too nonplussed for my liking but, reluctantly, agreed to return to the brief.

I must confess, from experience, that DJ's can be a rare breed, and Casper clearly thought that his musical integrity was being compromised. Thirty minutes later he returned to his House Music at maximum volume. At this stage, Lisa, who had clearly been enjoying our hospitality, decided to take the law into her own hands. She admonished both Casper and me in a way that would make a builder blush and insisted that Casper stuck to the agreed party classics. Fair play, her tone, while overly aggressive, did the trick and Casper stayed on plan for the rest of the evening.

I was crestfallen, however, as despite our meticulous planning and nurturing of Lisa, she was clearly raging and would not be recommending our venue to anyone else for sole use. The rest of the event, however, went without hitch and everyone seemed to be having a wonderful time.

As we were saying our final goodbyes, I could see, out of the corner of my eye, Lisa approaching me. Here we go, the final nail in my coffin. "Apart from the hiccup with your DJ, it was absolutely fantastic," she exclaimed. "I will be recommending you to all our business partners. Here is my credit card, please put £5000 on for your hard-working team. Happy Christmas."

WOW – we had somehow managed to snatch victory from the jaws of defeat! It just goes to show that if you stick to the plan, engage with your team and deal with whatever adversity comes your way, you will win in the end. The next day, the first of many five-star reviews started being liked and shared on our social media pages.

Two years later, I have been promoted to Area Manager while my previous site has gone from strength to strength as a single party venue. I will never forget Lisa and her party; however, I consider it a salient learning that I now share with my General Managers. Having said that, the hairs still stand up on the back of my neck whenever I hear House Music!

Shawn Grant

A Pint of Foster's, Please

No matter how much planning you put into your beer orders, a rush on any individual product can wipe you out in a surprisingly brief time. Most managers try to hold onto at least two weeks' worth of stock to prevent this happening, but you can still get caught out now and again.

It was such a rush on one product that left us short just before our delivery.

I remember it clearly even though it was several years ago. I was managing a pub in High Wycombe. The dray lorry had arrived a little later than normal and the pub was open.

Bill, a local, who had drunk in this pub all his life, was walking into the bar. Bill was a real character, almost part of the furniture and like many regulars he was 'very demanding' but very loyal to the business.

He came in daily and there were times when you could time your watch by his arrival. He drank only Foster's lager. I never saw him drink anything else for all the years I worked there. Except, by accident as unfolds below.

When he came in, Bill noticed that the 'Foster's' pump was covered with a sign saying, "Sold Out." The bartender, thinking that he was doing the right thing under the circumstances, poured a pint of 'Carlsberg' and apologised to Bill, as the Foster's had run out. Bill spat it out in disgust and complained that it was an awful taste. He said.

"The bloody dray is outside surely they've got Foster's on the load".

The bartender had not noticed that the wagon had arrived and said he would go and check.

The bartender disappeared but was back in no time at all. He removed the 'Sold Out' sign on the Foster's pump and poured a perfect pint from it. Bill gasped with delight, as he had finally got the pint that he knows so well.

I was at the bar signing the delivery note with the draymen and watched this unfold.

"Good job" I said to the barman when he got within range. "You handled that well".

He smiled at me and said, "thanks boss."

Once the dray had left, I had to go back down to the cellar to sort the delivery out and line it up for the week.

I noticed that all the Foster's were still at the bottom of the drop. It was not the biggest cellar in the world, and the draymen knew to leave it for me to sort out when they had left.

I looked at the connected kegs. The draymen had inadvertently put a Carlsberg in the line that usually had the Foster's in it. The barman, in his haste just assumed it was Foster's and, in a flash, had connected it without realising he had put Carlsberg through the Foster's Tap.

My heart missed a beat. Bill would go bloody mad. I at once disconnected the tap and went back up to the bar to face the onslaught. But there was none!

Bill was happily sipping away at his pint none the wiser. There was the man who only drank Foster's and nothing else, who only moments ago had spat out the offending Carlsberg in disgust, now enjoying that very brew. I was amazed.

I watched him finish the pint and he went on his merry way, no doubt as always, we would see him later that day.

Right away I put the Foster's out of stock sign up again. The barman looked confused.

"But I just reconnected it" he said.

"No, you made an error with the keg".

I let him know what he had done, and we both broke into laughter. Not at the error but the mutual understanding that Bill had not noticed the difference.

It is an offence to knowingly pass off one product as another. Not so in this instance as it was done totally by accident. I quickly flushed the line with water and restored the Foster's.

We decided it was best to let sleeping dogs lie and never told Bill.

Who really does like other lagers, but just doesn't know it"?

Norse Invasion

It was a hot mid-week evening in the summer. The sun had been beating down all day in the pub garden, and as a result, we had several groups of people drinking cocktails and enjoying the last rays of balmy sunshine outside in the smoking area.

Suddenly, out of nowhere, a middle-aged man entered through the gate. This would have been the usual everyday occurrence except for the fact that the gentleman in question was wearing a Viking helmet and carrying a large Sword.

I couldn't quite believe my eyes. I stood watching and waiting for the penny to drop, or for some sort of punch line in the form of a larger group following behind him, clad in Viking costumes, ready for a good old Norse knees up; but this did not materialise.

I was quite new to management at the time and, whilst being comfortable in dealing with unruly patrons, I hadn't been trained in how to handle someone brandishing an actual weapon, let alone a sword.

Although I was pleased to see he had left the bow and arrows, spear and axe at home, he still looked every part the 'Viking Invader'.

The gentleman in question walked over to a bunch of people who were quietly enjoying their drinks and, without consideration of his metal clad extremities, tried to sit down at their crowded table, as if trying to acquire safe passage onto a boat back to Scandinavia. They exchanged a few words, and through bemused faces and sympathetic giggles, the conquered table kindly and politely inferred to the invader, that his presence was no longer required, and he duly retreated taking refuge at our sister bar next door.

With customer and team safety in mind, (although on reflection perhaps too hastily and with too much emphasis on the word sword), the police were called and alerted of the pending Nordic invasion.

We were instructed to keep the offending gentleman in the pub and remain calm. He was now sitting at the bar, making random conversation with the bartender and probably looking for that day's edition of 'Runes of the

World,' his helmet perched on the bar top as if it were a handbag; because who doesn't need a swift drink after a long day of conquering the high street?

The bartender kept the gentleman engrossed in conversation, enquiring as to which of the newfound venues he would invade next, until the reinforcements arrived.

I expected perhaps two officers to arrive, but it ended up being like a scene from a Hollywood blockbuster. The armed police rocked up like an army of knights, eager to protect, and quickly exited their riot van in tandem, besieging the building and covering all doors. They quickly had the other customers leave hastily, and quietly through the back doors.

Thankfully, the police officers were able to thwart the invader and safely detain him. It later came to light that he had just had a few too many meads, one of the many perils of re-enactments at Viking festival days.

It turns out that contrary to folklore some Vikings have trouble handling their beer! It was one of the most exciting and bizarre encounters of my career!

Marianne Smith

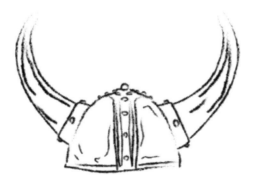

The Lockable Car Park

Working in a nightclub, in a city centre, with its own car park is an absolute blessing. At the end of a long night's work, not having to trudge around exhausted, trying to remember where you parked, just removes that bit of stress you do not need at 4am in the morning! However, it can also be a nightmare trying to prevent shoppers and local workers stealing the spaces from our team, and strong lockable gates are necessary to stop this from happening.

At the end of a particularly long evening, I was eager to get home, pop on the TV, and enjoy a cheeky bedtime beer. However, as always, I stopped my car just outside the gate, to check that the place was empty before leaving. Seeing no-one about, I locked the gates, put work out of my mind for the night, and began the short drive home.

An hour later, I was relaxing on the couch, and finally about to crack that beer open, when I received a phone call from a bewildered sounding police officer, informing me I had accidently locked someone in the car park. Unbeknown to me, a young man named Jack had parked directly behind the fire escape, the only blind spot in the car park, so he and his significant other could spend some quality time together.

I hurriedly drove back, cursing myself for forgetting to check the car park properly, and expecting to be met by an incredibly angry man furious that he had been stuck there for so long. Instead, I was firstly greeted by an embarrassed young chap, looking as though he wished the ground would swallow him up.

Secondly, an aggressive looking man in a boiler-suit and mask and waving a welding torch in the air, was attending to an expensive car with a missing front bumper. He looked like he had stepped straight out of a horror movie. Finally, two police officers were busy questioning a young, sparsely clad lady who appeared to be known to them. I paused for a moment wondering if I was part of a strange dream.

When the police officers had finished questioning the scantily clad young lady, they took me to one side and explained what had happened. Jack, on realising he was trapped in the car park, panicked. He was in his father's new car and had not realised that an emergency number was posted on the entrance. He discovered a rope in the boot of the car and tied it to both the bumper and the gate. His attempt to pull the gate off its hinges failed miserably and all, he succeeded in doing was removing the bumper from his father's car!

Still in a state of panic, Jack had called his good friend, Owen, who happened to be a welder. The plan was for Owen to remove the lock from the gate and enable Jack and the barely clad lady to make a not so swift exit.

Not surprisingly, the noise from Owen's attempt to remove the lock, woke up several neighbours who called the police on the basis that the nightclub was being broken into!

The whole escapade remains surreal, and I did feel that I had ventured onto a film set! The police officers eventually allowed everyone to leave with warnings for Jack, Owen and the hardly dressed lady, after having helped Jack with lifting the detached bumper onto the back seat of his father's pride and joy.

To this day, I have always wondered how Jack explained his "accident" and whether he and the scantily clad lady of the night were ever reunited!

Gary Joines

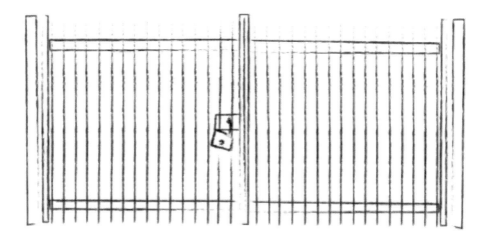

Blind to the Bowler's Tash!

Everyone has a friend like Michael. You know, one of those people that is very intelligent, but not much common sense or social awareness. Michael has always been lots of fun to spend time with, such as the time we were travelling the far east together and on seeing a statue of Gandhi, genuinely thinking it was Sinbad the Sailor.

Michael and I used to go to the gym at the Holiday Inn, in Leeds, as it was located in the town centre near where we both worked. After burning off some calories and pounds in the gym we would often visit the hotel bar, putting calories back on and putting pounds into the fruit machine.

At the time, the hotel was one of the newest and best in Leeds, had a great gym, and attracted celebrities and sports teams alike, who would stay at the venue when playing in the area.

Michael was a serious cricket fan. However, what I knew about cricket, you could write on the side of a cricket bail.

In the early 90's the Ashes were being played at Headingly, and the Australian team were in Leeds staying at the hotel. There was lots of excitement, with the entourage, big coaches in the car park, broadcasting trucks and so on. After our hard work out in the gym after work one day, during which all I heard from Michael was "cricket, cricket, cricket", we decided to go to the bar for a drink.

As Michael and I stood waiting to be served at the bar, it was totally empty apart from us and four, very tall, very loud guys with strong Australian accents in bright tracksuits. One of the four who stood next to Michael must have been over 6'4", had a very heavy Australian accent and a huge bushy handlebar style moustache, which you simply couldn't miss. Now even though I don't know one end of a cricket bat from the other; even I instantly knew this was Merv Hughes, who's moustache was as legendary as he was.

We grabbed our drinks and sat down. Just as the Australians left the bar. I could tell by his body language that Michael was excited to be amidst all the activity around the cricket. Michael turned to me and said, "I wonder if we will get to see any of the team staying here?"

"But you were just standing next to one" to which he registered a look of bewilderment. A brain the size of a planet but the sharpness of blunt pencil. You have to love him.

Thirty years on Michael and I are still best of friends and when I am home in Leeds we still go to the pub for a drink together. Michael still puts his foot in it, at every opportunity.

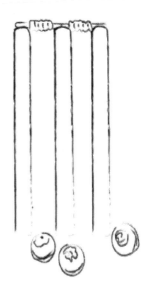

The Bargain Basement Hold Up

Working in pubs is a fun thing to do. From chatting and developing long lasting bonds with your regular customers, welcoming fresh faces to both the team and client base. The palpable energy that comes with match days to the high - octane nights out where everyone is having the best time. But it can have its risky, more sinister elements, due to sometimes holding a lot of cash at the end of the night and, obviously, involving a lot of alcohol.

I have had an extensive career in the pub industry. I have seen many things and experienced many changes to both my venue and the industry. You could be led to believe that with the vast catalogue of in-depth knowledge and experience, this makes you well prepared for most, if not all, eventualities. But you would be wrong! There is no preparation for the scenario that all Landlords dread, being held up by burglars! This has happened to me not once, not twice, but THREE times!

The first one was a terrifying experience. The knife wielding thugs had managed to force open a window and gain entry to the pub to realise their intentions. I still have no idea whether they expected the building to be empty, which would have made their task a little easier, but they unavoidably found me in the office, alone.

On discovering they were not alone, they ordered me to lie on the floor face down with arms and legs spread, whilst they ripped the office phone out of the wall. I got the impression these were professionals and that this was not their first outing into the criminal world.

Fortunately, we had an old fax machine with a phone attachment and, once the coast was clear, I hastily heaved myself up off the floor and was able to plug in the archaic fax machine and raise the alarm. My efforts, however, appeared to be in vain as by the time the police arrived the assailants had escaped with their loot. Having given up smoking some eighteen months previously, my first words on being released were "somebody give me a bloody cigarette" and this quickly became a running joke.

The second time consisted of a similar mode of operation, but with a lone assailant who had switched the sharp, flesh piercing knife for the blunt force of a hammer. I felt, again, that this was somebody who was not averse to using violence in their general day to day activities and the requirement for nicotine at the end of the ordeal made itself felt once again.

The most recent snatch and grab was, however, a vastly dissimilar experience altogether. It felt more like a bargain basement hold up as I was confronted by a young man, shrouded in nerves and frozen on the spot, wielding a mop handle which quivered violently between his hands due to the aftershock of the uncontrollable shaking that was happening all over his body.

It was clear to me, judged on my previous experience, that this was his first foray into the world of crime, and I was quite tempted to pull up a chair and provide guidance on the fact that this, clearly, was not the career for him.

However, with my safety in mind, I reluctantly handed over the money. Whilst the outcome was the same, I did not seek out nicotine to quash my overwhelming fear, but a simple bar of chocolate to keep my sugar levels up.

Hopefully, there will not be a fourth time but, if there is, I fear giving the sliding scale of competency it will be a puppy with a bone!

Gary Joines

A Rendezvous for a Memory

This story dates back to 2010, on a beautiful sunny day in the height of summer in a small seaside town on the south coast of England.

A standard day in my life as a pub manager in the tourist season regularly saw me helping out the team on the shop floor, clearing plates, serving food and drinks and making sure all was ship shape.

So, there I was going about my usual routines, when one of my staff informed me that a table wanted "to speak to me". Cautiously and internally praying this was going to be a simple question and not a complaint, I approached a table overlooking the harbour. As I arrived I was greeted by an elderly couple and two half eaten plates of fish and chips.

The gentleman introduced himself as Don and asked if I was the General Manager. Informing him that I was indeed the General Manager and awaiting what I thought was going to be an ear bashing, he went on to say how wonderful the food was, and how he and his wife were sorry they could not finish it. Breathing a sigh of relief, I thanked him and asked if there was anything else I could do for him? "Yes" he replied, going on to say, "do you live on site?" Taken slightly aback and not knowing where this was leading, I told him that I lived upstairs with my girlfriend.

"Oh, how wonderful" Don replied. "This was my childhood home," I was hooked.

After a short conversation I had found out that Don had lived here over seventy years ago with his mother, father and sister. His father had owned the building and their home was where my flat is now situated. Don and his wife were approaching eighty years old and were due to celebrate their diamond wedding anniversary the following day. In fact, they had travelled across the country that morning to see the place where he had grown up.

I knew I had the perfect anniversary gift for him, so I immediately asked if he would like to see his old home? Beaming; Don virtually leapt from his seat

285

and began to escort me upstairs. As we got into my flat and with tears in his eyes, he began to tell me stories from his youth as we moved from room to room. Some of the rooms had changed over the years; my living room used to be their winch room and their living room was now my bedroom. I refrained from giving many of my own tales from that room! The one story that stuck in my memory was of our kitchen.

The kitchen itself, apart from some electrical goods and modern appliances had not changed over the years. Don, told me a wonderful story of a cold, wet, rainy day when he and his sister were bored and longing for the beach. His mother, exhausted from the imprisoned sibling rivalry, had been to the beach, collected buckets of sand and allowed them to build sandcastles in the middle of the kitchen floor! My girlfriend put a firm stop to that idea when I suggested it later that evening.

I couldn't help but dig for more information as I was fascinated to hear such a wealth of history about the place that I lived, worked and loved. He went on to tell me that the building itself used to be a Market store called Lawrence's. His father had shared the business fifty-fifty with another gentleman. After some time, the gentleman in question wanted to move away and start a store of his own, so sold his share of the business to Don's Father.

This gentleman did indeed move away and ended up setting up a small shop with his wife, in what was at the time one of the poorest parts of London in Drury Lane. Being very proud of his achievement, he put his own name in bold letters across the frontage of his shop. The shop itself was quite the success and to this day carries the same name across the front of all its stores:

Sainsbury's

K.D. Treggiden

I Used to Run a Pub You Know

Many Moons ago, maybe a cryptic clue there, I used to run pubs. Both were in North London, but they were worlds apart. One was in the leafy suburbs, the other the exact opposite.

I have many a story or experience most other Pub Managers will identify with. On the most part, I loved my time as a manager. The good times outnumbered the bad, but God, it was physically hard and so tiring.

Let me take you back and set the scene. It was a time when customers could smoke in the pubs, even at the bar. It was lovely finishing your shift smelling of someone else's smoke..not! It was a time of working five and a half days a week and split shifts – either 9am to 3pm and back to work at 6pm to midnight, or 9am to 6pm and returning at 9pm to midnight or what we fondly call five AFD's (All F***ing Day).

We were spoilt on Sundays as the pubs used to close at 3pm and reopen at 7pm. We would average a sixty-five-hour week even before you had to get up early to take in the dray, or cover shifts for any staff that didn't turn up or were skiving, and my day off (whilst in training) would be spent at the Training Centre in another part of North London. I could sleep standing up or on a perch, and still, now over 20 years later the short mid-afternoon nap is often part of my daily routine, especially at the weekend.

Oh, the joys of getting up early to let those jolly Draymen in. 7am on the dot you would hear the reversing alarm of the dray lorry coming up the road to the back of the pub. Then came the crash of barrels as they dropped off the back of the lorry and were rolled with an extreme lack of care, through the back yard. Woe betide anything living or static that got in the barrel's way. Many a pound sterling was spent repairing and strengthening walls from the impact.

The one thing the Draymen wanted was to be back at the depot as soon as possible and nothing I did or said was going to stop them. One time they rolled the barrels down the wooden portable shoot, into the back of the pub and straight into the radiator. I heard the snap of the pipe and witnessed the

287

gush of water seeping all over the carpet. There was me, frantically trying to carve and trim down a cork from a wine bottle to plug the pipe. An hour's job turned into a morning of sweat and tears clearing the carpet ready for opening.

The barrels were rolled in, always faster than you could check them off, but my cellar was always ready for them, with my old stock pulled out furthest from the wall so I could easily check the correct amount had been delivered. As for crates, in those days it wasn't unknown for the bottles only to be around the edge of the crates, with the middle spaces all void of any bottles. It was like an episode of Police 5 - where you had to 'keep them peeled', always.

Then there was the stillage all ready to be stacked and stock rotation organised to a tee. When the last barrel from last week was empty, my newly delivered stock would be allowed to rest, be tapped and spiled, and the ale, once bright, would be ready to be served. I am proud to say that I never ran out of any stock, but how exactly do you safely get an eighteen-gallon keg of 'Directors' on top of a stillage? Well, we used the trusty barrel hoist.

The hoist's distant cousin, the supermarket trolley would be so proud of it, for when fully loaded with said barrel those wheels had a mind of their own as to which direction they wanted to go. I am sure the hoist had a phobia of metal as the more you would try to push it towards the racking, the more it would veer to the left or right. In the end I would give up using the hoist and just lift the barrel onto the stillage. No wonder my back is shot today.

As well as the brass in the pub itself, my cellar was my pride and joy. Everything in its place and a place for everything. It was so clean you could eat your dinner off the floor, as one Area Manager commented on an Audit.

Barrels were all marked up with a racking and tapped dates, and once bright, hard pegged with a big B embossed on the barrel. All my bottles of beer and tonics were neat in their crates, all taken from the front to the back, no taking them out of sequence - not in my cellar. I had many happy a morning and night-time doing my cellar checks. I miss those days.

Running a Pub would be joyous and rewarding experience but for one thing. The customers! I have got to be honest, most of them were fantastic. They would come in, have their drinks, enjoy a laugh and a joke with you and then leave with a fond farewell until the next time. But there were always the nightmare customers. Mine came in two different forms.

The first were the old boys at the bar. In my case there were three of them propped at the bar from 11am in the morning to 2pm in the afternoon Monday to Friday. I had to endure their chatting with no escape, especially the first hour. More often than not I would be on my own in the pub with no chance of leaving the bar. I became so knowledgeable of their stories I could finish them for them. The same drivel every day, but it kept them amused and they did no harm really - only to my sanity. Big John used to love to tell me at least five times a day "I used to run a pub." He was always on hand to 'advise me' on how to deal with customer complaints, how to unblock the toilets. He was a font of knowledge but all no good to anyone for anything.

Then there were the 'once a year' customers who would come in and complain about everything – trying to get a freebie. The food came from a microwave, so I don't know why they were expecting a dish created by Gordan Ramsay. Their favourite line was "I used to run a pub" and "this is how I would have dealt with this etc." I would have loved to have said "Well go and run your pub and leave me alone," but instead a smile and an "of course" would always save the day.

Between Monday to Thursday, we weren't a late-night bar. By 10 pm we would have bottled up with all the labels perfectly facing forward – a Marketeer's dream. We would have cashed off the spare till, emptied the ashtrays and wiped down the tables and I could set my watch by my four regulars who would come in at 10.30pm every night and with a wink and a wave they would always say "Quiet then?" and I would smile back and say, "Just waiting for you, Gents". Inside I was screaming "Change your pub crawl route and get here at 7pm!". Would they leave early? Would they heck. Everyday a pint at last orders which they would sip and slurp till 11.20pm – whilst I was shouting "Time please gents. Haven't you got homes to go to?

"How do you like your eggs, as I'm taking orders for breakfast?" The volume of my comical utterings getting louder and louder. Oh, what jolly japes we had, but inside all I wanted to do was to lock up, get upstairs and collapse in my chair and unwind. Of course, you couldn't go to bed straight away, not like normal nine to fivers, I still needed to relax and take in a couple of hours of TV, then five hours later I'd be ready to do it all again....

Tim Greaves

Acknowledgements

Originator

Colin Hawkins

Cataloguer and the 'Keeper of the Book'

Paul Cahill

Lead Editors

Colin Hawkins, Colin Cassels Brown, Tim Greaves, Paul Cahill.

Book Illustrator (cover and sketches)

Josh Warr

www.jjwgraphics.com

josh.jjwgraphics@outlook.com

Tel: 07803829639

Assistant Editors

Karen Hawkins, Lucy Dawson, Louise Wright, Aprile Jackson,

Angela Sinclair, Gabi Davis, Jason Lloyd, Kera Patch,

Andrew Jones, Edwina West, Caz Karlson-Douglas, Wayne Ince,

Ciara Nile, Alex Macey-Dare, Sarah Hark, Josh Elkington,

Denise Burke, Robert Thornton, Lucy - Jane Conner, Anita Chong,

Helen Marshall, Carl Burns, Adrian Diggory, Alfie Edge,

Ceri Hughes, Fearne Charles, Steven Lambert, Marc Baker,

Nina Marshall, Barry Garnham, Jordan Clark, Rebecca Pryor,

Paige Carter, Anya Czekeryla, Brianna McGeever, Natalie Moran

Amy Fox, Peter Hufton, Susan Smyth, Roksana Zym,

Marianne Smith, Susan Quinn, Grace Thomson, Diccon Burge,

Stacey Minnell-Gault, Ross Hughes, Briony Curran, Louise Woods,

Edward Moor, Milly McCarron, Paula Paylott, Jodie Ellis,

Annalie Davis, Courtney Pedersen, Gareth Eyton, Emma Mack,

Mark Willson – Pepper, Larrisa Goree.

Authors

While we were unable to accommodate every story, they are all cherished and share the same sentiment: A Love of the Great British Pub.

Anne McNamara, Ant Surtees, Aaron Wilson, Adam Hancox, Alan Armstrong

Andrew Younger, Annalie Davis, Barry Garnham, Chris Sturgess,

Catherine Banwell, Catherine Button, Iain Clark, Ciara Nile, Claire Bradshaw,

Clive Hawkins, Colin Hawkins, James Fox, Wayne Ince, Janne Sedgwick,

Sam Patrick, Neil Carruthers, David Lee, Spencer Bloomberg, Iain Turnbull,

Clare Milton, Colin Cassels Brown, Ian Payne, Jennifer Kuhn, David Sharp,

Mick "Face" Lee, Liz Appleton, Lord Simon Cant, Damian Maloney,

Daniel Manley, Darrell Appleby, Darren Earl, Dave Alebon, David Crow,

David Sharp, Tommy Cawley, Joanna Roberts, Colette Sarjant, Gareth Lane,

Gary Joines, Joanne Fuller, Vicki Phillips, Jamie McCann, Graeme Evans,

James Vann, Graham Davies, Helen Marshall, Iain Clark, Ian Coote,

Roksana Zym, Jason Lloyd, Jay Frostick, Joanna Roberts, Joanne Probert,

Jodie Ellis, John Cheetham, Jonathan Seed, Jacqueline Weston, Craig Southall

Julian Searle, Kate Vicary, Kate Wilton, Kelly Wright, David Peat,

Kirsty Pettitt, Lorna Galloway-Mccaroll, Louise Woods, Michelle Lawless,

Nick Scofield-Adams, Marianne Smith, Mark Quinney, Mark Willson-Pepper,

Matt Picker, Matthew Brown, Mike Glover, Mike Harrison, Paula Heneghan,

Stuart Ward, Susan Smyth, Oliver Sweetman, Alfie Edge, Paul Cahill,

Authors Continued

Tim Greaves, Keith Treggiden, Paul Harper, Paul Taplin, Paulo Jacinto,

Peter Hufton, Philip Preston, Rebecca Light, Rebecca Fryer, Dawn Hall,

Lisa Jeffs, Ross Hughes, Kate Lawless, Sally Tarling, Sandy Castle,

David Beveridge, Wayne Reeves, Shawn Grant, Simon Pac-Pomarnacki

Victoria Pac-Pomarnacki, Stacey Minnell-Gault, Ben Jones,

Stephen McMahon, Steve Skupski, Susan Quinn, Tim Painter, Neil Maturi,

Hesham Badra, Carol Clare, Paul Marshal, Victoria Rue, Zoe Hayward.

Got a Pub Story for us?

Fancy contributing to Volume 2?

100% of the proceeds from Volume 1 and any future volumes of this book go to the Licensed Trade Charity, (dedicated to supporting the lives and welfare of Pub, Bar and Brewery workers).

If you would like to submit any ideas or stories for future volumes (for free and in agreement that your work is a charitable donation to the project) then please send it to:

submit@memorybank.pub

and we will read and consider your story for future publications.

LICENSED
TRADE
CHARITY

Helping licensed trade people

0808 801 0550

www.licensedtradecharity.org.uk

support@ltcharity.org.uk